'So.'

'Yes.'

'And for some reason you think I might do?' Emma said.

Hunt winced. 'I beg your pardon if I gave that impression. But, yes, you do…er…'

'Fit your requirements?'

A long-forgotten burning sensation informed him that he had actually blushed. 'Something like that.'

'And along with your requirements are you also going to ask for references?' Her chin was up.

Hunt looked at her. The brief hint of laughter was gone. In its place was…bitterness? No, not that. Resignation. As if she expected rejection.

'If you will forgive the impertinence, Emma, I think your children are your references.'

She stared at him. 'Oh.'

And that lovely soft mouth trembled into a smile that shook him to his very foundations. Was he insane? He wanted a wife who would not turn his life inside out. Now it would serve him right if he found himself fronting the altar with London's most notorious widow! Only… Could she really have done anything truly scandalous? He was finding it harder and harder to believe…

Author Note

Somewhere in writing each book I start to worry about the next. Never mind that my current characters are still stuck in whatever mess I've concocted for them, I'm off on a tangent, worrying about what I'll write next. It's pointless. I know perfectly well from experience that well before I finish the next book will be running around in my head. Very often at least one of the characters is right there under my nose in the book I'm just finishing. This is one of those times.

If you read *In Debt to the Earl* you may remember James's friend the Marquess of Huntercombe. Hunt was grieving for his half-brother Gerald, who had been murdered. From the moment Hunt stepped—quite literally—out of the shadows to help James and avenge Gerald, I wanted to know more about him. And I wanted him to have his own happy ending. I hope you enjoy his story.

HIS CONVENIENT MARCHIONESS

Elizabeth Rolls

Published in Great Britain 2017
by Mills & Boon, an imprint of HarperCollins*Publishers*
1 London Bridge Street, London, SE1 9GF

© 2017 Elizabeth Rolls

ISBN: 978-0-263-93257-7

Our policy is to use papers that are natural, renewable and
recyclable products and made from wood grown in sustainable
forests. The logging and manufacturing processes conform to the
legal environmental regulations of the country of origin.

Printe
by CP

Elizabeth Rolls lives in the Adelaide Hills of South Australia with her husband, teenage sons, dogs and too many books. She is convinced that she will achieve a state of blessed Nirvana when her menfolk learn to put their own dishes in the dishwasher without being asked and cease flexing their testosterone over the television remote. Elizabeth loves to hear from readers and invites you to contact her via email at books@elizabethrolls.com.

Visit the Author Profile page
at millsandboon.co.uk for more titles.

For Anne, Linda, Lynn and Suzie.

Because you inspire me and keep me going.

And because we can put away more champagne,
cheese and tea at a critique group meeting
than anyone would ever believe.

You've seen a fair bit of this story over the past year.

Now it's yours.

Chapter One

Late October, 1803

The Fifth Marquess of Huntercombe perused the list in his hand with something akin to panic. He gulped. No, not *merely* akin, it was the thing itself: sheer, unadulterated panic. His hands were damp and a thin line of perspiration—damn it to hell—trickled down his spine. In his own library. All because of a list his elder sister had handed him. And he'd only read the first few names. That was quite enough.

He cleared his throat. 'Letty, this is not—'

'Huntercombe,' Letitia, Lady Fortescue, silenced him with an unnerving stare as well as his title. 'You acknowledge that you must marry again.'

She *always* called him *Huntercombe* in just that tone when she wished to remind him of his duty. As if he *needed* reminding. The Marquess of Huntercombe always did his duty. To the family, his estates and Parliament.

'And that it is a matter of some urgency. With which,' Letty added, 'I wholeheartedly concur. Gerald's death was a disaster.'

Hunt's jaw tightened. 'Yes, quite. But—'

'Caroline and I have listed *all* the eligible girls currently on the market.'

Market was definitely the right word. And *girls*. He accorded the list another glance—it reminded him of nothing so much as a Tattersall's sales catalogue of well-bred fillies, with said fillies paraded, albeit in absentia, for his consideration. Letty and their sister Caroline had included each filly's sire and dam, notable connections, looks, accomplishments including languages spoken, and fortune. Staying power wasn't included, although he sincerely doubted his sisters had heard of, let alone seen, Harris's infamous list of Covent Garden Impures. He looked again at the list, forced himself to read *all* the names…

'For God's sake, Letty!'

By the fire, his spaniel, Fergus, raised his head and cocked his ears.

'What?'

'Chloë Highfield?' He signalled for Fergus to stay put and the dog sank back with a sigh.

Letty looked affronted. 'Well, of course. She's—'

'My goddaughter!' Hunt could imagine the reaction if he attempted to pay his addresses to

Chloë. His imagination didn't merely quail; it turned tail and fled. Although not before he had an all-too-likely vision of his good friend Viscount Rillington's approaching fist.

'Oh.' Letty had the grace to look disconcerted. 'I'd forgotten. How very awkward. Cross Chloë off, then. It can't be helped.'

Cross Chloë— With a strangled curse, Hunt strode to the fireplace and consigned the entire list to the flames.

'Giles! Hours of work went into that!'

'I don't doubt it,' he said through gritted teeth. If only a similar amount of thought had gone into it. 'Letty, you wrote to me last month wishing me a happy birthday. Do you recall how old I am?'

Letty scowled. 'Since I turned fifty-six in March, it was your fiftieth birthday. Although what that has to say to anything I'm sure I don't know!'

Hunt stared at her in disbelief. What the hell did she think a man of fifty was going to do with an eighteen-year-old virgin?

Giving up on tea, Hunt walked over to his desk and poured himself a large brandy from the decanter there. The mere thought of taking to wife— and bed—a chit only a couple of years older than his own daughter would have been if she'd lived left him vaguely nauseated. Oh, it happened. All the time. But it wasn't going to happen with him. The very idea made him feel like an elderly satyr. An incestuous one to boot when he considered Chloë. For God's sake! He'd taken the child to

Astley's Amphitheatre for her tenth birthday and still took her to Gunter's for an ice whenever they were both in London. He would be one of Chloë's guardians if that was ever required. He took a swallow of brandy, felt it burn its way down. If Chloë was old enough to appear on anyone's list of eligible damsels, he'd probably bought their last ice cream. It made him feel positively elderly.

Letty leaned forward. 'Giles, marriageable ladies do *not* languish on the shelf for years on the chance that a middle-aged widower will exercise a modicum of common sense.' She scowled. 'If a woman remains unwed at thirty there is a very good reason for it! I acknowledge the difficulty, but—'

'A widow.'

'What?'

Hunt set the brandy down. 'Letty, a widow would be far more appropriate. A woman of some maturity would be a far better match for me.' A widow would be less demanding of his time, his attention…his affections. She would know how to go on and not require his guidance. And he wouldn't feel like a satyr.

Letty scowled. 'Well, I suppose so, but you need a woman young enough to bear children!'

'Thirties,' Hunt said. 'That's still young enough.'

It was rational. It was sensible. An older woman would not have stars in her eyes or romantic fancies he could not fulfil.

Letty pushed her tea away. 'You may pour me some brandy.'

He reached over and did so, passing it to her.

She took a healthy swig. 'No money with a widow, most likely. She may even have *children*.'

'No matter.' A widow's dowry usually went to her first husband's estate, or was settled on her children. Any jointure, in ninety-nine cases out of a hundred, ceased upon remarriage. And if she had children, at least he would know she was fertile. Any sons other than infants would be safely at school and very likely their paternal relatives would have guardianship. That was how it was done. As for daughters, they would be their mother's business. He frowned. Now he considered it, it seemed a cold way of doing things…

'Very well.' Letty swigged more brandy. 'Another list.'

Hunt cleared his throat. 'I think I can just about manage to find my own bride, Letty.'

She tossed off the rest of the brandy. 'I doubt it. Many widows do not move much in society. There's no need for them really.'

That sounded cold, too. But— 'All right. But for God's sake, be discreet.'

She fixed him with a look that would have sunk a battleship. 'Why don't we pretend you didn't say that?'

He grinned, despite his vexation. 'I beg your pardon.'

She gave him a blank look. 'My pardon? For what?'

'For—never mind. Don't know what I was thinking.'

Returning to his library after seeing Letty to her carriage, Hunt poured another brandy and sat down at his desk, clicking his fingers at Fergus, who came to him, tail wagging. This room, full of books, with lamplight glowing on the bindings, warm with the rich fragrance of leather, was his sanctuary. Here he could be private and as content as it was possible for him to be. The dog's head rested against his knee and he fondled the silky, drooping ears.

By the inkwell, where he saw them every time he dipped a quill, was the miniature of his first wife, Anne, and their children, Simon, Lionel, and his Marianne, and Gerald, his young half-brother. Now, instead of letting him slip back into the past, their silent gazes prodded him forward. He took a careful breath, reached out and picked up Anne and the children. Very gently he laid them in the drawer where he kept paper. What bride would want her predecessor on her husband's desk? The portrait of Gerald at nineteen remained, a reminder of his terrible failure.

'But we could buy a proper kite *instead* of paying the subscription, Mama,' Harry explained in a wheedling tone for what Emma calculated was the fiftieth time. 'It doesn't have to be just my kite. I promise I'll share with Georgie and you can use it and we'll—'

'No, Harry.' Lady Emma Lacy, a box of subscription books under one arm, released her daughter Georgie's hand and pushed open the door of Hatchard's Bookshop on Piccadilly. She gestured Harry inside. 'The weather for flying kites is over.' October was nearly gone and the weather had turned cool. At least at this time of year the likelihood of running into anyone she knew on Piccadilly was low. London had emptied of the *ton* after the Season ended. Some would return briefly for the autumn sitting of Parliament, but right now town was empty. Except for—she cast an edgy glance over her shoulder—the man who had walked behind them all the way from Chelsea. He was nowhere to be seen and she breathed a sigh of relief. She was being foolish. Other people lived in Chelsea. Perfectly respectable people for the most part and she had walked into town along the King's Road, the most direct route. It was hardly surprising that someone else should do so. She had seen this particular man rather often in the past weeks. But she knew most of her neighbours and she had never seen this man before, nor did he ever seem to *do* anything except simply be there—where she was. It was foolish, but she could not shake off the feeling that she was being watched.

'*Please*, Mama?'

She dragged her attention back to Harry, summoning patience. 'We can set money aside for a kite at the next quarter day. For Christmas.' Assuming no unexpected bills dropped into her lap. As it was, she had considered letting the Hatchard's Circulating Library subscription go back at Michaelmas, but the children had to be given their lessons and she needed the weekly selection of books to help with that. It simply meant that she could not save as much this quarter towards the day when she must send Harry to school.

'I hate quarter day.' Harry dragged his feet over the doorstep, his face sulky.

Emma opened her mouth to tell him not to scuff his new shoes, that they had to last until the next quarter day—and changed her mind. She hated quarter day, too. Hated the having to sit down and budget for the next three months, because there never seemed to be enough for new shoes and a simple treat like a kite for a ten-year-old boy. Hated having to worry about the cost when one of the children became ill and most of all she hated that Harry even knew what quarter day was. Even little Georgie had an inkling of the import of quarter day.

The struggle to make ends meet had not been so bad when Peter was alive. There had been more money and the children had been smaller, too. Georgie, now six, was still content with Emma's attempts at doll-making. Her effort at kite-making had fallen well short of the mark. Quite literally. The makeshift kite had ended up in the Serpentine.

'Papa would have known how to make a kite.' Georgie, holding Emma's hand again, looked up with complete assurance in her tawny eyes. Peter's eyes.

Harry looked back and scowled. 'Oh, shut up, Georgie. You're just a baby. You don't even *remember* Papa.'

Georgie stuck her tongue out. 'Do, too! And he would have!'

'Harry.' Emma frowned at her son. 'Don't be rude to your sister. Georgie, no lady ever sticks her tongue out.'

Georgie looked mutinous. 'It's only Harry.'

'Even so. And, yes, Papa would have known how to make a kite.' And how to help their rapidly growing son become a man.

Harry looked crosser than ever. 'Doesn't matter anyway.' He sulked ahead of his mother and sister, still scuffing his shoes.

Emma followed, Georgie's hand tucked into hers. Harry needed to be with boys his own age, but at the moment school was beyond her means. More, he needed a man's influence. Not, as her father had put it four years ago, to lick him into shape, but just to be there for him. Somehow she had to see to his education and—

'What book shall I choose, Mama?'

She smiled down at Georgie. 'Let's see what's there, shall we?'

Hunt told Fergus to stay and left the spaniel sitting beside Hatchard's doorstep. Fergus's plumed tail beat an enthusiastic tattoo on the pavement and, confident the dog would be there when he came out, Hunt strolled into the shop and breathed in the delight of leather bindings, ink and paper. One of the few things he missed about London when he was in the country was her bookshops, this one in particular. John Hatchard had only opened his business a few years earlier, but it had quickly become one of Hunt's favourites.

The dark-haired young man came forward to greet him. 'Good morning, my lord.' He executed a slight bow. 'Welcome back to London. You found us, then.'

Hunt smiled. 'Good morning, Hatchard. Yes.' He glanced around the shop. When he'd left London at the end of the spring sitting of Parliament, Hatchard had been further along Piccadilly. 'Your new premises are satisfactory?'

The bookseller smiled back. 'Oh, yes. I venture to say we'll be here for a while, my lord. May I help you with something in particular?'

'No, no. I'll just wander through to the subscription room and make my selection. Unless you've anything special for me look at?' Hatchard knew his collection almost as well as he did.

Hatchard's smile deepened. 'As it happens, sir, I do have a 1674 edition of Milton. I was going to write to you.'

Hunt hoped his expression didn't betray him. '*Paradise Lost?* That sounds interesting.' An understatement if ever there was one. Hatchard knew perfectly well that he didn't have the first edition of *Paradise Lost*.

'I'll fetch it for you. The subscription room is through there.' Hatchard pointed.

Hunt tried not to look as though Christmas had arrived early. 'Thank you, Hatchard. No rush. Call me when you're ready.'

Hunt strolled on through the shop, pausing to

look at this book and that, making his way towards the subscription room. He didn't know any of the other customers; late October was a little soon for most of the *ton* to return to London. He planned to head out to his house near Isleworth in a few days himself, rather than stay in town the whole time, but there were matters to discuss with his man of business and solicitors if he were to marry again.

He couldn't bring himself to care very much. *Paradise Lost* was far more enticing than marrying merely because male branches on his family tree were in distressingly short supply.

He stopped on the threshold of the subscription room and quelled his unreasonable annoyance at finding it occupied. A grey-clad woman and two children had claimed a large leather chair, the small girl snuggled in the woman's lap and the older boy—was he ten, eleven?—perched on one arm, kicking at the side of the chair. A governess and her charges, he supposed. The boy glanced up at Hunt, subjecting him to an unabashed stare from dark blue eyes.

Slightly taken aback, Hunt inclined his head gravely. 'Good morning.' A pang went through him. Simon had had just that direct, confident gaze.

The lad's eyes widened. 'Oh. Um, good morning, sir.'

The woman looked up sharply from the book she and the little girl were examining and Hunt forgot the boy. Deep blue eyes, very like the boy's, met his. His breath caught and he tensed, staring, startled by the unexpected and unwelcome heat in his veins. Her lips parted and for a moment he thought she would speak, but with the merest nod she returned her attention to the book and settled the little girl closer, speaking too quietly to hear anything beyond the question in her voice. The child nodded and the book was set aside.

Hunt forced himself to turn to the shelves. All he saw was a pair of midnight eyes in a still, pale face. He gritted his teeth, willing away the shocking heat. For God's sake! He was fifty. Not a green boy to be rattled by an unexpected attraction. And he didn't prey on governesses, damn it! Although…no. The resemblance to the boy was clear. Not the governess. Their mother and that meant she was married. Respectably married judging by her gown and the fact that she took her children about with her, rather than leaving it to a governess. Memory stirred. She had nearly spoken to him and he had seen those eyes before. It was not just that unwelcome flare of attraction. Did he know her? He started to turn back, but stopped. She had neither smiled, nor given any hint of encouragement. When a lady made it clear she did not wish to acknowledge an acquaintance, then a gentleman acquiesced. The Marquess of Huntercombe did *not* accost strange females in bookshops.

'Harry?' The woman spoke firmly. 'Will you have Mr Swift this week?'

At the musical, slightly husky voice, Hunt's memory stirred again.

'I don't mind.'

Perusing the bookshelves, Hunt thought that sounded remarkably like *I don't care.* He grinned. Understandable that the boy would far rather be out with friends playing cricket, than choosing books with his mother and sister. His own boys had been the same.

'Georgie, you had that stupid book last month!'

'Harry.' The mother's voice remained quiet, but it held steel enough to wilt a grown man, let alone a young boy.

'Well, she did, Mama.' Brotherly contempt oozed. 'Why can't she choose a proper book if we *have* to come here? Fairy tales are only for babies.'

'I'm *not* a—!'

'*Georgie.* I haven't noticed you choosing any book at all, Harry.'

Mama's clipped tones silenced the little girl and had Hunt wincing. The boy was dicing with death here.

'I chose Mr… Mr Swift!'

'No. I suggested it and you didn't mind. That's hardly choosing.'

A moment's sulky silence. 'Well, I'd rather have a kite. Not a stupid library subscription.'

'Harry—'

'I know! Because *she* was sick and had the silly doctor and a lot of medicine, *I* can't have a kite.'

'It wasn't my fault! You gave me the beastly cold!'

'Yes, but I didn't have the doctor, because I'm not a stupid *girl*! *Ow!*'

'Georgie! Don't hit your brother. You know he can't hit back.'

'Don't care! He *did* give me the cold and I'm not stupid!'

'Right.'

At the sound of upheaval, Hunt turned to see the woman rise from the chair, setting the little girl down gently, despite her obvious ire. Her face scarlet as she met his amused and, he hoped, sympathetic smile, she gathered up several books and stalked to the shelves. His gaze focused on the slender figure, caught by the unconscious grace in her walk.

'Mama?'

'While I am replacing these you may *both* apologise to his lordship for disturbing his morning.'

That jolted Hunt from a particularly improper fantasy about how the lady might move in another context. If she knew he was a lord, then he hadn't been mistaken. He *did* know her and he certainly shouldn't be fantasising about her.

'I can't have my fairy tales?'

It was almost a wail from the little girl, but the boy turned to him, his face crimson, and nudged his sister.

'*What?* It's all your—oh.' She shut up and looked at Hunt.

'I'm very sorry, sir.' She retained the merest lisp, utterly enchanting. Bright brown eyes, still with the glint of angry tears, gazed up at him out of a face framed with tawny curls and for a shattering moment he saw another small girl furious with an older brother.

'I beg your pardon, sir.' The boy was stiff with embarrassment.

Hunt regarded the flushed pair and nodded. 'Accepted. But—' holding the boy's gaze and keeping his face stern, he pointed to their mother's rigid back as she replaced the books '—no gentleman behaves badly to his mother.'

The boy bit his lip, but set his shoulders and went to his mother.

'Mama? I'm sorry I was so rude. Please let Georgie have the fairy tales at least. It was my fault. I shouldn't have teased her.'

The mother turned and Hunt saw bone-deep weariness in her face. And something else he recognised: love, unshakeable love for the child. 'No, you shouldn't.'

'I… I can go without pudding, too.'

Her smile looked like it might turn upside down and Hunt was sharply aware of a longing to do something about that, to lift whatever burdens weighed her down. 'I do have to fill you up with something. I'd rather you chose a book for yourself and promised to read it.'

'Yes, Mama. I really am sorry.'

She ruffled his hair, and gave a smile that made Hunt's heart ache. 'I know. Go on. Choose your book.'

'Perhaps I might help there?' The offer was out before Hunt even knew it was there.

The mother stiffened. He saw it in the set of her

slender shoulders, in the firm line of her mouth and his memory nudged harder, trying to get out.

'That's very kind, sir, but quite unnecessary.'

Hunt gave up racking his brains. 'This is most embarrassing, but I cannot recall your name, ma'am. We *have* met, have we not? I'm Hunter-combe, you know.'

'Yes, I know. I'm surprised you remember me, sir. It was years ago. Thank you for accepting their apology.'

He smiled. 'I think you were more bothered by them than I. Don't give it another thought.' So he *did* know her. Although from her clothes it was clear she did not move in society, nor was she eager to recall herself to him. She had avoided giving her name. Perhaps she *had* once been a governess. He would not have noticed a governess, but she might have remembered him if her charges had known his own children. He should not pry, but something about those expressive dark eyes held him, despite her obvious reluctance.

The little girl, Georgie, came and slid her hand into her mother's. 'Were you a friend of Papa's, sir?'

He smiled at her. 'We are not quite sure. Your mama and I were—'

'He was Lord Peter Lacy,' the child said. 'I'm Georgiana Mary and that's Harry.'

'Georgie, sweetheart.' Her mother took down the fairy tales again and handed them to her. 'Take your book and sit down with it.'

'Yes, Mama.'

Lord Peter Lacy. He was a younger son of the Duke of Keswick. Hunt wasn't quite sure *which* younger son; Keswick and his Duchess had been nothing if not prolific, although a couple of their sons had recently died. But Lord Peter had married in the teeth of his father's disapproval and dropped out of society. He remembered hearing something, but he had been mired in grief at the time and hadn't taken much notice. Just who *had* he married…? His memory finally obliged.

'Lady Emma Lacy,' he said. 'Of course. Dersingham's daughter.' It vaguely came back. Lady Emma Brandon-Smythe she had been. Dersingham had been furious, too. Granted, the match had not been a brilliant one for either party, but perfectly respectable. Keswick and the Earl of Dersingham had only objected due to their mutual loathing of each other. There had been whispers of star-crossed lovers.

'Yes.'

'He's well? I've not seen him since the spring sitting.' Not that he'd tried. He didn't like the Earl above half.

'I believe so, sir.' The polite smile did not so much as touch the weariness in her eyes. 'If you will excuse me, I must finish choosing our books.'

'Of course, ma'am.' Hunt stepped back with a bow. The child, Georgie, had referred to her father in the past tense and, given that Lady Emma was garbed in grey, it followed that… He took a deep breath and took a wild leap into the unknown.

'I was very sorry to hear of Lord Peter's death,

Lady Emma.' Lord Peter had been at least ten years younger than himself and he'd dropped out of society completely after his marriage. Hunt hadn't even heard that he'd died, but he'd been a decent sort, with little of Keswick's arrogance.

'Thank you, sir.' The unmistakeable shadow in her eyes was familiar. He'd seen it in his own mirror for long enough.

'Mama?'

Hunt glanced down at the boy.

He brandished three volumes. 'I've got this.'

Hunt nearly choked at the sight of *this*. 'Hmm. Rather dull, I thought it,' he said, dismissing all the wild extravagances of *The Monk*. Matt Lewis might cut him dead if it got back to him, but then again, he doubted even Lewis would consider his tale, in which a monk unwittingly raped and murdered his own sister, appropriate for a ten-year-old.

'Dull?' Harry's face fell.

'Yes. Beyond tedious.' Gently he removed the volumes from the boy's grasp. 'But I *can* recommend Swift's *Gulliver's Travels*. Very exciting. You'll like the talking horses.'

'*Talking* horses? Thank you, sir.' He looked at his mother. 'I'll get that then.'

'You do that.' Lady Emma's voice sounded a trifle strained. 'Thank you, sir,' she added very quietly, laughter quivering beneath the surface, as the boy headed back to the shelves. 'I wouldn't have let him read it, but—'

'Perhaps it was more palatable coming from me?' he suggested. Lord, she was pretty when her eyes danced like that. Like the sea near his Cornish home. A man could drown in eyes like that...

Her mouth twitched. 'Probably. Not that I would have been fool enough to tell him he wasn't *allowed* to read it, but I've no idea how I would have wriggled out of that.'

He cleared his throat, uneasy at the sudden camaraderie between them. 'Well,' he said stiffly, 'it cannot be easy for a woman to control a headstrong boy. Ought he not to be at school? Surely Keswick has something to say in that?'

The drowning blue froze to solid ice. 'That, sir, is none—'

'Excuse me, my lord?' Hatchard stood in the doorway. 'I have the Milton ready for you. Oh, good morning, Lady Emma.'

'Good morning, Mr Hatchard.' Along with her eyes, Lady Emma's voice had iced over, the dancing amusement winked out as though it had never been.

A reserved, sober matron faced Hunt, nose in the air. 'I won't keep you, sir.' She held out her hand. 'Goodbye.'

It was a dismissal worthy of a duchess. 'Ma'am.' He took her gloved hand. It fitted perfectly within his and, standing this close, he was teased by the warm fragrance of woman, despite the fury seething in her eyes. No scent, just soap and something that was Lady Emma.

'Au revoir.' Goodbye was a great deal too final. The French said it much better.

Chapter Two

Their selections made, Emma hurried towards the front door of the shop, the box of books tucked under her arm. How *dare* he criticise her management of Harry? No doubt *his* children had been brought up by an army of governesses and tutors. He probably saw them once a day, if that. Although his sons would have been at Eton or Harrow, learning to gamble as her own brothers had! And what on earth was she thinking to find the man attractive? For a start he was married and *years* older than she was and she was a *widow*. A widow who had loved her husband to distraction. Besides, it was ridiculous for her pulse to leap and skitter simply because an attractive gentleman had spoken to her and made her laugh. He had been kind. Polite. And stuffy and critical.

But he was married, which made it appalling that she had permitted herself to feel any attraction. And he was the first person from her past in years who had neither ignored her, nor let his contempt show. Although to be fair, not all the gentlemen ignored her, although their contempt took a different form to that of the ladies. To these gentlemen a widow with a shady reputation was just the thing to enliven a dull existence. Not that she could quite see Huntercombe trolling for a mistress in a bookshop, even if she'd been dressed in silks rather than this dreary grey wool. Even if he *had* thought she couldn't control her own children.

Harry shot ahead to open the door, something he hadn't done on the way in. *No gentleman behaves badly to his mother.* 'Shall I carry the books, Mama?'

Her breath jerked in. The man who followed them from Chelsea stood across the road, his expression insolent as he looked her up and down. She stiffened. Curse it! Who was he? It wouldn't be the first time someone had recognised her and followed, thinking she would be ripe for an affair. Lord Pickford had done just that in May, taking her rebuff in bad part.

'Mama? Shall I—oh, just *look*!'

Books forgotten, Harry rushed down the steps towards a brown and white spaniel.

'Harry!'

To her amazement Harry actually stopped and looked back. 'Oh, Mama, please may I pet him? I don't think he'll bite. Do look at him!'

Emma choked back a laugh. Judging by the spaniel's flopping tongue and insane tail, the only danger was that Harry might be licked to death. She doubted anyone could walk past the creature without stopping to pat him. However, to her amusement, although the dog raised a beseeching paw at Harry, he remained firmly seated.

'Yes. You may pat him, Harry.'

Harry was beside the dog in a flash, holding out his hand to be sniffed and approved.

'Do you think he's lost, Mama?' Georgie tugged at her hand. 'We could take him home and look after him until his owner finds him.'

Emma shook her head. 'I don't think he's lost. Look, he has a very handsome collar with a brass plate on it.'

'There's a name on it,' Harry announced. 'Fergus.'

The dog wriggled ecstatically, his tail a blur of feathered delight.

'He *might* be lost,' Georgie argued. 'Maybe his master is horrid and he's looking for someone nice. We're nice.'

'I am afraid, Georgiana Mary,' said a deep voice behind them, 'that Fergus is not lost at all. He's merely waiting for me.'

Emma closed her eyes on a silent curse, wondering if her children could possibly embarrass her any more in one day, as she realised precisely who the supposedly horrid master was. Huntercombe might be stuffy, but he wasn't horrid.

If Fergus had been pleased to meet Harry, his reaction to Huntercombe was nothing short of ecstatic. Still sitting, he quivered all over, uttering whimpers of delight.

'All right, lad.' Huntercombe clicked his fingers and the dog bounded to him, one wriggle of joy as he danced about his master's boots.

'He's awfully well trained, sir,' Harry said. 'He stayed sitting the whole time.'

Huntercombe's smile, even directed at Harry, left Emma breathless. 'Thank you, Harry. He's a good fellow. Looking forward to his run in the park now.'

Harry's eyes lit up. 'Really? We're going to the park. We always do after coming here. Don't we, Georgie?'

Georgie backed him up at once. 'Yes. We do. And we like dogs. Especially dogs in the park.'

'Oh. Well.' While not looking offended by this very unsubtle hint, Huntercombe seemed somewhat taken aback.

'Would you like to come with us, sir?' Harry asked, as though inviting a marquess for a walk in the park was the sort of thing one did.

Emma plastered a placating smile on her face. 'Harry, I'm sure his lordship has—'

'That's very kind of you, Harry,' Huntercombe said.

At least he's letting him down gently.

Huntercombe continued. 'Fergus is definitely looking forward to his run and I'm sure he would enjoy it more if he had some young legs to run with him. Ma'am, if you permit?'

Shock held Emma silent long enough to see

Harry's shining eyes. Both children loved dogs, as she did. Yet having one was simply impossible— a dog needed more meat than she could afford.

'May we, Mama?'

Georgie tugged at her hand. 'Please, Mama?'

Oh, devil take it! What harm could there be walking through the park with an acquaintance of her *father's* for goodness sake? A few more smears on her reputation were neither here nor there. And she knew Huntercombe's reputation. He was a gentleman and married to boot. He could view her as nothing more than an acquaintance's impoverished daughter.

She glanced up to see the man across the street walking away east along Piccadilly. Probably he had been put off by Huntercombe's presence. Her tension eased.

'Thank you, sir. Your company will be most welcome.'

For a short while she would enjoy the company of someone from her own world who viewed her as neither an embarrassing acquaintance, nor a potentially convenient widow. What possible harm could it do?

By the time they reached the park Hunt had concluded that Lady Emma Lacy was a conundrum. He discovered that she read the newspapers and was well informed, but unlike most ladies she was uninterested in the doings of society. She deftly kept the conversation general, avoiding anything that verged on the personal. In short, she held him at bay.

The moment they left the more populated areas of the park he took a well-chewed old cricket ball from his pocket—something his valet and tailor shuddered over—and hurled it. Fergus, ever reliable, had hurtled after it and brought it back to drop at his feet. Seeing Harry's delighted face, Hunt at once suggested that he and his sister might share the task. Harry having promptly handed Hunt the box of books, the children raced off, the dog leaping about them.

'How far do you wish to go before turning back?' he asked eventually. Fergus would run all day given the chance.

She frowned. 'Turn back?'

'Home.' He gestured back towards Mayfair.

'Oh.' She flushed. 'I live in Chelsea. We walked in.'

He wasn't sure why that brought colour to her cheeks. Quite a number of well-to-do people lived in Chelsea. Far better for the children than living right in town. 'Are you near the river?'

'Not particularly. But nowhere in Chelsea is very far from the river.' Her gaze followed the children and dog. 'Thank you, sir. They are enjoying themselves very much.'

'Every boy should have a dog,' he said.

Her brows lifted. 'I can assure you that Georgie would object heartily to the limitations of that statement. She would love to have a dog.'

He watched as Fergus, tongue hanging out, tail

spinning, dropped the ball at the child's feet. Georgie picked up the by now probably revolting ball between finger and thumb, managing to throw it about ten feet.

'But you don't have one?'

'No.' Her gaze followed Fergus's pounce on the ball.

'Why ever not?' He could have bitten his tongue out as her mouth flattened and the colour rose in her cheeks again.

'Because, my lord, I cannot afford to feed a dog.'

'Cannot—?' He broke off and several things registered properly. She was neatly dressed, but not in anything approaching the first stare of fashion. Furthermore, now he looked properly, beyond those tired blue eyes, he noticed that her pelisse was worn and rubbed, her hat a very plain straw chip trimmed with a simple black ribbon. And Harry had said something about Georgie being sick and the medicine costing too much for them to buy a kite as well.

'We must start for home,' she said. 'I'd better call the children.'

'May I escort you?' Why the devil had he asked that? Of course it was the polite thing to do, but she had clearly consented to his accompanying them for the children's sake. And wasn't that *his* motivation? Admittedly, he liked the children. Excellent manners, but not so regimented they couldn't engage in a good squabble. And he liked that they were so deeply smitten with a dog.

Her chin came up and she stiffened. 'There is no need, sir. It was very kind of you to bring Fergus this far for them.'

He raised his brows. 'Who said I came this far just so the children could enjoy Fergus?' Hadn't he?

'If you are suggesting, sir—'

'That I enjoyed your company? I did. And I should very much like—'

'No.'

He blinked. 'No?'

Her mouth, that lovely soft mouth, flattened. 'No, as in "no, thank you, I am not interested".'

Not interested? Not interested in *what*, precisely? What on earth had set up her bristles?

'Harry! Georgie!' She stepped away, beckoning to the children.

'Mama!'

Hunt cleared his throat. 'Permit me—' He stuck two fingers in his mouth—a skill his mother had deplored and his sisters still did—and let out an ear-splitting whistle.

Fergus, the ball in his mouth, bounded back, the children racing behind. Hunt made a grab for the dog, but Fergus danced out of reach, grinning around the ball. Hunt laughed. Fergus knew perfectly well it was time for home, but Hunt played his silly game for a moment while the children shrieked encouragement to the dog. At last, slightly out of breath, Hunt said firmly, 'Sit.' Fergus sat at once, the expression on his face saying very clearly *cheat*. He spat the ball out at Hunt's feet.

'Good boy.' He bent to pick up the now completely revolting ball between thumb and forefinger.

'Are you putting it in your pocket?' Georgie demanded. 'Like *that*? *Eeeww!*' She fished in the little embroidered pocket hanging from her waist and brought out a handkerchief. 'Here.' She held it out. 'You can wrap it in that, sir.'

'That's very kind, Georgie,' he said gravely, not meeting Lady Emma's eyes. 'But your mama will not wish you to lose your handkerchief.'

Georgie's expression took on an air of wholly spurious innocence. 'You could bring it back if you walked Fergus to Chelsea. We live on Symons Street, in the row behind the stone yard.'

If not for the frozen expression on Lady Emma's face, he might have laughed.

'Georgie.' Lady Emma's voice was very firm. 'His lordship does not have the time to walk all the way to Chelsea. You have other handkerchiefs.'

Georgie's face fell. 'Oh. It's all right, sir. I do have lots of hankies.' But her gaze lingered on the dog.

'One should never contradict a lady, of course.' Hunt accepted the handkerchief, wrapped the ball carefully and dropped it in his pocket. 'But I can always find time to walk Fergus and he very much enjoys Chelsea Common.' He raised his hat. 'Good day, ladies.' He held out his hand. 'Harry.'

Beaming, Harry shook hands. 'It was very nice to meet you, sir.'

Yes, excellent manners. He smiled. *'Au revoir.'*

He turned and left them, Fergus trotting beside him.

Georgie's clear voice followed them. 'He said *au revoir*, Mama. That means until we see each other again! He's going to come!'

Well, at least someone would be pleased to see him. But he still couldn't think what the devil he had said to make Lady Emma poker up like that. *No*, as in, *No, thank you, I am not interested.*

And he was damned if he could think why that annoyed him. It wasn't as if he'd been planning to see her again, had he? Just return the child's handkerchief, because she'd been so delightfully open about her desire to see Fergus again. That was all.

Hunt was turning into Upper Grosvenor Street when it dawned that a gentleman strolling with an impoverished widow might have less altruistic intentions than walking a dog and indulging two children…

'Bloody hell, Fergus,' he said. 'She thought I was trolling for a mistress!'

Fergus looked up, interested. Hunt shook his head. At the very least he was going to clear up that misunderstanding, but—

A carriage halted beside him.

He recognised the carriage, horses and coachman even before Letty put her head out of the window. 'Giles! How very convenient. If you stop in now I have that list.'

This list would be much more appropriate. Women of some maturity and dignity who would understand the advantages and convenience of a second marriage. But the thought of perusing that list under Letty's gimlet gaze and no doubt being expected to indicate a preference...

'Thank you, Letty. But I have Fergus with me. Perhaps you might send it around?'

That would buy time to consider the possibilities in private.

Letty gave Fergus a disapproving stare. 'I cannot think why you have a dog in town at all. Or, if you must, why a servant can't take it for an airing.'

'Well, you see, Letty,' Hunt said cheerfully, 'since he is *my* dog, *I* like to walk him. So, send your—'

Letty snorted. 'One can only hope that a wife will curb some of your bachelor habits. I dare say I can put up with the wretched animal in my drawing room. It appears well behaved enough. I shall see you in a few minutes.' She rapped with her cane on the ceiling. 'Drive on, Bagsby!'

Hunt stared after the carriage as it lumbered away from the curb. He glanced down at the dog. 'Much help *you* were! Couldn't you have misbehaved for once?'

Fergus just grinned up at him. Hunt snorted. 'It would serve you right if I *did* let a wife change some of my bachelor habits.'

Hunt, fortified with his brother-in-law's brandy, rose as Letty sailed into her drawing room a short time later. She gave Fergus, lying quietly by the hearth, a disapproving look, but said nothing. Hunt suspected that not a single woman on this new list would care for dogs in the house. Idly he wondered if Lady Emma minded dogs in the house.

Letty took the chair opposite him and arranged her skirts very precisely. 'Caro and I have given a great deal of thought to this.' She frowned. 'The last thing you want in a wife is any breath of scandal. I am sad to say that there is often far more than a breath about many widows.' She gave him a searching look. 'Are you sure you won't consider—?'

'No virgins,' he said. He cleared his throat as Letty's brows shot up. 'Your list?'

Letty scowled. 'It isn't a *list*, as such. Merely a suggestion.'

'*A* suggestion?' He stared at her. 'Just one? Do you mean that in the length and breadth of Britain you can only suggest *one* possible candidate? Who?'

Letty preened a little. '*My* goddaughter—Amelia Trumble.'

Hunt stared. 'Amelia? She must be well over thirty, surely!'

Letty bristled. 'Twenty-seven. And she is a very good sort of woman,' she said. 'You could hardly do better, especially since you already know her.'

Hunt didn't see that as an advantage. Amelia Trumble was about the most boring female of his acquaintance. Her late husband, eldest son of Baron Trumble, had been equally dull. How a young woman of twenty-seven contrived to make herself look and act forty, he wasn't sure, but...

'Dear Amelia is the very pattern of Respect-ability and Good Sense,' Letty pronounced.

He knew that. And Respectability and Good Sense were all very admirable. But did they have to be allied with Dullness?

'She would make you a most dutiful wife, Giles. She has every qualification—including an annuity that remains with her and would do for pin money. Nor will you be bothered with her son. As Trumble's heir he will remain in the custody of his grandfather.'

Hunt frowned. 'She would leave the child with Trumble?' He was surprised that it bothered him. Most men would be delighted not to have the evidence of a woman's previous marriage underfoot, but—he saw a woman wearing a neat grey gown, her daughter snuggled in her lap... He shoved the memory away.

'Trumble would not countenance otherwise,' Letty said. 'No doubt Amelia would visit the child, but she is not unduly sentimental.'

The memory of Emma's face as she accepted her son's shamefaced apology slid into his mind. *Unduly sentimental?*

But...he didn't dislike Amelia. She just didn't interest him. Did that matter? If Letty and Caro were satisfied he'd done his duty...

'Very well. I'll consider your suggestion. By the by, are you acquainted with Lady Emma Lacy?'

She blinked. 'Who is—? Good God! Emma Brandon-Smythe, you mean? Giles, she may be a widow, but you are *not* considering an alliance with *that* dreadful creature, are you?'

'What?' Hunt stared at her. 'No. Of course not.' *Dreadful creature?* 'I ran into her in Hatchard's, that's all. It took me a moment to place her.'

Letty snorted. 'No doubt the shameless hussy presumed upon your acquaintance with Dersingham and forced herself upon your notice. She ran off, you know—from the altar, no less!—to live openly with young Lacy. And *then* persuaded him to make an honest woman of her. Dersingham cast her off regardless and naturally the Keswicks do not recognise her.' Letty shuddered. 'If she approaches you again, you must ignore her as everybody else does. I wonder at Hatchard allowing her in the shop. I shall have a word with him about that. Disgraceful that she is permitted to mingle with her betters!'

'Oh, that won't be necessary, Letty.' Hunt's mind spun. Lived openly with Lacy? In sin? Ran off from the altar? That had to be exaggeration. 'I doubt she will approach me again.' Not after she'd come close to telling him to go to hell. In fact, she hadn't approached him at all. *He* had spoken to *her*. How the devil could he deflect Letty? The last thing he wanted was to have Letty force John Hatchard to refuse Emma admittance! 'Ah, is Amelia in town?'

Letty looked gratified. 'Dear Amelia is not in town just yet, you know. Would you wish me to—?'

'No. Absolutely not.' Hunt fixed her with a

steely look. 'You will say nothing whatsoever to anyone about this. Is that quite clear?' Thank God he'd deflected her from Emma Lacy. 'Just let me know when Amelia is expected in town.' Letty was right; for a man who wanted a convenient wife, Amelia would be the perfect choice. Convenience was often a trifle dull.

However, he *would* return Miss Georgie's handkerchief. He was going to make quite sure Lady Emma understood that the Marquess of Huntercombe only trolled for books in Hatchard's.

Chapter Three

Disappointment and rage lashed at Emma over the next two days. Disappointment that Huntercombe's apparently disinterested kindliness towards the children had been anything but disinterested and rage that he had used them in his attempt to get close to her.

Harry and Georgie could talk of little but Lord Huntercombe and Fergus. Emma even overheard Harry tell his sister what a jolly good idea she'd had with the handkerchief. 'Because no matter what Mama says, I'm sure he'll bring it back!'

Georgie, openly smug about the predicted success of her scheme, asked Emma, ever so casually, just how long it took to launder a handkerchief. 'In a big house, Mama.'

It might have been funny had Emma not been so angry. And if she were honest, angry with herself for feeling even for an instant that betraying flicker of interest. Had she accidentally encouraged him? Did she have to be rude to every gentleman who spoke to her to avoid this sort of thing? And somewhere in all that there was hurt. Why she had thought Huntercombe would be different, she had no idea. After eleven years she knew how society viewed her.

She did not have the heart to disabuse the children of their conviction that Huntercombe would call. How could she, without giving an explanation as to *why* she was so sure he would not? Six and ten was far too young for them to realise how gentlemen viewed their mother. Instead she took advantage of any dry weather to get them out for walks as much as possible, trying everything she could think of to keep them busy and distracted.

And yet walks inevitably brought on chatter of how fast Fergus could run, how he twisted in mid-air to catch the ball and when they might see him again.

So the knock on the door on the third morning was as unwelcome as it was unexpected. Nor did Emma appreciate the involuntary leap of her own pulse. Harry and Georgie, just sat down for their morning lessons, looked up, eyes bright.

'It might be *him*, Mama!'

Emma gave Georgie a quelling look. 'Him? The cat's father?'

'Fergus!'

She changed her snort of laughter into a cough. The Marquess of Huntercombe, outranked by his own dog. Bessie's footsteps hurried down the short hallway and the door creaked open. A velvet-dark voice spoke, the tone questioning, and Emma's pulse skittered. Anger, she assured herself. Unfortunately it didn't feel like anger, but that did not change how she was going to deal with this.

'Yes, yer honour. What? Right. I'll ask her then.'

'Mama!' Georgie and Harry jigged in their seats.

'Stay where you are.' She held them in place with a raised hand. 'It might be a complete stranger.'

More hurried steps and Bessie opened the door, face pink. 'It's a lordship, mum! Do I let him in?'

Despite her anger, Emma suppressed another laugh. The Most Noble Marquess of Huntercombe left kicking his heels on the doorstep…

'It *is* him!' Harry and Georgie let out a unison shriek of delight, surged from their seats and stampeded past Bessie and into the hall.

'Sir! Good morning!'

'Look! It's Fergus!'

Bessie held out a visiting card. 'Said 'is name was Huntercombe, mum. Not Fergus.'

'The dog,' Emma said. Damn his eyes! Must he make it so difficult? But it was not only Huntercombe who was making it difficult. She had repelled other men with ease. It was her own unruly attraction to him that was difficult. The others had been annoying. Huntercombe's approach infuriated her.

Huntercombe's deep, quiet voice returned the children's greetings.

'Come in, sir!'

His lordship's response to Harry's invitation

was dismissed by Georgie. 'Of course she won't. It's this way.'

A moment later his broad shoulders filled the doorway. 'I beg your pardon, Lady Emma.' A tinge of colour stained his cheekbones. 'I did ask your servant if you were at home, but—'

'We're nearly always at home,' Georgie said. 'Except when we aren't.'

Huntercombe's eyes crinkled. 'I see. The thing is, Miss Georgie, a gentleman should always give a lady the chance to send him to the right-a-bout if she does not wish to see him.'

The smile in the grey eyes as he looked at Georgie was completely disarming. Emma had to remind herself that he was married, that he had no business calling on her alone, disarming her— even unintentionally—or causing her pulse to skip with that smile that stayed in his eyes and warmed her from the inside out. And he was years older than she was, although that didn't seem to matter as much as it had when she was twenty. To Emma, at twenty, the greying hair on Sir Augustus Bolt, the man her father had decreed she was to marry, had horrified her. But now, curse it, on Huntercombe the greying dark hair—especially those silvery patches, just there at the temples— was simply gorgeous. And unlike Sir Augustus, who had run sadly to seed by forty-nine along with a pronounced stoop to his shoulders, Huntercombe was still straight, broad-shouldered and looked as though he kept himself fit.

She forced her mind to function. What mattered, she reminded herself, was that *he* was married and *she* had two children to protect. Very well. He'd called. So she'd take his advice and send him to the right-a-bout. And since there was no way she could be even remotely private with someone in a house this size—

'As it happens, sir, we are about to go for a walk,' she said. 'Would you care to join us?'

Harry stared at her. 'You said we had to do our lessons.'

Emma wondered why children always contradicted you like that. 'I've changed my mind. The sun is out now, but I wouldn't care to wager upon it staying that way.'

'But, Mama,' Georgie looked up from patting Fergus, eyes wide, 'When Harry said that at breakfast, you said—'

'Don't you want to come for a walk?' Huntercombe asked mildly.

'Of course we do,' Harry said.

Huntercombe nodded. 'Then stop reminding your mother about lessons. Her conscience may get the better of her.'

Emma stifled another laugh, wishing his dry sense of humour wasn't so wickedly appealing.

Harry grinned. 'Yes, sir. Come on, Georgie. We'll fetch our things.'

He'd meant to return the handkerchief, assure Lady Emma that she had been thoroughly mistaken and leave. But now he was going for a walk with the *dreadful creature*. Although he had to admit explaining Lady Emma's mistake in that tiny house with two children present might have been awkward.

Hunt noted that Emma again kept the conversation in the realm of polite generalities as they waited for the children. Nor by so much as a flicker did her demeanour suggest that she had received him in anything less than the most elegant drawing room.

Whatever he had expected of her home, Hunt realised, it had not been the reality of this shabby-genteel, whitewashed parlour. It was spotlessly clean and he wondered if she did the dusting herself. The floorboards—no carpet, just scrubbed, bare boards—were swept. The furniture, what there was of it, was polished to a gleam and books crammed a battered set of shelves beside the window. An elderly lamp stood on the table and a plain wooden clock ticked on the shelf over the clean and empty grate. The chill in the room suggested that the fire was lit only in the evenings.

Emma Lacy, he realised, lived on the edge of very real poverty and that puzzled him. Surely she had something to live on? Unless Lacy had muddled their money away. That was quite possible. Anyone brought up as Lacy and Emma had been would struggle to manage on much less. The younger sons of dukes, having been raised to luxury, then left with relatively little, were notoriously expensive and debt-ridden. A very pertinent reason why fathers preferred not to marry their daughters to them.

She invited him to sit down and chatted about

the renewed war with France. Not for long though. Harry and Georgie appeared in their outdoor things very quickly.

'We brought yours, too, Mama.' Harry had a brown pelisse over one shoulder and Georgie clutched a bonnet and gloves.

'Thank you.' Emma smiled at them. 'That was very thoughtful of you.'

'We wanted to have lots of time to throw the ball for Fergus,' Harry explained.

'Ah. Silly me.' Emma's eyes danced and something inside Hunt warmed as he saw again the open affection in her face. Whatever else this house might lack it was not deficient in love. And the thought crept up on him: this was not a woman who would leave her children to marry again.

'That reminds me—' He drew Georgie's laundered handkerchief—God knew what his valet had thought when handed it with a request for an immediate wash—from his pocket and handed it to her. 'Thank you. I've brought an extra one of my own today.'

'Oh.' Georgie looked crestfallen as she tucked the scrap of cambric into her sleeve. 'I wouldn't have minded lending you another.'

Emma cleared her throat. 'Georgie, Lord Huntercombe cannot keep visiting merely to return your belongings.'

Shards of ice edged her voice, but this was not the moment to launch into explanations. Time enough for that when the children were out of earshot. 'Shall we go?' he suggested.

* * *

The children raced ahead with Fergus, but obeyed Emma's injunction not to get too far in front. A biting wind whipped around them, bringing bright colour to her pale cheeks. She had ignored his offered arm, tucking her gloved hands into a threadbare velvet muff. He wondered just how old it was, if she had owned it before her elopement.

'You should not have come,' she said.

Hunt raised his brows at the cool, not to say imperious, tone. She had dropped the veneer of affability like a brick. 'No? Why not, ma'am?'

Anger flashed in her eyes. 'I told you the other day that I am not interested. And I resent you using my children to force my compliance this morning!'

He raised his brows. 'I am sorry to contradict you, ma'am, but I had no intention of going for a walk. *You* informed *me* that you were going for a walk and invited me to join you. However, since you have raised the issue, let us be very clear on one thing; I am *not* looking for a mistress!'

She stopped dead and he halted obligingly. Amused, he saw that her eyes were blank; he'd managed to shock her. 'That is what you thought, is it not?'

'Yes.' Her voice sounded strangled, as if she were having trouble getting any sound out at all. 'But, still, even if that is true—your wife, what will *she* think if anyone sees us together?'

He froze. 'My wife?'

She glared at him. 'Yes. I may have been out of society for a long time, sir, but I remember Lady Huntercombe perfectly well.'

'Do you?' How did this equate with the *dreadful creature* Letty assumed had accosted him boldly in Hatchard's? A woman furious with him because she believed he was about to make improper advances to her and doubly furious because she remembered his wife?

'Yes. I liked her. She was kind.'

He couldn't help smiling at her. 'She was, wasn't she?'

Emma stopped, stared up at him. *'Was?'*

He nodded curtly. 'I have been a widower for some years, Lady Emma.'

'Oh. I'm… I'm very sorry, sir.'

He felt himself stiffen. 'No need. A misunderstanding. As you said, you have been out of society. You weren't to know.'

'I meant,' some of the astringency returned, 'that I am sorry for your loss. She was lovely.'

It was a very long time since anyone had offered their condolences. Of course, it had *been* a long time since Anne and the children died.

'Thank you.' He let out a breath. Eleven years gone and he was thinking about marrying Amelia Trumble. Maybe. If he could screw his good sense to the sticking place.

'Mama! Watch this!'

They turned to watch Harry hurl the ball far and high. Fergus raced underneath, leaping with a lithe twist to take the catch in mid-air.

'See, Mama! Just like we said!'

Fergus came racing back, spat the ball out at Harry's feet.

Emma turned back to him, laughter dancing in her eyes. 'Thank you. I'm sorry I was so rude. But I'm not going to be sorry that I accidentally forced you to come for a walk. This is such a treat for them.'

A treat. Taking a dog for a walk and throwing a ball. And she had been about to give them their morning lessons when he arrived. Amelia had a child. A young boy who would remain in his grandfather's custody if his mother remarried, doubtless with a nanny and tutors, but still…without his mother. He hadn't really thought about it. Just that it was helpful to know she was fertile… He hadn't thought about the child, or children. Was it *right* for a woman to be forced to abandon her children? Would Trumble allow the child to spend time with them if he *did* marry Amelia? *She is not unduly sentimental.* Wouldn't Amelia *want* the child with her?

'Tell me, Lady Emma, if you ever remarried, would you consent to leave your children behind?'

'*What?*'

What insanity had prompted him to ask *that*? 'An academic question.' There. That was better—a calm, logical approach. 'You see, I am considering marriage and I wish to know what is reasonable to expect of a woman. *Should* she be expected to leave her children if she remarries? If, say, her father-in-law is their legal guardian?'

Those dancing blue eyes chilled. 'No. But the law doesn't agree with me. Nor would most men.' Her mouth flattened. 'You, for example, seemed to assume that Keswick must be my children's guardian. He is not.'

Hunt frowned. 'He is not their legal guardian?'

'No. I am. Keswick has nothing to do with them.'

He tried to imagine Amelia, virtuously conventional, spurning her father-in-law's authority at all, let alone so brazenly. He ought to be shocked that Lady Emma had done so. Instead, he was shocked that he *wasn't* shocked.

'So a gentleman offering you marriage would have to take the children?'

'A very academic question, my lord, but yes. And *I* would retain guardianship.'

An iceberg would sound warmer. Yet somehow all his calm, logical reasons for considering Amelia were sliding into ruin. And in their place...

No. Impossible. Emma Lacy was not at all the sort of bride he ought to consider. And if he *were* to consider her he would need to know her a great deal better. But how could he further their acquaintance without her believing that he was, after all, pursuing her with less than honourable intent?

He took a very deep, careful breath. 'I should make it absolutely clear, ma'am that I am *not*, at this moment, offering you marriage.'

'I never imagined that you—' She stared. *'"At this moment?"'*

'However, I must marry again and you fit my…
requirements.'

He heard the sharp intake of breath and braced.

'Requirements?'

He was not fool enough to be lulled by those
dulcet tones.

'A clumsy word, Lady Emma, but honest. I am
too old—' and too emptied out '—to be tumbling
into love, so I am not looking for a giddy young
girl. I require a woman of maturity, but still young
enough to bear children.'

There. That was perfectly logical and rational.
He'd touched on all the relevant points.

'I see. You want a proven breeder, not an un-
tried filly.'

His mouth opened. He knew that. Unfortunately
nothing came out.

'Speechless, my lord?'

He laughed. He simply couldn't help it as that
warlike glint in her eyes started to dance again.
Eventually he stopped laughing. '*Touché*, ma'am.
At this point I should probably do better if I cut
my own tongue out.'

'Yes.' She gave him a puzzled glance. 'So, you
wish to remarry—'

'Yes.'

'And for some reason you think I might do.'

He winced. 'I beg your pardon if I gave the
impression that it was a matter of *you might do*. I
was trying to be sensible, not insulting. But, yes,
you do, er—'

'Fit your requirements.'

The long-forgotten burning sensation informed Hunt that he had actually blushed. 'Something like that.' Why did the ground simply not open up and swallow him?

'And along with your *requirements* are you also going to ask for references?' Her chin was up. 'Because I am afraid I cannot offer any. Quite the opposite, in fact.'

He looked at her. Really looked at her. The brief hint of laughter was gone again. In its place was... bitterness? No, not that. Resignation. As if she expected a rejection. Letty's words burned into him: *'Dersingham cast her off regardless, of course. And naturally the Keswicks do not recognise her.'*

'If you will forgive the impertinence, Emma, I think your children are your references.'

She stared at him. 'Oh.' Just that. *Oh.* And that lovely, soft mouth trembled into a smile that shook him to his very foundations. Was he insane? Hadn't Letty warned him? He wanted a wife who would not turn his life inside out. Now it would serve him right if he found himself fronting the altar with London's most notorious widow! Only... could she really have done anything truly scandalous? He was finding it harder and harder to believe...

Emma swallowed. *Your children are your references.* Just words. Probably meaningless ones. Yet she was melting like a puddle! He had not offered for her. She had to remember that. 'Then this is in the nature of a...courtship.'

He frowned. 'I suppose so. In a way. I—that is *we*—would need to know each other better. If I *were* to offer for you, I would be offering a marriage of convenience. I need an heir. In return, Harry and Georgie would be provided for and you would have a generous settlement and jointure. However, I have *not* done so.'

She flinched. His voice was cool, unemotional, his eyes shuttered. Totally at odds with the man who had enchanted Harry and Georgie, and kept his dog's revolting cricket ball in his pocket. The man who had said the children were her references.

His mouth tightened. 'I did not wish you to think my intentions were dishonourable.'

'No. I quite understand that—' *Children... I require an heir...* 'Sir, you say you need an heir, but I thought—'

'Smallpox.' He said it in a very distant voice. 'My wife and all three of our children. Then my half-brother died last year.'

Sometimes distance was all that could protect you from pain. 'I'm sorry,' she said simply.

For a moment he was silent. Then, 'It was a long time ago. But you see why I must marry again.'

She did. It was exactly the sort of marriage her father had arranged eleven years ago, and that she had fled from. Or was it? Was Huntercombe really offering what Augustus Bolt had offered? She didn't think so and now was not the time to discuss that. But Huntercombe was a very different man from Sir Augustus. Bolt had been arrogant, condescending, seeing her only as a well-bred, hopefully fertile, vessel for his political ambitions… and Dersingham had approved Bolt as exactly the man to curb a headstrong girl… That brought her back to reality with a jolt. *Did Huntercombe know the whole story?*

She took a deep breath. 'Are you aware that I was betrothed to Sir Augustus Bolt?'

Huntercombe frowned. 'I knew there had been another betrothal. It was to Bolt? I dare say Dersingham wanted the match.'

She nodded. 'I might have agreed in the end, but I had met Peter, you see, and—'

'You fell in love.'

Emma heard the guarded tone. She could imagine what he'd heard and she doubted the truth would be any more acceptable to him, even if he believed it.

'The wedding with Sir Augustus was set for my twenty-first birthday. But when Dersingham delivered me to the altar I refused my vows and walked out of St George's.'

There. It was out. And judging by his stunned expression he *hadn't* known. In a moment, when he had recovered from the shock, he would take his leave politely and she'd never see him again. No well-bred young lady jilted a man at all, let alone literally walking out on him at the altar straight into the arms of another man. Only now, when she had burned all her ships and bridges, did she know exactly how much she had wanted this chance. How much she had wanted someone to understand. Not forgive. She had never considered her marriage to require forgiveness.

Hunt could only stare at the woman before him, her chin up, defiant. He tried, and failed, to imagine any other young lady he had ever known doing something so utterly scandalous. Letty hadn't exaggerated at all. For once the gossip had been literal truth.

Although… *Gus Bolt*? The man must have been nearly fifty at the time. Exactly the sort of marriage Letty and Caro had assumed *he* would make. If the idea had horrified him, how must it have looked to a girl of twenty-one?

He stuck to practicalities. 'Was Lacy waiting outside the church?'

She flushed. 'In a way. We *hadn't* arranged it, although my parents thought we had. He had no idea what I was going to do. He just wanted to see me.' Her eyes became distant, remembering. '*I* didn't know I was going to do it until I walked out. And, well, there he was. We didn't stop to think. He took me to his great-aunt, Lady Bartle. She loathed Keswick and I stayed with her while the banns were called.' She gave him a very direct look. 'No one ever remembers that, or that Peter went to my father, asked permission to marry me and was refused. According to most of the stories Peter and I lived openly in sin until he deigned to make an honest woman of me.'

Hunt was silent. She had handed him what any sane man would consider sufficient cause for withdrawing. She was not at all an eligible bride for the Marquess of Huntercombe.

But what about Hunt? Would she be a comfortable wife for *him*?

A little voice crept into his head… *What would you have done if Anne's father had ordered her to marry someone else all those years ago? What, more to the point, would Anne have done?*

Peter Lacy had not been a bad match. Except for the fact that Dersingham and Keswick hated each other. Some quarrel decades ago and neither could let it go.

Emma's voice dragged him back to the present. 'I have shocked you, sir, but I thought it better that you knew the truth.'

Hunt took a deep breath. Headstrong, managing and distressingly independent she might be, but Emma's honesty was bone-deep. She had told him in the full expectation that he would walk away without a backward glance. She would not even blame him. 'Do you mind dogs in the house?' he asked.

She blinked. 'No, but what does that—'

'Excellent.' There was really nothing to say about her scandalous marriage. It was not his place to approve or disapprove. After all, it was in the past and if it meant she did not wish to give her heart again…well, he wasn't offering his own heart. Just his hand in marriage.

Now she was staring, those deep blue eyes slightly suspicious. 'I just told you I'm a walking scandal and you're worried about dogs in the house?'

He *ought* to be scandalised at what she'd done. Such behaviour argued that she was ungovernable. He knew that. And, yes, it would definitely cause a stir if he married her. But somehow that didn't worry him. Emma Lacy was the sort who stuck to her word. She hadn't tried to sugar-coat what she'd done, let alone hide it. She'd thrown it in his face before he could commit himself in any way. And if she *had* married Gus Bolt she'd *still* be married to him and *he'd* be dodging Amelia Trumble. Or worse.

'Were you happy with Lacy?' he asked at last and caught his breath.

A tender smile softened the stubborn set of her mouth.

'Oh, yes. Although what that has to say to—'

'Good.' He possessed himself of her hand and tucked it safely into the crook of his elbow as they started walking again. It felt right there. Completely right. *This* felt right. Logical. As long as he didn't imagine her one day smiling that way at the thought of *him*. 'I don't think you would have enjoyed marriage to Gus. God knows I wouldn't.' Her jaw dropped. Now he thought about it, it would be as bad as being married to Amelia. 'The man's a dead bore,' he went on. 'You'll need time to consider, but while you do so you may as well know exactly what I am—what I *would be*—offering.'

* * *

She hadn't said no outright. Hunt told himself that as he walked them home in the lengthening shadows. A light drizzle had started, nothing very much, but no one wanted the children to take a chill.

She hadn't said no. Instead she had listened to his suggested settlement for herself and the children, and agreed to what he asked; that he be allowed to call on her while they considered. Walk with them, get to know her and the children. She had very firmly stipulated no gifts of any sort, whatsoever. Reluctantly she had agreed that he might buy the children a few sweets. He understood that; she did not wish to build hope in the children, only to crush it if either of them did not, in the end, want the marriage. He suspected that she fully expected *him* to step back.

So he escorted them home and hoped. This could work. There was no reason it would not. He was attracted to her; *more*, he liked her. He liked the children. She was of his world, familiar with it, if temporarily out of place. She had not leapt at the chance of marriage. Even now she employed no arts to attract. If anything she was rather quiet, as if thinking. And yet the silence between them was not awkward. It was…companionable, that was the word. They had said what needed to be said for now, so they could just enjoy each other's company. At least he hoped she was enjoying his company. Perhaps she thought he was boring, like Gus Bolt.

As they reached her front door, she looked up at him, her expression serious. 'Thank you for understanding that I need to think about this.'

'Of course,' he said. 'It is a huge step, marriage.' It was a good thing that she would take the time to think about it logically and rationally. As he had done.

She smiled. 'Most men would think that they were the only ones who need to do any thinking about it. That a woman, especially in my situation, should simply say thank you very much— yes, please.'

'Is that what Gus Bolt thought?'

She flushed. 'I suppose he might have. My father told me that Sir Augustus had offered and *he* had accepted. That it was all settled. Sir Augustus was presented to me as my betrothed. I doubt either of them expected me to say anything about it at all. As far as my father was concerned it was none of my business.' She bit her lip. 'When I protested my father said I was being missish. That the marriage would work well enough if I just did as I was bid.'

Would Anne's father have insisted on the marriage even if Anne had been repulsed? It didn't bear thinking about. And here he was, perilously close to pushing Emma into marriage just because *he* could see no reason against it. She knew next to nothing about him. For all she knew he could be the sort of bastard who beat his wife. She had no one to protect her and ensure that the marriage settlement was equitable, or that her children would be protected. Women took a far greater risk in marriage than men.

Predictably, the children were lagging behind. They came up, faces a little downcast. Georgie took his hand and tugged on it. 'Will you come again, sir?'

He smiled, his fingers closing on the little hand. That felt right, too. 'Oh, yes. Your mother has said that I may. The day after tomorrow? If the weather is bad we could have an indoor picnic.' Tomorrow he would see his solicitor and have the most careful and decent marriage settlement drawn up that he could devise. If he pretended that he was overseeing a marriage settlement for Marianne…he bit his lip. Or Georgie. Would he one day negotiate a match for Georgie?

'An indoor picnic?' Georgie giggled. 'How do you do that?'

The question pushed back the abyss. 'You spread a picnic rug on the floor and sit on that, and you eat picnic food,' he said. Surely if he sent a message to the kitchen for food suitable to an indoor picnic his cook would rise to the occasion?

'What sort of food do you have for an indoor picnic, Mama?' Harry demanded.

Emma opened her mouth and shut it again, clearly uncertain.

'That,' Hunt said, 'is a secret. You'll have to wait and see.' Along with himself.

'But Mama has to know,' Harry argued. 'Because she'll have to cook it with Bessie.'

Hunt shook his head. 'Not when I've invited you to a picnic. That means I bring the picnic, you provide the games and entertainment.'

Georgie brightened. 'Backgammon. Mama's teaching me. And Harry can play chess.'

'And what does Mama do?' Emma's voice was very dry, but there was a twinkle in her eye.

'You keep us all in order,' Hunt informed her. 'I have no doubt that you're very good at it.'

She sighed. 'Wonderful.' Laughter danced in her eyes, luring him. 'A managing female.' She slipped a hand into her worn pelisse and drew out the house key. Hunt took it from her gently. There was little enough he could do for her until she agreed to marry him, but he could do this. He could show her that the Marquess of Huntercombe would be a courteous, kindly husband.

'I'll do that.' And wondered if he had overstepped the mark. But she smiled, a little wistfully he thought, as he slipped the key into the lock and turned it. A courtesy and a minor one at that. But he liked the thought of doing things for her.

Emma made the children say their goodbyes as soon as they were inside. 'Off to the kitchen, both of you. Hang your damp things by the fire and tell Bessie I said you could have some hot milk.'

'And cake?' Harry wheedled.

'A small piece,' Emma allowed, as she pulled off her gloves. 'Say goodbye to Lord Huntercombe.'

Georgie knelt down, hugged Fergus and shrieked with laughter as he licked her face. She jumped up, gave Hunt a ravishing smile. 'You don't need my hankie, do you, sir?'

Laughter welled up at the child's certainty. He shook his head. 'Not this time, Georgie. Enjoy your cake.'

'Thank you, sir.' Harry held out his hand and Hunt shook it.

He watched the children as they rushed down the short hallway, waving at the door into the kitchen. It banged behind them.

That left Emma. He took a deep breath as he pulled off his own gloves. There was only one way to say farewell to a woman you had sort of asked to marry you…he caught her hands and his breath jerked at that first touch of his bare hands on hers. He felt the warmth of her skin, the slight roughness of her hands that told him she did indeed do some of the housework. Those deep eyes, drowning blue, widened as he drew her closer. 'You permit?' He wanted to kiss her. Every fibre in his body urged him to do just that. But she was not a woman who either gave herself, or could be taken lightly.

For a moment she looked utterly confused. 'Permit? Oh!' A flush crept over her cheeks. He thought her fingers trembled a little, or perhaps his did. Whichever it was, his heart was suddenly pounding. Yes, he was definitely attracted to her. Rather more than that if he were to be honest about it. He wanted her and every instinct clamoured for him to take her in his arms and show her that.

But this was supposed to be a polite, decorous courtship. A chaste kiss would be more the thing.

'I think… I think I may have forgotten…'

Heat shot through him at the soft confession. 'I haven't,' he assured her. Releasing her hands, he took her in his arms and drew her closer until their bodies touched and his blood hammered in a rhythm he had thought lost. It was not as though he had been a monk these past few years, but this was different. And not merely because he was thinking of marriage. It was just…different. She felt *right* in his arms, soft breasts against him, her eyes dark in her flushed face. She smelled of soap, just soap, rain-damp wool, and warm, sweet Emma.

'My lord—'

'Hunt.' He put his hand under her chin. Lord, she was soft. Peach soft, silk soft. 'My friends call me Hunt. Will you be my friend for now, Emma?' He stroked the delicate line of her throat, knew the leap and quiver of her pulse under his fingers. And wanted. Burned. *A chaste kiss.*

'Yes.' It was no more than a whisper, yet he heard it in every corner of his being as he lowered his mouth to hers and feathered the lightest, briefest kiss over her lips. It nearly broke his control, because her lips flowered under his, opening on the sweetest, softest sigh, inviting him in. Everything in him leapt to meet her response and he took the kiss deeper, tasting the warmth and shy welcome of her mouth. She met him, took the rhythm from him and their tongues matched, danced. Her body moulded to his, supple and pliant under his hands. He found the curve of her bottom, pressed to bring her more fully against his aching shaft and heard the soft gasp of shock.

A kiss. Just a kiss. This was more than just a kiss.

And he was going to want more than just sex... *Damn.*

Somehow he broke the kiss, released her and stepped back, his body taut with protest. Just a kiss. He would not give her the least reason to think he subscribed to society's usual attitude to widows with a shady past. Even if his body had no discretion, he didn't have to give it free rein. Not until he had her to wife. And even then, this was to be a marriage of convenience. The sort where a gentleman visited his wife's bed, then retired to his own.

'*Au revoir*, ma'am.' He raised his hat, put his gloves back on and left. Before he could change his mind. The door safely closed behind him, Hunt used the short walk back to the inn where he had left his carriage to remind himself exactly what a marriage of convenience entailed. An alliance of mutual benefit. A contract, an arrangement that would not require any changes to the routine of his life. Except for regular sex. As enjoyable as he could make it for both of them. But not passion. They would be friends with an affectionate regard for one another. Not lovers in any more than the physical sense of the word.

Emma only permitted herself to think about Hunt's not-quite offer after she had kissed Harry goodnight. She went back down to the parlour and tried to consider it dispassionately.

There were no logical arguments against. Not if he could accept her past.

Hunt was offering a future for the children. Without even waiting to be asked he had said that he would dower Georgie as if she were his own daughter and named a sum that had nearly made Emma's jaw drop. Harry could have a good tutor, go to school, university and be trained for a profession. There would be money settled on him as if he were Hunt's younger son. Money would be settled on her to provide for her in the event of Hunt's death.

I'm not precisely a spring chicken. She smiled at the memory of his wry voice. How old *was* he? She was no spring chicken herself.

He offered passage back into the world from which she had been exiled. She had never regretted the exile for herself, only the difficulties of providing for the children. But now she had a way back and a future for her children. All she had to do was marry him without love on either side. Instead she would have respect, some affection and kindness. And the title of Marchioness of Huntercombe.

She liked him. He was a good man, honourable to the core. She had enjoyed his company both the other day and today. But she had *loved* Peter. Passionately. If she married Hunt she would be marrying for advantage. Though she could not pretend it would *only* be for the children's sake. She wouldn't insult Hunt by wearing pretty clothes again and accepting jewels from him, while pretending they were sack cloth and ashes she wore for the sake of Harry and Georgie. Nor could she pretend that she would not enjoy sharing her bed with a man again.

No. Not just any man—Hunt. Her breath caught. She wanted him. Her whole body hummed at the memory of that kiss. Hours later and the shock of awareness lingered, with the faint enticing odour of sandalwood soap, damp wool and warm male. She could still feel the fierce strength of his arms as he held her and her breath hitched at the remembered taste of his kiss, hot and male, as her mouth had trembled into that swift, shocking response. Heat crept over her cheeks at the memory of his erection pressed against her belly. Had her response shocked him? Would he think her a wanton or, even worse, desperate to have responded so fast? So freely? He had called her *ma'am* afterwards and left immediately, but—she was being foolish. *He* was the one who had initiated the kiss. If he didn't want a response then he should have delivered a chaste peck to the cheek. *He* was the one who had pulled her against him.

But she had wanted him, still wanted him, and it bothered her. Other men had made advances to her in the last few years. None of them had interested her and not just because they had offered nothing more than an affair. She hadn't even been attracted, let alone tempted. If Hunt had wanted an affair, well, she hoped she would have refused, but she could admit to herself that without the children to consider it would be tempting.

He had asked her to be his friend, but with very little encouragement, or perhaps none at all, she could do very much more than simply *like* him. There was something about the quiet confidence, the dignity that was far more than his rank—that was simply *him*. And he was kind. Not in a patronising sort of way; that could annoy. His kindness was bone-deep. And, she smiled, there was something very appealing about a man so obviously fond of his dog. He had been open with her, honest. She would be a fool to refuse…*if*, in the end, he offered for her. Because he had *not* offered marriage as yet. He had asked to court her, to have a chance for them to become acquainted.

And there was the other thing that bothered her; she already knew her answer. Just as she had with Peter almost from the first moment of meeting him at that house party so long ago. They had ridden out in a large group, but somehow it had been as if no one else existed from that moment. And she had known, just as she knew now. Although it was a little different. With Peter she had known that she was falling in love; with Hunt she simply knew that she wanted to marry him, that she could be happy with him.

She who, according to her parents, had flung her life away for love was now prepared to marry for convenience.

For safety. For her children's future.

Only there had been that kiss… Something inside her fluttered, something she had thought if not dead, then asleep.

Chapter Four

In the ensuing week Emma was careful not to allow the children to think of Hunt as anything more than a friend of their father's. He called three times, including two indoor picnics, and by the end of the third outing—a walk, since the weather relented—Emma had no doubts at all. If he offered she would accept. How could she do otherwise with a man who read fairy tales to Georgie on a rainy afternoon? And the way he slipped on his reading glasses was ridiculously attractive in a bookish and scholarly way. Under his tutelage Harry's chess had improved greatly. He had lent Harry a small book on tactics which Harry had his nose in whenever permitted.

They had not discussed marriage, but she assumed if he was still visiting, then he was still considering it. Only…he hadn't really kissed her again. Oh, he kissed her goodbye each time, a careful, chaste brush of his lips on her cheek. Exactly as he might kiss a sister.

That bothered her more than she liked. Not that she wanted him making advances to her, but when he had kissed her that first time…

Perhaps he *had* thought she was too eager and wished to indicate that their marriage should be conducted along more decorous lines. She hoped she could take a hint, but while she thought she could manage a marriage of convenience, she wasn't sure she would be entirely happy in a marriage where she would be expected to curb her enjoyment of the marriage bed. On the other hand, in a perverse way, she might feel less disloyal to Peter if she wasn't looking forward to the marriage quite so much in quite that way.

But she liked Hunt and looked forward to his visits, perhaps a little more than was wise. But now, sewing in the parlour while the children played upstairs, she wondered if he would raise the subject of marriage again this afternoon. When he had left the day before yesterday he had said that they should talk next time…they *had* talked, just not about marriage, so presumably that was what he wanted to talk about. As long as they could be friends, if Huntercombe preferred a marriage where the marriage bed was only for the procreation of heirs, then she would accept that.

So the thrill that shot through Emma at the knock on the door was less than welcome as well as unexpected. It was barely two o'clock. Hunt was early and that embarrassing little leap of delight rubbed in the fact that she had been watching the clock for the past hour.

'Be the door, mum.' Bessie appeared in the doorway, wiping her hands on her apron. 'You want me to get it?'

Emma rose. 'No, it's all right, Bessie. It will be his lordship, so—'

Harry and Georgie clattered downstairs. 'Is it Lord Huntercombe, Mama? And Fergus?' Georgie demanded.

Emma smiled. 'Why don't I open the door and find out?'

'It's not raining,' Harry said. 'We'll be able to walk Fergus again.'

Emma thought ruefully that it would be his dog as much as himself that would render Hunt acceptable to her children as a stepfather.

She opened the door and blinked at the liveried footman.

He looked down his nose at her. 'The residence of Lady Emma Lacy, if you please.'

Emma took a proper look at the livery. It was only too familiar. 'This is it.'

The young man's expression registered shock, then condescension. 'Inform her ladyship that she has a visitor, my good woman.'

Emma narrowed her eyes. The impudent puppy couldn't be more than twenty. 'Do you always take that tone with your elders?' She used an imperious voice she never bothered with for Bessie.

His jaw dropped.

'Straighten your shoulders!' She knew an unholy glee as he snapped to attention. 'You may tell me yourself who is calling.' She knew perfectly well, but saw no reason to let him off the hook.

He looked winded. 'Ah—'

'Roger! Do they know the correct address, or not?'

The querulous voice had not changed in the least. 'Good day, Mother.' Emma stepped around the goggling Roger and walked to the carriage. 'Whatever brings you here?'

Lady Dersingham stared in disbelief, first at Emma then the house. 'I thought I must have the direction wrong. What a hovel!'

Emma took a firm grip on her temper. 'It's lovely to see you, too, Mother. Won't you come in?'

Louisa Dersingham actually hesitated, then said in wilting tones, 'The steps, Roger.'

Emma moved aside as the footman opened the carriage door and lowered the steps. She gritted her teeth as her mother descended as though tottering to her doom. She fixed the footman with a steely glare. 'Take her ladyship's bricks to the kitchen and ask my servant to reheat them.'

She knew her mother. Hell would freeze over before Louisa ventured out to Chelsea in November without hot bricks to her feet.

'Really, Emma.' Louisa's voice quavered piteously. 'If you *must* live out here, surely a nice villa by the river would be a more eligible situation. I believe they can be had quite reasonably.'

'No doubt. Come in, Mother, and have a cup of tea to warm you.'

Louisa shuddered. 'Tea?'

'Yes.' Emma offered her arm to support Louisa across the pavement to the house.

'And what, pray, is that *dreadful* noise?' Louisa demanded as they reached the doorstep.

For a moment Emma could not think what she meant. 'Oh. That's the stone yard behind us.' She was so used to the banging that she scarcely heard it any more.

'A *stone yard*?' Louisa made it sound slightly less respectable than a brothel. 'Well, Roger must step around to ask them to make less noise. Indeed, I am sure they can stop work completely for a little while.'

Emma didn't quite roll her eyes. 'Mother, they have their livelihoods to earn.'

Louisa stared. 'What on earth has that to say to anything?'

Emma reached for patience. 'All that will happen is that Mr Adams, who is my landlord, will tell Roger to get out of the way.' In fact, she thought the stonemason would probably tell Roger to go to hell. She ushered Louisa over the threshold. 'Welcome, Mother.'

The children had disappeared, but a stifled gasp from upstairs told her that at least one pair of small ears was flapping.

Bessie appeared in the kitchen doorway. 'Tea, mum?' She cleared her throat. 'I can see as how ye've got a *special* guest.'

'Yes, Bessie.' Emma knew exactly what the maidservant was asking; should she re-use the breakfast tea leaves, or use fresh? 'A very special guest—my mother, Lady Dersingham.'

'Oh, well, I'm sure I'm pleased ter meet yer ladyship.' Bessie dropped a very respectful curtsy.

Louisa looked pained. 'Yes, yes, my good woman.'

Quelling an insane desire to laugh, or just scream, Emma said, 'A *nice* cup of tea will be most welcome, Bessie. And her ladyship's footman needs to reheat the carriage bricks.' Difficult to judge who was the most outraged—her mother or the footman. 'Come into the parlour, Mother.'

Louisa gave a shuddering glance around the parlour. 'Oh, dear. Emma, please see that *Roger* brings the tea in. Really! That woman! Of course creatures of that sort never know their place.' She eyed the battered sofa to which Emma had conducted her with grave suspicion and sat as though she expected it to bite.

Thinking that Hunt had not shown by as much as a blink that he had noticed her shabby parlour, nor been rude about Bessie, Emma spoke through gritted teeth. 'Bessie gives complete satisfaction, Mother, and I certainly will not offend her in any way.'

Louisa closed her eyes and spoke in failing accents. 'My dear Emma, if I am obliged to set eyes upon that creature again—'

'Then keep them closed.'

Louisa's eyes snapped open, all pretence of languor gone. 'Really, Emma! Is that any way to speak to your mother?'

'This is my house, Mother.' Emma sat down. 'What brings you here? You haven't visited me since Peter died.' Emma's fingers curled to fists at the memory. 'Nor have you acknowledged any of my letters, including the one that informed you we had moved.'

Louisa dismissed that with an airy wave. 'I am afraid I am but an indifferent correspondent. I am sure I *did* write. Perhaps my maid neglected to put a letter out for Dersingham to frank. And really, after the dreadful way you have behaved—!'

The door opened to admit Bessie bearing a tray. 'Here we are, mum. Lovely, fresh cuppa. Had the kettle nice an' hot. Don't take a minnit, then.' Adorned in a clean apron, Bessie set the tray on the table. 'An' I put a little plate of biscuits besides.'

'Thank you, Bessie.'

Bessie beamed, addressing herself to Louisa. 'An' the bricks is heatin' up nice on the fire, me lady.'

Louisa winced. 'Er...very good.'

'Nippy, it's turned,' Bessie said, cheerfully unaware of shibboleths shattered and taboos toppled. 'Not but what ye'd be as cosy as a bug in that big carriage.'

'*Bugs?*' Louisa's mouth fell open. 'I assure you, my good woman, there are no bugs in my carriage!'

A second knock on the front door deflected whatever Bessie might have replied. 'I dessay that'll be his lordship, mum.' She smoothed her apron and hurried out.

Louisa sank back on the sofa, encountered the very hard back and straightened. 'For goodness sake, Emma! If you cannot conduct yourself with greater discretion, you cannot wonder—'

'Now, that's real kind, yer lordship. Reckon me lady'll be right pleased!'

Huntercombe's deep voice responded cheerfully as Louisa shuddered. 'Whatever possessed you to hire that creature?'

'This way, yer lordship. Me lady's mam is here, an' a fine lady *she* is.'

Emma bit the inside of her cheek to stop the laughter escaping. 'High praise, indeed, Mother.'

The door opened. 'His lordship, mum,' Bessie announced. 'An' I'll bring another tea cup as quick as quick.'

Hunt strolled into the room, hat and gloves tucked under his arm, Fergus at his heels. His brows lifted at the sight of Louisa, but he smiled at Emma. 'Lady Emma. How do you do?' He bowed over her hand.

'Ah, Huntercombe. It *is* you.' Louisa's voice was delicately pained. 'Rather an odd hour for you to call.'

Hunt gave Louisa a puzzled glance and said to Emma, 'I thought this was a perfectly acceptable time to call on Georgie.' He glanced at the battered old clock on the chimneypiece. 'I am a little early, I confess.' He smiled and Emma's pulse skipped. Oh, foolish! A marriage of convenience was what he wanted. Convenience and some liking and affection. Not this girlish *fluttering* at the mere sight of him.

He bowed to Louisa. 'How do you do, ma'am? Is Dersingham well?'

'Perfectly, thank you.' Louisa's brow creased. 'Who, may I ask, is *Georgie*? Is that the dog's name?'

Hunt simply stared and Emma couldn't blame him. 'Georgie is my daughter, Mother. Your granddaughter,' she added, in case there was any confusion. And couldn't resist saying, 'You were invited to her christening over six years ago.'

Louisa's mouth pinched. 'Oh, I dare say. But one has so many things to take up one's time, I am sure keeping track of—' She broke off as Bessie came in with another tea cup.

'There y'are, your lordship. Pretty, ain't it, with all them flowers round the edge.'

He took it with a smile. 'Thank you, Bessie. I'm sure the tea will taste even nicer in such a lovely cup. Would you take Fergus to the kitchen with you?'

Bessie beamed. 'Oh, yes, yer lordship. Be a pleasure. And proper, fresh tea it is. Made special for her ladyship.' She bobbed in Louisa's direction.

'Thank you, Bessie,' Emma said. 'Could you please tell Master Harry and Miss Georgie that I am unable to take them for their walk just now?'

'Yes, mum. Come along now, Fergus.' Bessie

curtsied and closed the door behind herself and the dog.

Emma turned to Hunt. 'I am so sorry, sir, but we will be unable to go for our walk.'

There was a faint, a very faint, twinkle in his eye as he handed her the tea cup. 'Of course you can't. Not with such a delightful, and I think unexpected, visitor.'

'Quite unexpected,' Emma agreed. The less said about delightful the better.

A twitch of Hunt's lips suggested he had noted the omission. 'But,' he went on, as Emma poured his tea with just the tiny splash of milk he liked and handed it to him, 'perhaps once I have done justice to the tea and this cup, and the children have made their bows to their grandmother, I could take them out while you enjoy a quiet visit with Lady Dersingham?' He smiled at Louisa. 'Your grandchildren must be such a pleasure to you, ma'am. No doubt they will be delighted to see you.'

If Emma had harboured doubts about his acuity, the edge on those final remarks would have put them to bed with a shovel.

Louisa frowned. 'I do hope their governess has taught them better than to enact a great deal of vulgar nonsense over—'

The door burst open and Georgie and Harry rushed in. Georgie flung herself at Emma. 'Mama! Bessie says we mayn't go for our walk! Please, Mama!'

'Georgie.' Hunt's firm voice drew the child's attention. 'We will have our walk, but first you must make your curtsy to your grandmother.'

'Grandmother?' Harry stared at Louisa, who bridled, in obvious shock.

'Well, really! I must say—'

'Yes, Harry.' Emma cut Louisa off without hesitation and gave her son a warning glance. 'You will remember my mother, Lady Dersingham.'

'Oh, yes, of course.' Harry took the hint and executed a bow. 'Good afternoon, ma'am. How do you do?'

Louisa sniffed. 'Harry? There is no Harry in the family.'

'He is named for his godfather,' Emma said, through gritted teeth. 'Harry Fitzwalter, a friend of Peter's.' Much notice any member of either family had paid to Harry's birth. Or Georgie's for that matter.

Georgie slipped her hand into Emma's, staring at Louisa. 'So if she's your mama, then that makes her our grandmama?'

Louisa tittered. 'Good heavens! Is the child backward?'

Harry beat Emma's choking rage into speech. 'She is *not*!' He glared at Louisa. 'She's only six and she didn't even know we *had* a grandmother!'

Louisa opened her mouth and Emma braced for battle.

'Harry?' Hunt's voice was quite calm. 'Would you take your sister upstairs and get ready?'

His face crimson, Harry nodded. 'Yes, sir. May Fergus come with us?'

Hunt glanced at Emma. 'If your mother says so.'

Saying a silent prayer of thanks for a storm delayed, if not averted, Emma nodded. 'Yes. That's all right. Off you go.'

Harry took Georgie's hand. 'Come on. Let's get Fergus.' He tugged her along, then seemed to remember something. Executing a very stiff bow in Louisa's direction, he said, 'Good day to you, ma'am. It was very nice to meet you again.'

Having drunk a cup of tea she barely tasted, in an atmosphere brimming with arctic ice and unvoiced feminine outrage, Emma saw Hunt off with the children.

'Mama, I didn't mean to be rude,' Harry whispered, none too softly. 'But—'

'Papa would expect you always to stand up for your sister, Harry,' Emma said, checking his gloves.

'And I *didn't* know we had a grandmama!' Georgie was sucking her thumb, her gloves clutched in the other hand.

Emma hugged her. 'Never mind, sweetheart.' She removed the thumb from Georgie's mouth and tugged on the worn little gloves. 'Enjoy your walk.' She rubbed Fergus's silky ears and he licked her hand enthusiastically. 'You have fun, too,' she told him.

Straightening, she looked at Hunt. 'Thank you.' There was so much more she wanted to say, but with the children listening it was impossible.

His eyes were grave, but he took her hand—the

one Fergus had *not* anointed—and kissed it. Her
pulse did a great deal more than skip at the touch
of his lips, and her breath caught.

His fingers tightened for an instant, but he said
only, 'You'd better not rub *my* ears.'

She managed a weak chuckle as Harry shouted
with laughter. Georgie smiled around her thumb.
Her glove was off again, the thumb back in her
mouth.

'Right.' Hunt looked at the pair of them. 'Fergus is in charge, so stay close until we reach the
Common. Come along.'

Emma closed the door behind them and leaned
on it for a moment, resisting the temptation to
abandon her mother and bolt out the door after
them. After not bothering to write or visit since
just after Peter's death, Louisa had to pick this
afternoon.

Summoning up all her restraint, Emma went
back to the parlour.

Louisa was poking into the drawer of Emma's
little kneehole desk. She looked around unblush-
ing and shut the drawer.

'Well, I'm relieved you know better than to
keep incriminating letters, but you should not
permit Huntercombe to visit in broad daylight!'

Emma took a very careful breath. 'He came to
take the children for a walk.'

Louisa snorted. 'Oh, the pair of you did a creditable job of passing it off, but when one already
knows—' She waved an airy hand.

'Knows what, Mother?' Did Louisa think she was having an affair with Hunt?

Louisa's laugh tinkled. 'Why, that Huntercombe is your latest paramour. Everyone is talking about it.'

'What?' She tried to think. *Latest?* Of course it was possible people had seen them together and she supposed Hunt's servants were as likely to gossip as anyone else's, but *latest*? 'Just to be clear, Mother,' she said flatly, 'Huntercombe is *not* my lover. Nor,' she added, her temper rising, 'has anyone else been my lover!'

Louisa's amused smile sliced to the bone. 'Emma, we're both grown women—we *all* have lovers after we marry, but it's best if we are discreet.' She sat down again. 'I was quite in demand in my day.'

Emma could not find a single coherent thought, let alone word. She didn't want to think about Louisa—her *mother*—having sex at all, let alone with a parade of faceless and nameless—*please, God, let them remain nameless*—gentlemen.

'Your mistake, dear,' Louisa continued, 'was to insist on marrying Lacy. No one, including Bolt, would have minded in the least had you conducted a discreet affair once you were safely *enceinte*. And he would not have cared about any other *petits pacquets* once you had provided an heir and a spare.'

Sickened, Emma found something that resembled her voice. 'Is that what you did?'

Louisa shrugged. 'Of course. I couldn't swear that you are Dersingham's get yourself.'

Emma struggled with that for a moment. 'And my brothers?'

'Oh, *they* are. Naturally I made sure the first two were his. So convenient that they were *both* boys, so I had the heir and the spare out of the way.'

'And who do you think *might* have sired me?' Emma demanded.

Louisa appeared to give that serious thought. 'Oh, well. Eltringham comes to mind as the most likely. But it could have been Havelock. Or even Dersingham for that matter. Although that is not very likely.' She pursed her lips. 'He was quite taken up with that dreadful Amaranth Hayes-Boyle at the time.'

Belatedly Emma recalled that she didn't want to think about her mother having sex, or know the names of her lovers, let alone Dersingham's lovers. She pulled herself together. 'Mother, surely you didn't call merely to inform me that the world believes me to be engaged in an affair with Huntercombe.' She'd be damned if she'd tell Louisa why Hunt was calling on her. It was none of her business.

Louisa's mouth thinned. 'Your father—Dersingham, that is—is renewing his offer to take you back. We both feel that you have had sufficient time to come to your senses. He is willing to reinstate your dowry.'

Emma stilled. 'In return for what?'

'That you sign over guardianship of both children to him.' Louisa's lip curled. 'Hardly a sacrifice one would think. Then you may make a marriage of sorts. Dersingham has some merchant in mind. You will have to be a great deal more discreet than you have been with Huntercombe and Pickford, of course.'

'Pickford?' She had stamped on Pickford's insulting offer with less thought than she would have accorded a cockroach.

Louisa sighed. 'My dear Emma. *Everyone* knows that Pickford was your lover earlier in the year. *He* certainly makes no secret of it. Now, this merchant has agreed to the marriage, but he refuses to be bothered with the children. You couldn't expect that.'

'No?' She heard the snap in her voice and took a steadying breath.

Louisa shrugged. 'A widow in your circumstances cannot be choosy. Dersingham will arrange schools for them.'

Emma was startled to find herself on her feet, fists clenched. Fury burned in every fibre of her body. A clear, cold voice spoke at a slight distance, telling her mother that she might go to hell and take Dersingham, along with his offer, with her.

Chapter Five

Georgie lagged behind. Thinking her shorter legs couldn't keep up, Hunt adjusted his stride, but nearing Chelsea Common a glance at her small, flushed face and over-bright eyes told him otherwise. For the second time her right glove was off and her thumb in her mouth. His heart twisted as he stopped, stripped off one glove, and held out his hand. 'Too fast for you, Georgie?' She said nothing, but removed her thumb from her mouth and tucked her small, cold hand into his. He closed his fingers gently, fiercely aware of the weight of trust as they started walking again.

Harry came racing back with Fergus as they reached the Common. He took a careful look at his sister's face. 'You can throw the ball first, if you like, Georgie,' he said, all generosity.

No answer.

Hunt raised his brows at Harry, who looked

at Georgie again. 'Is your throat sore?' He cast a glance up at Hunt. 'She gets awful colds, sir.'

Another shake of the head and the little fingers in his clung tighter. 'Does…does backward mean I'm stupid?' The very wobbly whisper ripped straight through him.

Hunt bent down and swung Georgie to his hip in a move he'd thought he'd forgotten. 'Certainly not. It means your grandmother is stupid.' Then, as Harry's eyes widened, he heard what he'd said and waited for the heavens to fall or at least produce a healthy thunderbolt. One should not criticise other adults to a child.

Georgie's lower lip trembled and he consigned Louisa to the devil in the need to comfort and reassure. 'Tell me, sweetheart—how often does your grandmother visit?'

Georgie stared. 'She doesn't. That's why I didn't know.'

'Well, she *has* once,' Harry said apologetically. 'But you were just—' He cleared his throat. 'It was ages ago. At the old house, just after Papa died, and I know you don't remember that.'

Once? Their grandmother had visited once? He'd realised Louisa wasn't a frequent visitor, but *once*? Even his own parents, formal though their lives had been, had adored their grandchildren.

'How old were you when your papa died, Harry?' He knew the answer, but he wanted it spelt out for Georgie.

'Six.'

And he was ten now.

'So your grandmother has a perfectly charming granddaughter and—' he gave Harry a considering look '—a quite reasonable grandson—' Harry just grinned '—but she hasn't visited you in how long, Georgie?'

She thought. 'Four years,' she whispered.

'Well, there you are,' he said calmly. 'You aren't stupid at all. She is. How should you know her if she doesn't have the good sense to visit you? Now, are you going to throw that ball for poor Fergus?'

'Yes, but Mama would be awfully cross if we called a grown up stupid.' Georgie laid her head on his shoulder and Hunt held her a little closer. Right now he would cheerfully have dumped the principles of a lifetime and slapped Louisa Dersingham. And not just for her unkindness to Georgie. What mother, living close enough, didn't visit her widowed daughter in four years? Didn't try to help her when she so obviously needed help? However angry the Dersinghams had been over Emma's marriage, surely they didn't have to be this vindictive?

'You didn't,' he said. 'I did. So your mama will be cross with me.' If she had room for more crossness with what she was probably feeling towards her mother.

Georgie shook her head against his shoulder. 'No, she won't. We won't tell. It can be a secret.' She wriggled and Hunt set her down, laughing.

'Worse and worse. Now we're keeping secrets from your mother. Don't worry, Georgie. If I confess properly, she may forgive me.'

Harry nodded. 'She never gets really cross if you just own up. I mean, she'll still make you go to bed early, or miss pudding, but she's not mean about it.'

Hunt chuckled. 'A very reasonable approach. Now, who's throwing this ball?' He handed it to Georgie, trying *not* to think of ways to have Emma order him to bed early.

There were a thousand and one things she ought to be doing, but Emma could not persuade herself to get up from her chair and do them. She felt drained, exhausted. She did not understand why her mother's visit, and Dersingham's offer, had hurt so much. Dersingham—*was* he even her father?—had made it very clear when she married Peter that he was cutting her off. After Peter's death he had made the same offer—that she grant custody of the children to him and marry according to his wishes. She had shown him the door, as she had just done to her mother.

So none of this was surprising, really. And yet it still hurt.

Pickford! Emma shut her eyes. He had made a complete nuisance of himself. Buying posies, pestering her in Hatchard's and in the park when she walked there with the children, offering to *set her up in style*. She had declined, but no doubt people had noticed him. He had persisted for a few weeks, but she had refused to admit him when he called and eventually he had given up. Apparently he had boasted of success rather than admit to failure with her.

She was still sitting, numb, when she finally heard the uproar of the children's return.

'Mama! Mama!' They rushed into the room with the dog bouncing around them and Hunt bringing up the rear.

'Safe home,' he said, removing his hat. 'We braved the wilds of Chelsea Common, but saw nary a single highwayman. Very disappointing. Harry assured me it was infested with masked bravoes.'

'Silly!' Georgie wriggled on to Emma's lap. 'He said they only come out after dark.' Her warm weight was a tangible comfort.

'Is that what he said?' Hunt's twinkle made Emma's heart ache. 'Sit, Fergus,' he said to the dog who was sniffing around the table where a single biscuit remained. 'We do not beg for biscuits in a lady's parlour.'

Fergus sat, panting, and then curled up with an exhausted sigh.

'I wish you'd come, Mama.' Georgie sounded tired but happy. 'I thought we'd have to throw the ball for ever, because Fergus just kept running.'

Emma laughed. 'A spaniel will do that. I imagine in season Lord Huntercombe uses Fergus to put up birds. He can probably run all day.'

Harry scowled. 'I wish Grandmama, I mean Lady Dersingham, had not come.'

'Harry.' Emma could not find it in her to say any more in reproof. *She* wished her mother had not come. Quite apart from anything else, she could not forgive what Louisa had said to Georgie.

Harry flushed. 'I'm sorry, Mama. But we wanted you to come. It was fun and you missed out.'

'Perhaps…' Hunt sounded perfectly diffident '…you might permit me to take your mother for a walk now?' He looked at the dog. 'I think poor Fergus is far too tired for another walk. Maybe you could look after him for me?'

'Oh, *yes*.' Georgie sat up so suddenly that she bumped Emma's chin. 'We could do that. Please, Mama?'

Emma took a careful breath. What she needed to say to Hunt had to be said privately. 'I should like that, sir.' And, oh, if only the pleased expression on Hunt's face didn't lure and beckon. It made this even harder. How pathetic to be so…so *needy* as to want someone—an adult someone—who wanted to spend time with her. Someone who liked and accepted her. A lover.

How was it that she had grown accustomed to Hunt so quickly? To his smile. To the way he tucked her gloved hand into the crook of his elbow and set his own gloved hand over it. Not possessive in any proprietary way, but somehow protective. And there was that knot of need in her. The need to feel his arms about her, to know his weight upon her, to know *his* body with her own.

After Peter's death she had ached for him with her whole body, wept for his loss in terrible loneliness and grief. That grief was, incredibly, a memory now. Had been, she realised guiltily, for a long time. Still painful, but it was memory. The loneliness remained. She knew the difference now because she wanted Hunt, knew he could banish that loneliness, and that made her feel even guiltier. But there was no need for guilt now. Her decision was made.

Patches of watery blue shifted and danced between dark, scudding clouds. Leaves, dying yellow and red, whirled ghostly in the breeze as they fell to earth. It had rained that morning and the lane was slippery, but Hunt's arm held her safely. Somehow she felt warmer just having him beside her and Harry and Georgie had enjoyed their walk so much. She knew it wasn't just Fergus, although that was part of it; it was Hunt himself. They liked him, accepted him. He had intervened with her mother, deflecting whatever Louisa might have said after Harry leapt to Georgie's defence. She could have hit Louisa for what she had said to Georgie. Georgie had gone out silent and upset; she had come back glowing, happy again. Hunt, she suspected, had been responsible for that.

'Thank you for taking them out, sir. And…and for everything.'

The moment she had mentioned fetching her pelisse, gloves and a bonnet, Harry had rushed upstairs at Hunt's raised brows and the jerk of his head and brought them down. She wanted to thank him for that; for taking Harry a little further along the path to manhood. But if she said that, how could she explain the decision she had made?

Hunt glanced at her, his expression quizzical. 'Were we not agreed that friends might use each other's names, Emma?'

'Yes.' Oh, God. How could she do this if he persisted in looking at her like that? As though he wanted *her*, not just a convenient wife who wouldn't bother him overly.

'Good.'

His smile shook her heart. It was just a smile, for heaven's sake! How could a smile—*his* smile, the one that started in his eyes—brighten a grey day so that it seemed the sun had come up with a shout at dawn and been shining ever since? She had to remember that he needed a bride society would accept. Not her.

They strolled on towards the river while she tried to think of some way to broach the subject of his proposal. She could not simply let this drift on when her decision was made. But how did you ease into such a conversation?

'Hunt?'

'Have you given any thought to my proposal?'

He laughed. 'I'm sorry, Emma. You first.'

She dragged her courage together and forced it to the sticking place. 'That was what I wished to speak to you about.'

'Ah.' He cocked his head, looking at her. Then his mouth twisted and the smile died from his eyes. 'I think from your expression that you do not have the answer I want.'

She shook her head, a lump in her throat. A gentleman to the core, he was making it easy for her. Or as easy as it possibly could be.

'I am very sorry, Hunt, but I… I cannot marry you.'

There. It was out and please God he would not ask why not. She wasn't sure she could explain the tangle of emotion and shame Louisa's visit had left behind. She was not even quite sure who she *was* any more. Was she Eltringham's, Havelock's or Dersingham's daughter? How many others had speculated on that over the years? Only one thing was clear: Hunt's reputation would be severely dented if she allowed him to marry her. The world might overlook the Marquess of Huntercombe marrying his mistress—might brush it off as a mere anticipation of marriage vows, but he could *not* marry a woman of soiled reputation, and if the world believed she had been Pickford's mistress, her name was mud. She knew Hunt did good work, conscientious work, in the House of Lords that would be compromised if he married unwisely. Worse, he might call Pickford out. She would not allow him to risk that for her.

'May I continue to call?' he asked. 'As a friend? If I promise not to pester you?'

Longing trembled deep inside. To have a friend. A kindly, undemanding friend. She put temptation behind her. 'Hunt, you must see that is not possible. You have to—' She forced words past the choking lump in her throat. 'You have to find another woman to court.'

His mouth flattened. He actually scowled at her. 'At least allow me to meet you when you change your books.'

She could hardly stop him entering Mr Hatchard's shop, but— 'Hunt, the children are already fond of you. If they continue to see you, when you disappear from their lives, as you eventually must, it will be much harder for them.'

'That,' he said, 'was a low blow.'

'But true.' She clung to the knowledge that he would do nothing that might hurt the children.

His mouth twisted as he inclined his head. 'Very well. Neither of us wants them hurt. But—' He stopped, gripped her shoulders and swung her to face him and her heart stuttered at the sudden fierceness in his eyes. 'You certainly have the right to refuse my offer and even to refuse to see me.' His jaw hardened. 'You do not, however, have the right, much less the ability, to make me court some other female until I'm damned well ready to do so.'

He cast a quick glance around, hauled her into his arms and his mouth was on hers. The reticent gentleman had been swept aside and something wilder unleashed. For an instant shock held her frozen and then everything in her leapt to meet him as it had the first time they kissed. This was heat and fierce demand, his mouth possessing hers deeply, his taste flooding her, igniting every forbidden delight, skimming along every nerve. Madness. But she clung to him, returned his kiss and offered her own, letting her tongue dance with his until she thought she could never forget the taste and heat of him, the strength of his arms or the hard press of his body.

At last he broke the kiss, his breathing as ragged as her own, and set her away from him.

'In case that didn't make it clear; I'm *not* ready.'

Not ready? Her wits had scrambled and she could only blink up at him, every defence melted, scorched, desire an open flame. Heaven help her, but *she* was.

With a muttered curse he swung her around and started walking. Movement, the lash of the wind on her cheeks, cleared her wits.

Not ready to court another woman.

He might never be ready.

Walking home with Fergus trotting beside him, Hunt realised he'd been a fool and a coxcomb to boot. Not for one single moment had it occurred to him that she might not accept him. He could have kicked himself—an arrogant fool at that. He had trotted out his offer as though all he had to do was ask and a woman like Emma, proud, capable and independent, would fall at his feet. As though he were the Lord God Almighty offering salvation.

He saw that now. But how else could he have couched his offer without dishonesty?

She does not want what you are offering.

He could understand that. What he didn't understand was why it bothered him so much. Why the idea of courting any other woman, let alone Amelia, revolted him. It wasn't as though he had formed an attachment. He just…wanted Emma.

Physically. Perfectly convenient, if she hadn't refused his suit. But how could he court another woman when he wanted Emma in his bed, Emma's taste in his mouth?

He reached Hyde Park Corner and turned north in the dying light. Link boys were lighting lamps and a light rain drizzled. He turned up his collar, opened his umbrella and walked faster. Logically, Emma was perfectly right. If she were set against marriage to him, then she had made the only possible decision.

And yet... Was he really coxcomb enough to imagine a woman's liking and attraction? He bit back a curse. She *was* attracted to him. Her response the first time he kissed her, *and* just now, had been real. He had believed she would accept because she had seemed in favour of the marriage. Understandable that she had wanted time to consider it, time for them to know each other better. He'd suspected she had wanted *him* to be perfectly sure. But between his last visit and this afternoon, something had changed *her* mind.

A month. That would bring them to early December. He would call on her again before leaving London after the autumn sitting. He had promised not to pester, but he would call in a month. One calendar month. No cheating and calling four weeks a month. It wasn't February. One visit. If she refused again...well, he would take the children for a walk, say goodbye to them and that would be that. He would return to London in the spring for the Season. By then he should have forgotten her taste, her fragrance and the wild, bone-deep response between them.

Chapter Six

It rained solidly for the next two days and Emma found herself constantly questioning her decision. *Had* she done the right thing? Almost she wished that Hunt had been furiously offended and withdrawn his offer in anger.

And how foolish to wish that he had behaved badly! Just for her own peace of mind. Because the more she thought about it, the more she thought that Hunt would be very angry at her reasons for refusing.

'Harry.' She dragged her mind away from Hunt and back to the present. 'Concentrate on your sums and leave Georgie alone.' The rain had made it impossible to take them out for any length of time and Harry at least was showing all the symptoms of confinement.

'She's only *sewing*.' Thus the male disregard for female pursuits.

'Really?' Emma laid down the shirt she was sewing for him. 'And of course you sew your own shirts, do you, Harry?'

He blinked. 'Georgie's sewing a sampler, not my shirt.'

Emma nodded. 'An excellent point. She can practise on your shirts instead of me doing them.'

Harry flushed and Georgie set her sampler down with a thump.

'I'm not sewing Harry's shirts!'

A heavy knock on the front door forestalled the inevitable fight.

Harry's face brightened. 'It might be Lord Huntercombe and Fergus.'

'Then make sure he finds you doing your lessons properly.' Emma ignored the pang of guilt. She hadn't told them Hunt would not call again. Perhaps it would be kinder to tell them rather than let them realise slowly, but she had not been able to do it. Nor had she been able to forget that kiss. She dreamed of it at night and woke up aching.

Bessie's footsteps sounded in the hall, followed by the groan of the rain-swollen door. Bessie's cheerful voice and—

'Out of my way, wench! Where's her fine ladyship?'

'Beg pardon, sir, but—ooh!'

Bessie's startled gasp was followed by uneven footsteps thumping along the hall. The parlour door crashed open and a stooped, elderly gentleman, supported by a cane, stalked in. Rheumy brown eyes scowled from beneath heavy brows.

Emma's breath seized, but she lifted her chin. 'Good day, sir. Were we expecting you?'

Apart from being eleven years older, the Duke of Keswick looked much the same as ever, disagreeable and disdainful of mere mortals.

He glared down his considerable nose. 'I do not choose to advertise my doings to the scaff and raff. This is your...*home*?' His scornful gaze swept the shabby parlour.

'As you see,' Emma said coldly.

Keswick was looking not at her, but the children, particularly Harry. 'So that's the boy. No doubt he's spoiled without a man's hand, but that can be mended.'

Mended? By whom? Emma rose. Beyond Keswick's totally unexpected appearance, there was something very wrong here. 'Harry, take your sister upstairs and remain there until I call you.'

Bessie appeared in the doorway. 'I'm that sorry, mum. Shoved right past me, he did.'

Emma gave her father-in-law a derisive glance. 'Of course, Bessie. Good manners are for lesser mortals, not dukes.'

Bessie blinked. 'Right. Well, young Jem Adams were passing and I told him to ask his dad to step around. Be here in a jiffy, he will.'

Adams, the master mason and her landlord. Emma readjusted. 'Thank you. Take the children to the kitchen and keep them there with Mr Adams when he arrives.'

'Yes, mum.'

'Harry, Georgie—*go.*'

'The boy stays.' Keswick rapped it out.

Harry hesitated and Emma stepped between them. 'Harry, do as you are bid.'

'Damn your eyes, woman—!'

'And yours, Keswick,' Emma snapped. 'I order my house and my children as I see fit.'

'As their legal guardian,' Keswick growled, 'they'll do *my* bidding!'

Fear ripped at her. 'You are not their legal guardian,' she said. 'I am.'

'Rubbish,' Keswick sneered. 'Their father was my son. Although I have not chosen to exercise it, the guardianship is mine, so—'

'Peter's will, duly witnessed and probated, named me sole guardian and specifically disbarred you from guardianship.' At the time she'd thought Peter's dying determination to ensure Keswick could not take the children was a waste of his time and strength. Now she thanked God for his foresight.

'Harry! Go!' Deliberately she stepped between Keswick and the door and gestured the children past her.

Heavy footsteps sounded in the hall.

'What's all the fuss, Lady Emma?' Hugh Adams, solid as one of his own masonry blocks, filled the doorway. 'Young Jem said some oaf pushed Bessie over and forced his way in.' His shrewd eyes looked over Keswick. 'This him?'

Some oaf...she would treasure that. 'Mr Adams, would you please take Georgie and Harry to the kitchen and keep them safe there?'

'Aye.' Hugh had removed his cap. 'I can do that, ma'am. You call if you need aught else.' He held out his hand. 'And how's Miss Georgie?'

Harry and Georgie hurried out to him and Emma shut the door. 'You will deal with me, Keswick.' She pointed to a chair. 'Be seated if you wish.' She resumed her own seat.

Keswick remained standing. 'I'm here for the boy, but I'll take the girl as well.'

'No.'

He stared. 'No? Do you dare refuse me?'

'Yes.' *Show no fear.* 'You have no claim. Their father's will makes that clear.'

He snorted. 'You think that can't be set aside? A court given evidence of your loose morals will deem you unfit and hand them to me without hesitation.'

Her stomach roiled. 'There is no evidence of anything of the sort!'

'Hah!' His triumph was palpable. 'Pickford has a pretty tale to tell. And now I'm informed you're waving your tail for Huntercombe!'

Her mind caught on that. Informed. Not that he'd heard gossip, but he'd been *informed*. As if— had the man following her been Keswick's spy?

He watched her, his expression scornful. 'Huntercombe was a bonus, but Pickford did enough that with a little help the gossip spread. No one will believe you innocent.'

Fear twisted, sick and cold, in her belly. 'Why? Why, after all this time, do you want them?'

He banged his cane on the floor. 'Don't play

games, girl! You must have known as soon as Thirlbeck died!'

The icy knot tightened. 'Viscount Thirlbeck is dead?' Thirlbeck had been Keswick's eldest son and heir to the dukedom and Peter had been the second son. Panic lodged in her throat.

'Harry is your heir.'

'And being raised in a pigsty!' Keswick sneered at the parlour. 'God knows I tried, as soon as Thirlbeck was buried, to have Peter's marriage disproved!'

'You *what*?'

'That prating parson wouldn't budge, nor Fitz-walter. Sent a damned impertinent answer, too!'

Harry's godfather, Major Harold Fitzwalter, had been Peter's groomsman. As far she knew he was with his regiment abroad, but he probably didn't know where she was or he'd have written to warn her.

Keswick went on. 'I've no choice but to take the boy and raise him properly. And the girl for good measure.'

Through the churning fear, she forced herself to breathe. 'Sir, this does not have to be a battle,' she said quietly. 'If you wish to see that Harry attends a good school, well, thank you. Of course I will bring him to visit you in the holidays so that he may know—'

'The hell you will!' Keswick's face was mottled. 'Out for what you can get! You ruined my son! Do you think I'll let you near the boy?

Or have you teaching the girl to whore herself? How much?'

'What?'

'How much for you to hand them over without a fuss? One thousand? Two?'

Rage ripped the fear to shreds. 'My children are not for sale!'

His knuckles whitened on the cane. 'You think you can rear a duke? Look at you! Dressed like a drab. Very well. I'll apply to the magistrates and you'll get not a penny from me.'

She raised her brows. 'Really? I dare say a court would be most interested in a letter, penned by your secretary, in which I was informed that Peter's annuity from his grandfather had died with him and categorically denied any interest in his children, stating that it was all one to you if we ended in the gutter where we belonged!'

He stared at her in shock and she knew a savage satisfaction. In her disgust she had nearly burned that letter, sent in response to hers informing Peter's parents of his death. Fortunately she had kept it.

'You think you can fight *me*?' Keswick demanded. 'By God, I'll see you in gaol for denying my right to my lawful property.'

Emma stood firm, her chin up. 'You'll have to prove that right first, Keswick. Now get out.'

He laughed. 'Once you're proved morally unfit, that letter won't matter.'

Her stomach churned. 'Difficult to prove what

never happened. Even Pickford won't lie under oath, so—'

'Pickford,' Keswick said coldly, 'will say exactly what he's told to say. I'll return with a magistrate in day or so,' he went on. 'You'll have the boy and his sister ready if you do not wish to end in Newgate for kidnapping.'

He rose and stumped out, slamming the door. Fear icing every vein, Emma rushed to the window and watched the carriage drive away. Her stomach churned. There was not a magistrate in the country who would support her against Keswick.

'Mum?'

Emma swung around. Bessie stood in the doorway, Adams behind her. 'You heard?'

'Couldn't help but hear,' Bessie said. 'Master Harry's saying he don't care who the old gent is, they ain't leavin' you.'

They would have no choice unless she could find a way to prove that she was *not* an unfit, immoral—she looked at the shabby parlour. Who was she deceiving? Even if she could prove that, any magistrate would judge that the children would be better off in Keswick's custody.

A clap of thunder heralded a downpour of rain, streaming on the windows and blotting out the street.

'Mama!' Harry and Georgie rushed in.

'We won't go!'

'We'll run away!'

They clung to her and she hugged them. 'I

wouldn't let you go. Ever.' And knew it for a lie. She would not be able to prevent it.

'I wish Fergus had been here,' Georgie said. 'He could have *bitten* that nasty old man.'

Emma froze. Not at the unlikely prospect of Fergus biting anyone, even Keswick, but at the thought of his master.

By the time Emma reached Mayfair the rain had eased slightly. Her umbrella had kept the worst off, but her skirts were soaked below the knee and her half-boots sodden, despite her pattens. The wind sliced through her as she squelched around from Upper Grosvenor Street into Grosvenor Square.

Shivering before the imposing façade of Huntercombe House, she hoped the note she had written for Hunt was dry under her pelisse. Even if he was home, his servants were unlikely to admit her. Once she would have taken such a house, if not quite for granted, as nothing out of the common way. Now, tugging on the doorbell, it looked forbidding, something from another world and time.

To her jangled nerves it seemed for ever until the door opened. The servant's brows shot up as he took in her shabby but genteel soaked self and the lack of servant or carriage.

'Yes, madam?' His tone suggested that he was merely covering his bets with this form of address.

'I have a message for Lord Huntercombe.'

The man's face blanked. 'I believe his lordship

is not home, madam. If that is all—' The door began to close.

'Wait!' Emma stuck her foot in the door. 'I do not ask you to admit me.' She drew the note, thankfully dry from under her pelisse. 'Merely to give him this as soon as he returns.'

He hesitated, frowning, and Emma lifted her chin. She knew better than to beg. 'I doubt that his lordship will thank you for interfering with his private correspondence.' She held out the letter as one who expected to be obeyed, her expression imperious.

'Ah, very good, madam.' He took the note. 'Who shall I say called?'

'Lady Emma Lacy. Good day to you and thank you.'

She turned away as the door closed. Please God, he would give it to Hunt.

Hunt looked up from the Parliamentary papers he was going through with his secretary as Bentham entered the library. 'I'm busy, Bentham. Whoever it was—'

'Lady Emma Lacy, my lord.'

'What?' Hunt stared at his butler, tamping down the leap of hope. He'd spent the past two days hiding from Letty. 'Show her in immediately!'

Bentham actually winced and held out a note. 'She didn't precisely ask to *see* you, my lord.'

'She's *gone*?'

'Ah, yes—'

Hunt was on his feet. 'Barclay—finish reading these. Make notes.' He shoved the papers across the desk at his startled secretary and sprinted for the door.

Drizzle and an icy wind slapped at him as he flung open the front door and stared around the square. There! At the south-west corner by Upper Grosvenor Street—

'Emma!' He pitched his yell to carry over a storm at sea as he leapt down the steps. The figure in the familiar brown pelisse stopped, turned back and he breathed a sigh of relief as he strode along the wet pavement. What was she *thinking* coming out in this weather? His longer strides had him meeting her over halfway to the corner.

He took one look and swore. Her face was pale, the soft lips blue with cold. 'Emma, you idiot!' He took her hand. The worn leather glove felt like a wet, half-frozen fish. 'You could have sent me a note through the post if you have changed your mind.' He started walking her briskly towards the house. 'You must have known I'd come!'

'It wasn't that.' Her voice shook. 'I… I need help. I didn't dare wait.'

'*Wait?* I asked you to marry me less than a week ago! If you think I'm that bloody inconstant—' He broke off. She'd said she needed his help. Fear stabbed. 'Emma, is one of the children ill?'

Her breath shuddered out. 'No. But I need your help. For them. Please.'

Once he knew the children weren't ill, he refused to hear another word of what she had to tell him until he had her seated in front of a roaring fire in the library. He sent Bentham scurrying for more coals, a tea tray and towels. Barclay, showing all the discretion for which Hunt employed him, had swept up the Parliamentary papers and departed without a word.

He'd just about ripped her damp pelisse off, noting with relief that her gown was dry underneath except for the skirts which clung wetly to her legs. Her hands—he'd peeled the sodden gloves off—were frozen and he doubted her feet were any better.

He knelt, shoved her skirts to her knees and began unbuttoning one of her boots, trying very hard not to notice the slender curve of her calf, or the sweetly turned ankle as he drew the boot off.

'Hunt! What are you doing?'

He gave her a withering look. 'What does it look like I'm doing?'

She flushed. 'You're taking my boots off, but why?'

'Because—' he tossed the first boot aside '—even if you won't marry me, it doesn't suit me to have you expire of an inflammation of the lungs!'

A throat cleared behind him. He looked around. Bentham stood there with the tea tray, his expression bemused. 'Good. Set that down on the table there.'

The porcelain on the tray rattled. 'Very good, my lord.' The tray met the table with what sounded nothing like Bentham's usual finesse. 'I took the liberty of adding the brandy decanter, my lord. Brandy being a warming thing on a cold day.'

'Excellent, Bentham.' Hunt started on the second boot. 'Now go away and find a cloak, or anything that isn't damp, for Lady Emma. We'll need the carriage in half an hour.'

Emma stiffened. 'I can—'

'No, you can't.' He chopped off Emma's protest ruthlessly. 'Half an hour, Bentham, and leave the door open.' That was all he could do to safeguard Emma's reputation without having his housekeeper in and he very much doubted Emma wanted that.

'Ah, warm slippers for my lady?' Bentham suggested.

'Oh, yes, Bentham. Thank you.' Emma beamed at the butler who looked gratified.

'A pleasure, my lady.' Bentham bowed and hurried off.

Hunt removed the second boot and peeled off her stockings.

'Right.' Hanging the stockings over the brass foot fender, he stood up. 'Tea.' He poured two cups, added cream, sugar and a liberal splash of brandy to each. He handed her one and sat down.

'Now. Tell me what this is all about.'

'Were you aware that our *affaire* is the talk of society?'

Our what? All he could do was stare at her.

Her cheeks flamed. 'According to my mother it's all over town that we are engaged in an affair.'

Hunt found his tongue. 'Nothing like being the last to know. Is that what brought you here?'

'No. Not exactly.'

Chapter Seven

His temper smoked, his control smouldered and he clenched his fists as Emma stumbled through Keswick's visit, wishing his Grace's neck was there to twist into a choking pulp.

She looked up when she had finished. 'I'm sorry, sir, but will you help me?'

'*Hunt,*' he got out. 'And sorry for what?'

'Hunt, then. This mess I've dragged you into.'

'I dragged myself into it,' he said. *And Emma.* His visits had given Keswick the hammer with which to break her. 'Keswick intends to refuse you all access to the children?'

She nodded. He saw her swallow, heard the rattle as she set down her cup and saucer, and knew just how frightened she was, how close to despair. Faced with losing her children, she'd had no one to turn to but him.

He thought it through. 'You want me to appear

in court as a witness. To deny we had an affair, but tell them I was courting you. That I made you an offer of marriage which you ultimately refused.'

She went white and bit her lip. 'Yes. No. I'm sorry. I see now you can't. It would make you look a complete fool.'

He took a very deep careful breath. 'Emma, that doesn't matter. I'll bear witness willingly, but—' He doubted it would work.

'Will it be enough?'

'No.' He drew a deep breath. 'The surest way for me to protect you and the children is by marriage.'

'*What?* But—'

'I know my offer was not very romantic, but I hoped we could be friends.'

'Yes. I understood that.'

Her eyes were huge and was that a glint of tears? He wanted to hold her, kiss them away, but if she didn't want to marry him…besides, he was offering convenience, not kisses and moonlight. A solution was needed here.

'My offer did not insult you, then?'

She shook her head.

'Then why did you refuse me?' He swallowed. 'I know I must be close to twenty years older than you. Does that repulse you?'

'What? No!' Her breath jerked in, her eyes wide and horrified. 'You *can't* think that! I… I *wanted*—' She broke off, biting her lip.

Something in him loosened. *I wanted to marry you?* Was that what she had been about to say?

Or even *I wanted you*? In either case, why had she refused?

He gritted his teeth. 'I'm old enough to be your father.'

She glared at him. 'I sincerely doubt *that*. Dersingham is sixty-five and he had a paunch even eleven years ago.'

He choked back a surprised laugh. He might have thickened in the waist, but he definitely didn't have anything remotely resembling a paunch, thank God.

She eyed him thoughtfully. 'How old *are* you?'

He braced himself. 'Fifty, two months ago.'

She nodded, apparently unconcerned. 'I'll be thirty-three in January. I hope that puts you out of the might-have-been-my-father category?'

He couldn't help grinning. 'It does. I wasn't quite that precocious.'

'How old—?' She broke off, blushed.

He laughed outright. 'The first time? Twenty. And damnably clumsy, I've no doubt.'

'Oh.' She looked disconcerted. 'Well, the thing is, Hunt, if you want children—'

She didn't have to say it. He was being an idiot. Under the circumstances their age difference was unavoidable.

'Then why did you refuse me?'

She flushed. 'Do you think I *want* to ruin your life? You need a wife who won't scandalise society. A marquess does not marry his mistress!'

He managed not to snarl at her. It was her mother and Keswick who deserved that. 'Let's pretend you didn't say that. At my age a man is reasonably sure about what will and will not ruin him. Marriage to you doesn't even come close. You weren't my mistress and I'll not allow society's idiocy to influence my choice!'

She took an audible breath. 'There's more. Do you know Lord Pickford?'

'Sadly, yes.' Pickford was the sort of scum that gave ponds a bad name. 'What about him?'

She told him.

'What?'

'I… I didn't, but, Keswick—'

'Damn it all to hell, Emma!' Hunt found himself on his feet again, rage searing every vein. 'You think I need to be told that?' he demanded. 'When you thought I was trolling for a mistress you gave me a flea in my ear that makes me itch just remembering it. And then you refused marriage? Hardly the behaviour of a loose, scheming widow.'

'No, I suppose not. But my mother knew—'

'Just like she knew about *our* supposed affair?'

'—and Keswick is certain that Pickford will swear to it in court, that I…that I—'

'Is he now?' Hunt's brain edged around his smoking temper. 'How very interesting. Just when did Pickford approach you?'

She stared, clearly not seeing what he had seen. 'Last May.'

'Thirlbeck died in March, as I recall,' Hunt said. 'God knows why *I* didn't put it together that Harry is the heir now, but Keswick knew at once.

And Pickford is one of his toadies. All very convenient.'

Emma's jaw dropped. 'He said he'd tried to have the marriage disproved.'

Hunt nodded. 'That would have taken a little time and he must have known it was unlikely to succeed, so he set Pickford on to stir up gossip to make claiming the children easier now.'

Her eyes widened. 'Oh, my God! *That's* why Dersingham tried to get custody of the children.'

'He did *what*?' Hunt crouched beside her and took her hands, enclosing them safely in his own. 'When?'

Her fingers clung. 'The other day. My mother relayed the offer. He'd give me my dowry and arrange a respectable marriage if I signed over custody of the children.' It came out in a croaking whisper. 'He tried to use them to get at Keswick! I'll kill him!'

'Marry me first and I'll help you with that.'

She stared at him in patent disbelief and he realised that as a marriage proposal, no matter the provocation, an offer to help kill her father wasn't really appropriate. He dragged in a breath, reaching for control.

'Hunt—'

'Emma, I can protect them as their stepfather and co-guardian. If the only reason you refused me the other day was a misguided attempt to protect me, will you do me the honour of accepting my hand in marriage?'

That was better. He was even on his knees in the prescribed manner.

Emma stared, those blue eyes wide and shocked. 'Yes,' she whispered. 'Yes, please.'

He raised her hand to his lips, pressed a kiss to her trembling fingers. Her fragrance, Emma, just Emma, broke through him, shattering every defence, desire storming in behind it. He took a careful breath and gritted his teeth against the urge to kiss her, taste those soft lips again, feel them tremble and part for him. This was to be a marriage of mutual convenience. Desire was all very well, even desirable. This leap of joy was anything but. No matter how much he wanted it, kissing her senseless the way he had the other day wasn't what was needed here. He had to be practical, logical. Exactly as their marriage would be. 'Excellent. That's settled. I'll have Barclay in and we'll get this arranged properly.'

She stared up at him, a slight frown creasing her brow. He touched it lightly. 'Don't worry. We'll sort everything out. You'll see.'

Logical. Rational. A partnership.

Hunt put Emma into his town carriage, wrapped in the warmest fur cloak he could find, with every available hot brick and told her to expect him later. 'I'll bring supper,' he said. 'Enough for all of us, including Bessie. You get back to the children.' He didn't like to think of Harry and Georgie wondering where Emma had gone, frightened their grandfather might come back and snatch them.

'I'll have to tell them about our betrothal.'

He shook his head. 'Not yet.'

She frowned. 'It might be best if I—'

'Wait for me. I'm not trying to wriggle out of it, you know.'

'I know *that*! But—'

'Trust me.'

She immediately gave way. 'Very well. Do you wish to tell them?'

'Something like that.' He wasn't sure what he intended. All he could think of was the kiss he hadn't taken in the library. He cursed. He was betrothed to her. Was he really going to let her go without kissing her at all? She was safely in the carriage. Surely he could kiss her now? He leaned in and kissed her gently. Her breath caught and those soft lips parted just as he'd imagined. Unable to help himself, for an instant, he deepened the kiss, tasted her. Then he stepped back and closed the door. He glanced up at his coachman, whose back radiated discretion. 'Drive on, Masters.'

'Aye, sir.'

The amusement in the man's voice left no doubt he knew exactly what had been going on behind his back. The carriage rattled away from the curb and Hunt watched until it swung around the corner. Then he stalked back inside. Several people, starting with his soon-to-be father-in-law, were going to be extremely sorry for themselves.

He held his fury in check, while he went through all the arrangements. Letters had to be sent. Most notably the one Barclay had already written for him to his Grace, the Archbishop of Canterbury, requesting a special licence. Since his cousin, David, on his father's side was attached to Lambeth Palace, he sent the letter under cover to him. He needed Emma and the children under his protection before Keswick could act.

Having seen the letters off with various footmen and a groom, and ordered his carriage to be ready for him when it returned from Chelsea, Hunt walked around to Dersingham House in Berkeley Square.

Dersingham received him, with rather heightened colour, in the library. 'Huntercombe. This is...er...an unexpected surprise.'

Hunt raised his brows. 'Aren't they all?'

Dersingham blinked. 'Aren't they all what?'

God only knew where Emma had got her brains from, but Hunt seriously doubted it was Dersingham. 'Surprises. If they were expected, they wouldn't be surprises. Would they?'

The Earl took a moment to work that out, then essayed a feeble laugh. 'Very amusing, Huntercombe. Will you not be seated?'

Hunt took a seat by the fire. 'Thank you. I fear, Dersingham, that I am guilty of an impropriety.'

Dersingham made a noise trapped between a turkey's gobble and a squawk. 'Oh, well. As to that, she's nothing to me. As long as you're discreet—' And he waved away the supposed debauching of his daughter. 'Dare say the gossip will soon die down.'

Hunt reined in the urge to knock Dersingham's

teeth down his throat. 'You misunderstand me. I am pre-empting your demand to know my intentions towards your daughter.'

'Your intentions?'

'Yes. And not only that, I have completely missed the bit where I am supposed to ask your permission.'

'My *permission*?'

Hunt permitted himself a chilly smile. 'Yes. Lady Emma has done me the very great honour of accepting my hand in marriage.'

'*Marriage?*'

Hunt sighed. 'Dersingham, try not to echo my words. Someone might think you a halfwit.'

Apparently debarred from any response at all by this remark, Dersingham simply goggled.

Hunt went on. 'Speaking hypothetically, because I am sure the situation will not arise, should any man ever again level an insult at Lady Emma and it comes to my ears, he will need to cough his teeth back up the next time he wishes to use them.' Hunt settled a cold gaze on Dersingham. 'I will not be taking account of his age, nor his relationship to Emma.'

Dersingham found his voice. 'You're going to marry her?' Some colour returned to his face. 'Why?'

Hunt looked him up and down. 'That's very close to my definition of insult.'

'Damn it all!' Dersingham blustered. 'She's my daughter.'

Hunt let out a crack of scornful laughter. 'Having failed to defend her from insult, nor demanded to know my intentions towards her and, worse, having attempted to snatch custody of her children when you realised you could use the boy to score off Keswick, it's rather late to remember she's your daughter.'

He rose to leave. 'One thing, Dersingham— Emma's dowry.'

'Her dowry?' Dersingham sneered. 'She doesn't have a—'

'Oh, yes, she does,' Hunt said. 'The dowry she would have had if she'd married Gus Bolt as you planned. How much was it?' He caught a calculating look in the Earl's eyes, and added, 'Or should I ask Bolt?'

Dersingham scowled. 'Twenty thousand. But I had to pay out five thousand to Bolt.'

Hunt shrugged. 'More fool you, trying to force her into a distasteful marriage. The dowry—the full amount—is to be settled upon her daughter, Georgiana Mary Lacy.' Under other circumstances he would have stipulated half for each child, but Harry wouldn't need it.

Dersingham's jaw dropped. 'Settle it on *Lacy's* get? Keswick's granddaughter?' His face mottled. 'Damned if I will!'

'It's rather damned if you don't, Dersingham,' Hunt said softly as he strolled towards the door. 'Have your solicitors contact mine for my instructions. Don't bother your butler. I'll show myself out.' It wasn't that he wouldn't have provided for Georgie as generously himself. But by God he wanted Dersingham to pay for what he'd done to Emma. As he closed the library door behind him, he thought that Lord Peter Lacy would have appreciated the irony.

Chapter Eight

Dusk was falling as Emma reached home and the chill cut to the bone despite hot bricks and a fur travel rug. The footman opened the carriage door and let down the steps.

'Thank you.'

He went ahead of her to the door. 'His lordship said I was to see as nothing was amiss, m'lady.'

'Amiss? Oh.' Emma's stomach clutched. Surely Keswick wouldn't have returned already...

The door flew open and Harry and Georgie tumbled out.

'Mama!'

'We're *all* going to run away!' Georgie's thumb was in her mouth.

Harry was holding Georgie's free hand. 'We planned it with Mr Adams, Mama. If we move they can't find us and—'

'It's all right, Harry.' She turned to the footman. 'Thank you. Everything is safe, tell his lordship.'

A faint smile flickered. 'Yes, m'lady. Good day to you, young master and miss.' He gave a little bow and went back to the carriage, swinging up behind.

'That looks like fun,' Harry said. 'Do you think I could do that one day?'

'We'll see.' Emma shepherded them indoors.

'Mama, where did you go?' Georgie spoke around her thumb. 'Should we pack?'

'Not quite yet, sweetheart. I saw Lord Huntercombe. He is sorting it all out.'

Georgie's thumb popped out. 'Did Fergus bite that horrid old man?'

Emma bent down and swung her up. 'No. But I'm sure he would have.'

'Mama?' Harry's eyes still held fear. 'Are you sure it's all right?'

'Yes,' she said simply. 'Lord Huntercombe is coming to explain.'

The tension ebbed from Harry's slight frame. 'Oh. All right then.'

Georgie positively beamed. 'Did *he* hit the horrid man?'

With a pang, Emma realised the confidence the children already had in Hunt. 'No, he didn't.'

'But he *could*,' Georgie insisted. 'And Fergus could bite him and then he'd know he had to leave us alone.'

Emma hugged her. 'Lord Huntercombe will tell him that you are staying with me.'

'Good.' Georgie snuggled in and Emma rested her cheek on the soft curls, fighting the urge to weep. The time for weeping was past. The children were safe. Safe because of Hunt's kindness and decency. All her problems vanished, as if they had never been. The only thing left to worry her was how to maintain the sort of marriage Hunt wanted—a marriage of convenience when her heart was anything but convenient.

Full dark had come. The children had helped set out plates, glasses and cutlery. Emma grimaced, remembering Hunt's elegant, unchipped porcelain. The luxurious furnishings which once she had taken for granted. And yet when Hunt had visited here he had appeared not to notice what his tea was served in, nor that the chair in which he sat was less than comfortable, that the fare was plain.

She could hear the gossip now...

Married him for his money, you know...

Eager to claw her way back, of course...

She let out a breath. Perhaps it was true. Amazing how everyone almost without exception married for money, but only recognised the fact when someone else did it. Someone they disapproved of. If they approved of you then you had made a *very good marriage*, or an *excellent match*. She wouldn't let it matter. Gossip was always a nine days' wonder and died if you refused to feed it.

She had made the only decision possible, for herself and for the children. That was all that mattered. Not snide comments and sneers. And right now, faces and hands washed, Harry and Georgie stood at the window, behind the shabby curtain, speculating on how soon Hunt might arrive.

'I hope he doesn't meet a highwayman.'

'He could hit him.'

Silent laughter shook Emma. Georgie wouldn't be happy until Hunt had hit someone apparently—hoof beats sounded, drew closer, slowed and halted.

'Oh. He's riding, Mama, and—no, wait!'

Georgie scrambled out from behind the curtain, eyes wide. 'It's someone else!'

Harry appeared, his face white. 'It's another man!'

She stood up, summoned every scrap of courage. 'If he's riding he can't take you away. But go upstairs and wait there.'

'I'll stay with you, Mama.' Harry's voice wobbled, but his chin was up, shoulders braced.

Through her fear, pride swelled. 'No. Look after your sister. That's what Papa and Lord Huntercombe would expect. Go.' She gave him a little push.

'Come, too, Mama.' Georgie's thumb was back in her mouth.

Emma shook her head. 'No. I'll see him. Go with Harry.' She hurried them out and pushed them towards the stairs as the visitor pounded on the door.

Bessie came out, wiping her hands on her apron. 'Mum?'

'Upstairs with the children,' Emma said. 'I'll deal with it.'

Bessie looked uncertain. 'Could run for Mr Adams again.'

'No. Stay with the children. His lordship is coming soon.'

Bessie's face cleared. 'Right. Up with the pair of you, now!' She shooed the children upstairs before her as the imperious knocks continued to rattle the door.

Arming herself with cold disdain, Emma jerked the door open, holding the lamp high. 'Whoever you are—oh, my God!'

It was like seeing a ghost. The same unruly dark hair, the bright, tawny eyes she saw daily in Georgie's small face. Her mind blank and throat thick, she could not speak as the years dissolved and memory poured through her in a painful flood.

She had never met this man, but she knew who he must be: Lord Martin Lacy. Peter's youngest brother, ten years his junior, had been a school boy when she married. Peter had spoken of him often, been fond of him, enough to visit him a couple of times at Eton. He had been bitterly hurt when Keswick forbade contact with the boy.

'You're Martin.' Even breathing was hard. His expression was cold as she had rarely seen Peter's, but the face was painfully familiar. 'He never mentioned how alike you are.'

'No?' Lord Martin's voice was as wintery as his

expression. 'I'm surprised he bothered to mention me at all after you seduced him.'

Anger burned through the pain. 'Of course. Your brother was a complete fool who couldn't think for himself. The sort of idiot who can't avoid a scheming hussy.' To her intense satisfaction, he looked as though a mouse had roared at him.

She stepped back, gestured him inside. 'I've had quite enough of your family for one day, but no doubt you wish to air your views.' She stalked ahead, not waiting for him to open the parlour door for her. Any politeness would be a sop to convention; she could do without it. Even his voice hurt, tearing at memory.

She heard the door close behind them as she walked to the fireplace and turned to face him. He hadn't bothered to remove his hat and she bit back the automatic invitation to sit. She was sick of returning courtesy for discourtesy.

'Say whatever you have to say, Lord Martin, and then leave.'

'You dragged him down to this.' Lord Martin's gaze flicked over the parlour.

Rage licked at her, but she kept her voice cool. 'No. This is where I moved after he died.' *After your father refused to continue the annuity to help his grandchildren.* She bit that back. Her own father had been just as culpable.

He gave a harsh laugh. 'M'father said you'd squandered Peter's money, had no notion how to manage.'

'Did he?' She reminded herself that Peter had

loved Martin, that he wouldn't want his brother to know how their father had behaved and, apparently, lied.

'For God's sake, woman! You can hardly imagine that this is the proper place to raise Peter's children, let alone a duke's heir!'

She raised her brows. 'At least he'll have a notion of the value of money and the privations his tenants may face.'

Lord Martin scowled. 'Look, it's obvious you aren't raising the children properly. You married Peter for his money and—'

'What?' Emma's temper snapped. 'I married your brother because I loved him and I jilted a wealthy suitor to do so. You may accuse me of anything else, but not that!'

He glared at her. 'How much will it take for you to release the children into my father's care without the necessity of a court case that can only bring scandal to you and distress to them?'

Her breath came in hard. 'Sell my children?'

His mouth flattened. 'He wishes only to protect them!'

She laughed, a bitter sound that scraped her throat raw. 'Odd that he hasn't wished to do so before. And there is hardly a need to protect them from me!' She could end this by telling him of her betrothal, but her own children did not know yet and some instinct warned that it would be better to hold that ace close to her chest.

'Lady Emma, I promise you, any magistrate will award custody to my father. A court appearance can only damage your reputation.' His lip curled. 'What there is left of it. If you will not think of your own best interests, consider my mother's distress at being denied her grandchildren.'

'And I am to be denied my children?'

He frowned. 'Nonsense.'

'Those were your father's terms.'

He cleared his throat. 'Look, I'll tell him you wish to see the children, ah, every so often and—'

'Get out, Lord Martin.' She held his furious gaze.

He stalked towards her. 'Do you think I'll leave my brother's children to the care of a harpy who didn't even tell his family they existed?' Scorn spat from his eyes. 'Or aren't they his, after all?'

'That's enough, Lacy.'

Hunt's deep voice sliced with bone-chilling anger.

Hunt wasn't well acquainted with Martin Lacy, but knew he held a position at Whitehall involving the Foreign Office. No one seemed to know quite what it was that he did.

He gestured to the footman following him, laden with a large basket. 'Set that down, Philip, then wait in the hall, if you please.'

'Yes, m'lord.'

'This is none of your business, Huntercombe!' Lord Martin cast Emma a sneering look. 'Just because you're tupping—'

Fergus let out a growl, took a step forward.

'Fergus—*sit*. Lacy, you're half my age, but that won't stop me calling you out.' Hunt spoke very precisely, his temper in a death grip. 'You will apologise to Lady Emma and leave.'

Lord Martin snorted, a wary eye on the seated, still-growling dog. 'Oh, I'll leave all right.' He glared at Emma. 'But I'm damned if I'll offer an apology! I hoped to appeal to her better nature and spare my brother's children the distress of being removed forcibly by a magistrate tomorrow morning, but—' At Emma's frightened gasp, he laughed. 'Yes, madam. A magistrate has agreed that the children should be in my father's custody until the case is heard. Does that give you to think?'

Hunt glanced at Emma. Her white face stabbed at him. 'Out. Lady Emma and her children have suffered enough from your family for one day.'

Lord Martin clenched his fists. 'All my father wants is to protect the grandchildren she has denied him! You can't possibly believe that they should be raised here!'

'As a matter of fact, I don't,' Hunt said in equable tones that slid over the searing anger. 'Neither do I know how Dersingham and Keswick have reconciled it with their consciences all these years. But you'd need to discuss that with them. Goodnight, Lacy.'

'All these—?' Lord Martin's eyes widened. 'Are you suggesting—?' He cast Emma an icy glare. 'I'll bid you a good evening. No doubt the magistrate will get to the bottom of who is lying!' He turned on his heel and walked out past Hunt with a curt nod. 'Huntercombe. My compliments on your dog.'

As the front door slammed, Hunt bit back several curses. He held out his hand. 'Emma— don't—'

She was in his arms before he could get another word out. His arms closed around her trembling body and the world seemed to stand still for an instant. How long had it been, he wondered, since there had been someone for Emma to turn to, to lean on? And how long had it been since anyone had turned to him in such trust and confidence? Or since a woman in his arms had felt so utterly right, as if she anchored something that had been adrift. As if he had needed her as much as she had needed him.

This wasn't what he wanted.

Of course he wanted her to trust him, turn to him for help. But this sensation of rightness…it threatened to grab his serene, ordered existence by the scruff of the neck and shake it like a terrier with a rat. His life was comfortable as it was. He wasn't supposed to need her.

He drew back a little, brushed a kiss over her mouth. 'Get yourself and the children packed.' Her jaw dropped as he went on. 'If Keswick has a magistrate in his pocket we need to act.'

'But—'

'Emma, possession is nine-tenths of the law. If he takes the children, even once we're married it will be the devil's own job to get them back and our betrothal won't be enough to stop him.' Fear flashed into her eyes and his gut twisted. He took her hands and realised they were shaking. 'Better to get them out of here tonight,' he said.

Be practical, concentrate on the problem and a solution.

'Not knowing where they are will slow him down and give us time to marry.'

Those midnight eyes stared up at him. 'But— where? Where can we go?'

'Grosvenor Square.'

Her hands tightened on his. '*What? Your* house? But—'

'They don't know we're betrothed,' he said. 'Grosvenor Square is the last place Keswick will look for a woman he believes to be my mistress. I've already applied for a special licence. We'll marry as soon as I have it in my hand.' They could weather the inevitable gossip. What mattered now was protecting Emma and the children.

Panic still gripped Emma as they bundled the children into the carriage with their belongings. This was too soon, too fast. She had counted on a week or more for the children to become accustomed to the notion of her marrying Hunt... Oh, why deceive herself? *She* had counted on a week or more to become accustomed. They hadn't even told the children yet. Only that they were moving to Lord Huntercombe's house. Hunt had embraced Harry's reiterated suggestion they should all run away.

'Excellent idea, Harry. That's exactly what to do.'

Now they were all, Bessie and Fergus included, crammed into the carriage. Bessie had been stunned, muttering that she'd go bail his lordship had hundreds of servants.

'None for the nursery and the children know you.'

The children, far from being scared, now viewed the entire situation as a high adventure. With Hunt in charge, apparently nothing could go wrong. Emma could see plenty that could go wrong, but the devil had the whip hand here. The first priority was to remove the children. She could worry about what came later…well, later. How long *did* it take to get a special licence?

Georgie was snuggled on her lap with her favourite doll, all fright forgotten in the excitement. Harry sat quietly, but she could feel him wriggling occasionally.

'Mama, how long can we stay with Lord Huntercombe?'

'For ever,' Georgie said confidently.

Oh, Lord! 'Let's talk about that when we arrive,' Emma suggested. She sought Hunt's gaze and he nodded slightly. Thank goodness. That was one conversation she'd rather not have in a carriage.

* * *

Georgie and Harry stared around the entrance hall of the Grosvenor Square mansion in shocked awe. Emma knew exactly how they felt. Despite having grown up in almost equal splendour, the gleam of black and white tiles, the glitter of crystal and mirrors, the blaze of light from wax candles and the discreetly liveried footmen made *her* feel out of place.

Fergus however, damp with the steady rain, shot past them and shook himself with cheerful disregard for any consideration of his master's dignity or the grandeur of the house.

'Fergus—*sit*!' A footman stepped forward armed with a towel as the dog sat and grinned up expectantly.

'Thank you, Mark.' Hunt smiled at Emma. 'They're all used to him.'

Emma glanced to where the footman was being enthusiastically licked as he rubbed the dog dry. 'I can see that.'

'You really won't mind him in the house?'

She tried not to laugh at the diffident tone of his voice. 'Even if I did, I'd be outvoted. Hunt, I don't mean to change your life.'

He looked relieved. 'That will disappoint my sisters. They deplore what they refer to as my "bachelor habits" and hoped that poor Fergus was one thing my bride would change.'

Emma swallowed hard, wondering what other 'bachelor habits' he might have, and glanced at the children, but Harry and Georgie were helping the footman with Fergus and appeared oblivious to all else. She did not imagine that Hunt had lived like a monk for the past eleven years. It was different for a man. Gentlemen, married or otherwise, frequently had mistresses and no one cared. No one referred to a man's loss of virtue—unless he cheated at cards.

Except she would care. And, given the terms of their agreement, she really had no right to. He was not offering love. Neither was she. She doubted that he would want it. But, she wanted *something*. A loyalty beyond the bargain they had been forced to strike. Something they could choose to give and had not been forced to offer.

'I'm afraid they'll be disappointed, then,' she said lightly. In all likelihood that wasn't the only way in which she was going to disappoint his sisters. Especially when they found out that she had moved in to his house already.

Hunt's staff decreed the library to be the best place for an informal supper. Very quickly a table was placed by the fire and the cold chicken, ham, bread, cheese and plum cake he'd taken to Chelsea were set out.

Bentham, having left the footmen to this task, reappeared and drew Hunt aside. 'Mrs Bentham wishes to know what sleeping arrangements should be made for Master Harry and Miss Georgie.'

'Ah…' Hunt stared at Bentham. 'The nursery? Surely that—'

'The nursery, my lord, is under holland covers and much is packed away in the attic. I fear it will not be possible to use it tonight. The children's nurse and Mrs Bentham have assured me they can have it ready tomorrow.'

Hunt had no idea what was necessary to make a nursery habitable, but if Bentham said it was impossible, then it was impossible.

'Perhaps, my lord, her ladyship might have a solution?'

Hunt could only nod. 'Bentham, you're a genius.' He glanced at Emma, catching her eye. She rose from where they had been showing the children a large globe and came over.

'Is there a problem?'

'The nursery will not be ready tonight,' Hunt said. Would she be upset? Annoyed? He knew so little about her, he realised. Certainly not enough to predict her reaction to a domestic problem.

Emma smiled at Bentham. 'Of course it won't. Put a truckle bed in my room for Master Harry. Miss Georgie may share my bed.'

Bentham blinked. 'Very good, my lady. There is already a truckle bed in the Marchioness's dressing room if that would suffice.'

Emma nodded. 'Excellent. There is a room for the children's nurse?'

'Certainly, my lady. The nurse's room in the nursery is being made ready for Mistress Hull.'

Hunt took a careful breath. Putting Emma in the Marchioness's rooms, which adjoined his, while the right choice, created all sorts of issues.

Namely issues of propriety, although having the children in there should take the sting out of any gossip.

'And Lord Cambourne called while you were out, my lord.'

'He did? He's in town?' He'd thought James out at Chiswick with his wife.

'Yes, my lord.'

'Good. You can take a note over.'

A few minutes later, the servants dismissed and a discreet note dispatched to Cambourne House, the four of them were seated at the impromptu supper table. Emma served the children while Hunt served her and himself. Bentham had placed a bottle of champagne in a bucket of ice and Hunt poured two glasses.

'Don't we have some?' Harry asked.

Hunt raised his brows. 'Certainly not. Mrs Bentham will be wounded to the quick if you don't drink the lemonade she made for you.'

'Lemonade?' Georgie wriggled in delight. 'Mama said she used to have lemonade at parties. Is it nice?'

'You tell me.' Hunt poured some for her and Harry.

Georgie sipped and beamed. 'It's awfully nice. Thank you, sir.'

Harry tried his. 'It's very good, sir.'

Memory stabbed at him. Sitting here with Anne and the children, enjoying an informal supper when their schedules had permitted it, usually a Sunday night. Harry, sitting where Simon had once sat, eyes shining in the lamplight, devoured a chicken leg as if half-starved. Something rose up inside him, hard and painful. Resentment. Shocked, he forced it down, shoved it away. Shameful to resent the boy sitting there. But the wave of longing for his own children, something he thought he had come to terms with long since, washed over him, threatening to drown him… He fought free of the wave, cleared his throat of the bitter lump.

'Harry?'

Harry swallowed a large mouthful of chicken. 'Yes, sir?'

'I have something important to ask you—and Georgie,' he said, thinking that his own daughter would have been deeply annoyed at not being consulted. 'I should like very much to marry your mother. Will you mind if I do?'

Opposite, Emma's eyes widened and in them he read her unspoken question: *What would he do if one of them objected?*

Georgie's eyes lit up. 'Will Fergus come and live with us, too?'

'Don't be silly, Georgie.' Harry didn't take his eyes off Hunt. 'A marquess can't live in a house like ours. We'd have to come and live here.'

'Oh.' Georgie thought about that. 'Well, Fergus would still live with us, so that's all right.'

'Harry?' Hunt watched the boy. He was old enough to know there was more to marriage than that.

'Would *we* still live with Mama?' Harry twisted

his napkin. 'I—we don't want to go and live with the Duke.'

'You'll live with us,' Hunt said calmly. No need to tell the boy that was why Emma had agreed, but— 'In fact, it would make it very hard for the Duke to argue that your mama can't look after you.'

'But she does,' Georgie said. 'Even when we don't want her to!'

Harry bit his lip, glanced at Emma and back at Hunt. 'May I speak to you, sir? In private?'

'Of course.' Hunt laid his napkin beside his plate and rose. 'In the hall?'

Harry nodded and followed him out.

Hunt glanced at the footman on duty. 'Mark? A moment's privacy if you please.'

'Yes, m'lord.' He retreated to the back of the hall.

'Go on, Harry.'

Harry faced him, chin up. 'I… I don't mind, sir. Not if Mama is happy. And of course, we like you—'

He stopped, obviously uncomfortable, so Hunt prompted. 'But? I doubt you can anger me, Harry, or offend me. Just take a deep breath and say it.'

'I don't want to call you *Papa.*'

Hunt swallowed. 'I see.' God help him, he hadn't even thought of that. And the idea of being called *Papa* again, by another man's child…there was that shameful resentment again. 'Well, that's all right,' he said carefully.

'So, do we just keep calling you Lord Hunter-combe?'

Hunt thought. 'Rather a mouthful. When it's family you can call me Uncle Hunt. In more formal company, or with strangers, you can call me Huntercombe or sir. Like any other gentleman would.'

Harry mulled that over for a moment. 'All right. It's…it's not that I don't like you, you know…it's just—' He flushed.

'Just that you remember your papa and miss him,' Hunt said quietly. His own father had been gone for twenty years—he still missed him at times, and his mother. 'I do understand and I'm glad you asked me.' If only there wasn't that little sigh of relief hiding away inside him.

'You really don't mind?'

'Not at all.' Hunt held out his hand and Harry put his in it to shake.

'Do you have children, Uncle Hunt?'

There was a note of hope in the boy's voice and longing for his dead children gouged a little deeper. 'I'm afraid not.' Seeing Harry's disappointment, he summoned a smile. 'But my friend Lord Cambourne has a young brother-in-law about your age. Fitch.'

'Oh.' Harry looked uncertain. 'Is he very grand? I don't know any lords.'

'Fitch?' Hunt let out a snort of laughter at the idea of anyone finding the boy Cambourne had adopted from the streets grand. 'He's not a lord and he'll probably think *you're* very grand. And you know me.'

Harry nodded. 'Yes, but that's different.'

Hunt hesitated. 'Not so very,' he said at last. Time enough later to tell the boy he now held the courtesy title Viscount Thirlbeck, that one day he would be a duke. 'Shall we go back?' he suggested. 'Your mother is probably worried about all the untold rudeness you might be inflicting upon me.'

Harry grinned. 'I thought you *would* think I was being rude.'

Hunt shook his head. 'Not at all. Just settling things between us, one gentleman to another. But be warned; you don't have to call me Papa, but I do have to carry out his job—that's my responsibility to both him and your mother.'

Harry wrinkled his nose. 'All right. But you can't spank Georgie. She's a girl.'

Hunt laughed. 'Understood. Come along.'

Emma breathed a sigh of relief as Hunt and Harry returned, clearly at ease with each other.

'He's not going to be Papa, Georgie,' Harry announced.

Emma's stomach dropped until she saw the laughter in Hunt's eyes.

'I'm to be Uncle Hunt,' he explained.

Harry sat down at the supper table again and helped himself to a piece of cake. 'And he's not allowed to spank Georgie, because she's a girl.'

Georgie smiled beatifically. 'But can we have a puppy? Mama wouldn't say.'

Hunt opened his mouth and Emma cleared her throat, catching his eye. 'Uncle Hunt and I will discuss that,' she said firmly. 'Finish your suppers.'

Hunt sat down, poured the merest drip of champagne into the children's glasses and rather more into his own and Emma's. 'A toast—to our new family.'

Chapter Nine

By the time they finished supper it was so far after the children's bedtime that Georgie was yawning, all the while insisting that she was not in the least bit tired.

'Of course not,' Emma said. 'But you will like to see where we are to sleep tonight.'

'Oh.' Another yawn. 'Where does Fergus sleep?'

Hunt cleared his throat. 'Ah, there is a basket in my bedchamber.'

Emma viewed with interest the faint tinge of colour that stole along his cheekbones, noting that he hadn't actually said *where* the dog slept...just that there was a basket.

'When we have a puppy it could have a basket, too,' Georgie said.

'Uncle Hunt and I can discuss that *after* you're in bed.' Emma rose, held out her hand. Georgie took it. 'What do you say, sweetheart?'

'Goodnight, Uncle Hunt. Thank you for a lovely time and marrying Mama.'

Not so much as a twitch betrayed amusement as Hunt also rose. 'It was very much my pleasure, Georgie. Goodnight. And you, Harry.'

'Goodnight, sir.' Harry flushed. 'Uncle Hunt.'

Hunt watched as they left with Emma. Somehow his house felt a great deal fuller than it had that morning. An odd thought, that. How could a mansion the size of this feel full simply because of the addition of two children to the nursery and their mother? He let out a breath as he faced the truth. It wasn't the house that felt fuller. *He* felt fuller, in a way he hadn't expected and didn't want. What on earth had he let himself in for? When he'd decided on taking a widow, he hadn't expected this feeling of *involvement*. Which was ridiculous. He'd intended to be involved, to be a husband, a kindly guardian to any children. But he hadn't intended *this*. Whatever this was. It was more. More than he and Emma had agreed on. More than either of them wanted. And he couldn't see any way to avoid it.

Emma hesitated outside the library. Bentham had assured her that Hunt was still there. The question was—should she join him? Was the library his private preserve? A place where a wife was only invited? In her parents' marriage the drawing room was Louisa's domain, the library Dersingham's. She took a deep breath. There was only one way to find out how Hunt preferred to live. She opened the door.

He was seated by the fire reading. She saw his surprise as he looked up and hesitated. *Was* she overstepping the bounds?

But he rose, set the book on a wine table and came towards her, smiling. 'I thought you'd stay until Georgie at least fell asleep.'

Emma smiled. 'She was asleep about two minutes after her head hit the pillow and Harry wasn't far behind. I shouldn't stay long though, in case either of them wakes. But I need your advice, if... if you don't mind me coming in here.'

'Mind? Why should I mind?' He handed her to a chair opposite his. 'Emma, this will be your home—indeed, as far as I am concerned, it is your home now. Shall I ring for tea? Or will you have a brandy with me?'

Plenty of men disapproved of a female taking anything stronger than ratafia, but if he'd offered... 'Brandy, please.'

He poured a glass and handed it to her. 'What's bothering you?'

'Harry.' She sipped the brandy, felt it burn its way down. 'I haven't told him that he's Keswick's heir.' It weighed on her. Harry's future glittered golden. She ought to be delighted, glad his future was assured.

Instead it terrified her.

'You haven't had time to arrange your own thoughts, let alone tell Harry.' Hunt looked at her closely. 'Ah. You're still frightened of losing him.'

'Yes.' She forced back the fear, managed a smile. 'Silly, but—'

'No.' Hunt shook his head. 'Even with us married, Keswick will probably do his damnedest to insist on custody. Trust me, Emma. I can protect you and the children.'

She looked up at him. He stood beside her chair, tall, reassuring in his quiet confidence. Her heart ached for the bargain they were making. He deserved so much more…except he did not want more. She had to remember that and respect it. She had to be a conventional, sensibly married lady, not headstrong Emma Brandon-Smythe who had flung her cap over the windmill for a younger son and never regretted it. She had *loved* Peter, had believed she would never truly desire another man. But apparently she did. She desired Hunt. Was she a wanton to want it to be more than duty? Even if love was forbidden, she wanted him to want *her*. Emma. She wanted to desire and be desired. Not to submit out of duty to a man who only bedded her out of duty.

'Emma?'

He had asked her to trust him. 'I know you will.'

She rose on her toes, intending only to brush her lips over his jaw.

She intended a kiss on the cheek. Chaste, completely non-sexual. But he didn't want that. He took her into his arms and captured her mouth. He felt her shock, felt her quiver to utter stillness against him. But then her body softened, the lush, soft mouth trembled under his and opened in invitation. He stroked his tongue inside and she tasted exactly as he remembered: spicy-sweet, tart and wild. She responded on a sigh of pleasure, her tongue answering his, their mouths melding. Heat poured through him and his arms tightened. Soft, supple curves, warm and so damn tempting under his hands. Her mouth a miracle of wild delight, answering his need with her own. He could taste it, feel it. Desire, welling up in her to meet his head on. He wanted her. Wanted her now. And the sofa was right there... *No*. Some semblance of honour reared its head, struggling for a footing in the surging riptide. Not like this. No matter how much they both wanted it.

Somehow he broke the kiss and wondered if part of him had ripped away. Emma blinked up at him, her eyes clouded and fathomless, mouth swollen from his kisses. He eased her back a little, his whole body rebelling, demanding that he sweep her up, lay her on the nearest horizontal surface and finish what he, what *they* had started. Because it had been *they*. Not just him. She wanted as much, as deeply, as he did.

'No.' He scarcely recognised his own voice. Rough, shaken.

Emma flinched. 'I'm sorry. I didn't mean to—'

'Don't apologise.' His hands tightened on her shoulders for an instant before he released her and stepped away. 'That was my fault. I shouldn't even be here.'

'Shouldn't be here? This is your house.'

He drew a careful breath. How the devil had a kiss reduced him to burning need? 'Regardless, I've arranged to stay across the square with the Cambournes until we marry.'

'Oh.' She looked as she might have argued, but sighed. 'I'm sorry to cause you so much trouble.' Her cheeks flushed. 'Choosing someone without all these complications would have been a great deal easier for you.'

'No.' He turned away, picked up his brandy and drained it. That wasn't true. With another woman it would have been easier to keep his life untrammelled. But he had met Emma and now he didn't want anyone else. He wanted Emma. It just meant he had to work harder to keep everything on an even keel.

He gave her a kindly smile, setting the empty glass down. 'I'll bid you goodnight, Emma. My staff will look after you.'

'Of course. Goodnight, sir.'

Emma stared at the door for a moment after it closed. Something had changed in Hunt. Was he regretting his offer of marriage? She probably shouldn't have come in here after all and he was too polite to have said so.

A marriage of convenience. That was what he had offered. What he wanted. She had to accept those boundaries. And if something in her didn't want those boundaries, then that was her problem. She could not make it his.

* * *

Entering the breakfast parlour of Cambourne House at an unconscionably early hour the next morning, Hunt was not surprised to find James, Earl of Cambourne, enjoying a plate of ham and eggs. He had seen neither James nor the Countess last night since they had been dining with friends.

James finished a mouthful and set down his knife and fork. 'Morning, Hunt. Penfold mentioned that we had a house guest. Sheets not aired to your satisfaction across the square?' He gestured at the coffee pot. 'It's fresh. I trust you passed a comfortable night?'

'Thank you.' A restless night was nothing unusual and certainly couldn't be blamed on the bed. Hunt took refuge in the coffee pot and niceties. 'Lucy is well?' He poured a cup of coffee, added cream.

James's mouth curved. 'She's very well. And just as curious as I am to know why you slept here last night.'

Hunt sipped his coffee. 'Propriety. My betrothed moved in last night.'

James's coffee cup rattled in its saucer as he set it down. 'You have my undivided attention.'

Although almost twenty years younger than himself, the Earl was one of Hunt's closest friends and Hunt had no hesitation in explaining the situation to him and the hastily summoned Countess, and issuing a very open-ended wedding invitation.

'I can't say when it will be,' he said. 'A day or so. I hope you'll attend.' Letty and Caroline were going to be furious. A couple of friendly faces would be very welcome.

James nodded. 'Since you aren't marrying Amelia Trumble we'll stay in town for a few more days.

Hunt and the Countess stared at him.

'James—' Lucy Cambourne sounded puzzled '—why would you think that Huntercombe was going to marry Mrs Trumble?'

James grinned. 'Because Letty Fortescue cornered me last night after dinner, singing the Virtuous Widow's praises as a suitable bride. At first I thought she'd forgotten I was married, but when I reminded her about you, she clarified.' He poured more coffee.

Hunt regarded him balefully. 'You didn't think to say something earlier? Warn me, perhaps?'

'Of course, but you broke your news first.' James sipped his coffee. 'And if you've already installed Emma Lacy in the Marchioness's suite and moved in here to keep it all above board, then you're safe. Letty's left holding the baby, or rather the Virtuous Widow, and there isn't much she can do.'

Hunt thought it was a fairly safe wager that Letty, and Caroline, would find something. If not to do, then to say. Repeatedly.

'Hunt?'

He turned to Lucy, sipping her tea by the window. 'Yes?'

She gestured out the window. 'You're always welcome here, but it might be time you went home.'

Hunt strode over, glanced across the square and choked back a curse.

Following breakfast in the nursery, Emma took the children down to the library. Routine was important and since lessons followed breakfast, the library seemed the best place with the schoolroom still being readied. The housekeeper had assured her the room would be ready later that day and that his lordship's secretary, Mr Barclay, was working not in the library, but in his office.

Both children had been fascinated by the large and detailed globe in the library and it seemed a good way to frame a lesson for Harry. She set him down at the table with paper and pencil to produce a map of Europe, complete with capital cities. Fergus, clearly at home, settled himself by the fire and went to sleep, his chin on the fender.

A quick glance at the bookshelves found something she thought Georgie would enjoy. She sat down, the child in her lap, and began to read slowly. In French.

Georgie scowled, but chewed on her lower lip, listening hard. After a moment her face lit up. 'It's Cinderella!'

Emma laughed. *'En Français!'*

Georgie wriggled, looked hard at the print. *'C'est Cen... Cendrillon!'* She snuggled closer, listening happily.

Harry looked up as the doorbell clanged. 'Should we see who it is, Mama?'

'Bentham will see to it,' Emma said absently.

'Oh.' Harry sounded impressed. 'Don't we ever have to answer the door?'

Emma looked up from Cinderella. 'No. Not here.'

'But what if Mr Bentham lets someone in we don't like?' Georgie asked.

Emma smiled. 'He won't. He's very good at his job.'

A few moments later a carrying female voice was heard. 'Nonsense, Bentham. If his lordship *is* out at this unlikely hour we shall await him in the library.'

Emma's stomach turned to lead. Only a family member would presume to such familiarity... Fergus had raised his head and was looking intently at the door.

Emma turned to both children. 'Not a word out of either of you.'

Harry scowled. 'But, Mama, you said—'

'Not a word.'

The door opened and Fergus uttered two loud barks.

'*Don't* tell me he leaves that wretched dog inside unsupervised!'

A tall, commanding woman, whom Emma remembered to be Hunt's sister, Lady Fortescue, stood in the doorway, her disapproving gaze on the spaniel. 'Bentham, what is this creature doing in—and *who*, may I ask, are *you*?'

Lady Fortescue's expression switched from disapproval to outrage as her gaze shifted from the dog to Emma.

Extricating herself, Emma rose, fiercely conscious of her plain, not to say shabby, gown, simply dressed hair and complete lack of a cap.

Another fashionably dressed lady entered the room and raised a quizzing glass. 'Good heavens!' she uttered in pained accents.

Emma gritted her teeth and summoned a smile. 'Good morning.' She remembered both Huntercombe's sisters perfectly well. The younger was Lady Caroline Chantry, wife of an M.P.

'But who *are* you?' Lady Fortescue demanded, ignoring the greeting. 'What are you doing here and where is his lordship?'

Emma kept her face impassive and her voice polite. 'Lady Emma Lacy. My children and I are guests.' Behind Lady Fortescue and Lady Caroline she could see Bentham, his face purple. 'Bentham, please send a message to his lordship that Lady Fortescue and Lady Caroline are here.'

'Lady Emma—?' Lady Fortescue's jaw dropped in a most unladylike fashion. 'I *warned* Huntercombe how it would be!'

'Uncle Hunt *invited* us. Didn't he, Mama?' Georgie, clutching the book of French fairy tales, had come to stand beside Emma and was staring at Lady Fortescue with open curiosity.

Emma dragged in a breath, touched a protective hand to Georgie's shoulder. 'Yes, Georgie. He did.' She faced the formidable matron. 'Huntercombe will be home very shortly, Lady Fortescue.'

Feathers trembled in Lady Fortescue's bonnet

and her nostrils flared. 'My brother must be lost to all sense to have admitted you to this house!'

'Quite so!' Lady Caroline ranged herself beside her sister.

Emma caught sight of Bentham, still in the doorway. 'Bentham, a tea tray, please, and milk for Master Harry and Miss Georgie.'

Lady Fortescue whipped around. 'Do no such thing, Bentham!' She glared at Emma. 'You have no right to be issuing—'

'She has every right, Letty.'

Emma's breath jerked in as Hunt strode in. His deep voice was icy, all the more lethal for its very quietness. 'Add coffee to that tray, please, Bentham.'

Hunt assessed the situation in one swift glance. Letty and Caroline had never quite lost the habit of treating his house as though it were still *their* London home to walk in and out of as they pleased. His not having a wife for the past eleven years had reinforced the tendency since occasionally one or the other acted as hostess for him. But it did not excuse them invading his library when he wasn't even home and—

'Huntercombe, *what* is this woman doing here? Have you lost your—?'

'Lady Emma has done me the very great honour of accepting my hand in marriage.' He viewed the results of this bombshell with satisfaction.

Letty's startled squawk was counterpointed by a

horrified moan from Caroline, who collapsed back on to the sofa in a suspiciously artistic fashion.

'Oh, for heaven's sake, Caro!' Letty snapped. 'Stop play-acting!'

Caroline sat up at once, her mouth sulky. 'Have you *no* sensibility, Letty? The shock—!'

Letty ignored this. 'Giles, have you lost your mind?'

'No,' Hunt said. 'But you and Caro appear to have mislaid both manners and dignity.'

'Huntercombe.' Emma's quiet voice held gentle reproof. 'This must be a very great shock for your family—'

'It certainly is!' Caroline struck in, her vapours forgotten. 'In fact—' She wilted under Hunt's glare.

'Caro, I was under the impression that you were fixed in the country for now.' He didn't miss the nervous look she sent Letty.

'Naturally, Giles, when Letty informed me that you were, ah, considering a change in your *estate*...'

If he hadn't been so annoyed, her floundering would have been funny. 'Yes, Caro?'

She scowled. 'Well, I, that is, Letty and I, felt that it was of the *first* importance that—' She broke off.

'Giles.' Letty fixed him with her best chilly stare. 'If you are so lost to all propriety as to have installed your—' She seemed to collect herself. 'Your *betrothed* in this house already, then—'

'I'm staying with Cambourne,' Hunt told her

and took an unholy satisfaction in her dropped jaw. 'Quite acceptable. Now perhaps you might like to congratulate me and wish Emma happy?'

Into the outraged silence another voice dropped. 'Are we interrupting?'

Hunt turned and barely suppressed a heartfelt *Thank God!*

James stood in the doorway, his Countess on his arm, and an amused quirk at the corner of his mouth.

Hunt strode forward. 'Cambourne. Ma'am.' He shook James's hand and bowed over Lucy's as though he had not recently quitted their breakfast table.

'Emma, my dear, permit me to present Lord and Lady Cambourne.' His gaze fell on the young boy hovering behind them. 'And Master Philip Fitzjames—Cambourne's ward.' He held out his hand to the boy, better known to his intimates simply as Fitch, who shook it with an expression of surprise.

As a diversionary tactic it was superb. While James bowed over Emma's hand his pestilential sisters regained their control.

'I think that Caroline and I should take our leave.' Letty spoke in calmer, if still arctic, tones.

James straightened. 'Not on our account, I do hope, Lady Fortescue. Hunt announced his happy news at breakfast and we thought to come and pay our respects to Lady Emma. I don't believe you are acquainted with my ward?' He turned to the boy. 'Lady Fortescue, Fitch. And Lady Caroline Chantry. And of course, Lady Emma Lacy.'

Lady Fortescue gave a visible shudder. 'I had heard something, I believe.' She fixed the boy with a basilisk stare. 'Lady Cambourne's brother, is he not?'

Not noticeably abashed, the boy made a very passable bow to Letty. 'Yes, ma'am.' He repeated this for Emma and Caro's benefit.

'Well done, Fitch.' Hunt tried not to laugh. 'This is Harry Lacy and his sister, Georgie. No need to bow to them. Why don't you accompany them out to the stables with Fergus? You know the way. Tell Masters that I sent you.'

'Yes, sir.'

The Countess cleared her throat and Fitch scowled at her. 'I hadn't forgotten.' He looked back at Hunt. 'Congratulations, sir.' He looked at the Countess. 'That was what you said, wasn't it?'

She looked pointedly at Emma. The boy grimaced. 'Oh, right.' He turned to Emma. 'I hope you'll be very happy, ma'am.' Cocking his head on one side, he added, 'He's not bad for a toff.'

'The stables. *Now*,' James muttered.

Hunt inclined his head to Fitch. 'Thank you. I believe that was a compliment?'

The boy gave Hunt a cheeky grin, and headed for the door. 'Yes, sir. You're pretty good in a tight spot.'

Hunt laughed. 'I could say the same of you. Off you go.' He smiled at Harry and Georgie. 'Go with Fitch. Obey Masters and you won't get kicked.'

* * *

Emma heaved a sigh of relief when Bentham and a footman arrived with tea, coffee and cakes. The atmosphere could have chilled champagne. She could only hope hot tea would thaw Hunt's sisters out a trifle.

Bentham set his tray before her. 'I took the liberty, my lady, of sending the milk and cake out to the stables with the children.'

'Thank you, Bentham. I'm sure Harry thinks breakfast was a very long time ago.'

Lady Cambourne laughed. 'Poor Fitch always thinks his last meal was far too long ago. Tell me, when are you to be married? We were so pleased to hear Hunt's news.'

Emma had no answer for that, but Hunt stepped in. 'With Lady Emma's agreement, we will be married as soon as the special licence is granted.'

Lady Fortescue cleared her throat in a very decided fashion. 'My dear Huntercombe—'

'Tomorrow if it arrives today,' Hunt continued.

Lady Caroline looked pained. 'Really, Huntercombe! Surely there is no need to be in *quite* such a hurry. After all—'

'I am sure that I have any number of important engagements this week,' Lady Fortescue announced. 'And next week. Perhaps next month would be better. I shall provide you with a list of my engagements and Caroline will do the same—'

'Thank you, Letty,' Hunt said gravely. 'Your lists are always so enlightening. I'll send you a note when the marriage has taken place, shall I?'

Lady Caroline looked as though she had swallowed a brick. 'You will surely wish us to attend!'

'Certainly,' Hunt said. 'But—'

Hunt's secretary, Mr Barclay, entered unannounced. 'Sir, these have arrived from his Grace, the Archbishop.' He held out a thick bundle of documents.

James grinned. 'Lucy, my love, I believe we're attending a wedding tomorrow. Remind me to have my own secretary clear my day.'

Hunt broke the seals and glanced at the documents. Relief flooded him. 'All is in order. And a private note from my cousin, David.' He glanced up at Emma. 'David is attached to Lambeth Palace as a chaplain. The old chap has offered to perform the marriage.'

Emma blinked. 'How very kind of him.'

Hunt didn't dare glance at his sisters. 'More a case of David saving his own skin actually. He's seventy, unmarried and my extremely reluctant heir.'

Chapter Ten

Hunt scowled into the looking glass the following morning as he tied his cravat with even more than his usual care. A wedding should be special. Not rushed, not entered into in any hole-and-corner fashion. Although he thought there was rather more ground between hole-and-corner and the pomp and circumstance his sisters considered his due. He suspected they had hoped, given a month, that they might scuttle the marriage.

His jaw hardened. Even without the threat of Keswick he wouldn't have been prepared to let them try to frighten Emma out of it. But a woman should have time to feel like a bride. She should not be rushed from proposal to betrothal to marriage in the space of two days. Well, a couple of weeks if he counted from their initial discussion of marriage.

For God's sake! He inserted a finger between

neck and collar. His cravat felt too tight, just as it had at his first wedding. He'd known Emma for three weeks. Oh, he'd known her by sight when she made her come-out years ago. Enough so that he'd greeted her at parties and chatted to her a couple of times. She had been one of the flock of young ladies in whom he had no interest beyond his acquaintance with her father. Now he was dragging her to the altar in less than an hour. He hoped she had found something pretty to wear at least. Lucy had taken Emma shopping yesterday afternoon with carte blanche to order whatever was needed for herself and the children. It was the very least she deserved.

He liked her children. He liked *her*. He was attracted to her.

It terrified him.

What if he failed them? Emma was marrying him to protect her children. What if a magistrate deemed him insufficient as a guardian? In itself Keswick's claim was undeniable. It all came down to his own reputation and influence. And a little bit of luck as to which magistrate Keswick had in his pocket.

What did he have to offer Emma if he couldn't protect Harry and Georgie?

He made the final adjustments to the folds of his cravat and stared critically at the greying, middle-aged gentleman in the looking glass. Fifty. Hell. He had not paid a great deal of attention to his birthday for the past ten years. He had said he was too old for birthdays. He had always made sure he did something for Gerald's birthday when his half-brother was a child, had taken his god-daughter out on her birthday if possible, but he had shied away from any mention of his own birthday. Better not to remember...

He held out his hand for the pearl pin his valet was holding. 'Thank you.' Carefully he set the pin in place in his cravat. Precise, neat. Exactly where it ought to be.

He had nothing to offer because there was nothing left. He had already given it all and been hollowed out, emptied, eleven years ago. What little had been left had shattered last year when Gerald died.

All that was left was the empty shell, an automaton who was geared to do the right thing, the decent thing, and tie his cravat perfectly. It was safer that way.

He caught his valet's eye in the looking glass, holding his coat ready. 'Thank you, John.'

The valet eased the coat on. Dark blue superfine, it was one he kept for occasions when it was important not to look as though he'd shrugged himself into his coat. Not that he'd been thinking of a wedding when he ordered it.

John gave the shoulders a tweak and stepped back. 'There. That will do.' He cleared his throat. 'Congratulations, my lord.'

Hunt met the man's eyes with a brief smile. 'Thank you. I'm a lucky man.' He was. He had to remember that. And remember how to keep everything perfectly in its place. Like the pearl in his cravat.

John nodded. 'You are now that you've looked for a bit of luck.' He smiled. 'Nice to have some young life in the house again, too. Not but what Mrs Bentham is muttering about the eating capacity of young boys.'

'Is she now?' Hunt glanced at the clock, preferring not to think about John's previous comment. 'I'd better not be late. Thank you, John.'

Hunt left his dressing room, wondering exactly who would show up for his wedding.

He got part of the answer at the door into the music room where he and Cambourne were supposed to wait until they got word the bride was coming down. Then they would go through to the drawing room.

Dersingham met him at the music-room door. 'I received your invitation, Huntercombe.' His scowl threatened to leave indelible evidence of its presence. 'If invitation it could be called.'

Hunt inclined his head. 'Naturally we wished you to attend, Dersingham.'

Dersingham huffed. 'Well, it's a nice thing when a man is *invited* to his daughter's wedding!'

Hunt raised his brows. He'd merely informed Dersingham of the time of the wedding. It hadn't been an invitation, as such. How *did* one invite the parents of the bride to their daughter's wedding? 'Lady Dersingham is here?'

The scowl assumed epic proportions. 'Certainly.' Dersingham adjusted his cuffs. 'Now if one of your servants would be so good as to show me *where* I am supposed to be, I'll get there.' He shot a filthy glance at the footman further along the hallway.

Following his glance, Hunt beckoned to the footman. 'Robert, do show his lordship to his seat.'

Dersingham's teeth ground. 'In case you have forgotten, Huntercombe, a man is supposed to escort his daughter down the aisle.'

Hunt's control teetered. 'No, I hadn't forgotten. But since *you* forgot that the last time Emma married, I believe other arrangements have been made.'

Dersingham stared at him. '*What?* Are you insane, Huntercombe? Other arrangements? What will people *say*?'

Hunt shrugged. 'I have no idea.' Over Dersingham's shoulder he saw Barclay, wearing his *This is urgent* expression. 'You will excuse me, sir. There is something I must attend to. Robert—' he gestured again to the footman '—his lordship's seat, if you please.'

Ensuring only that Dersingham was in Robert's capable hands, Hunt turned to Barclay. 'What is it, William?'

Barclay spoke very quietly. 'The Duke of Keswick has arrived with a magistrate. Demanding the return of his grandchildren. He knows they're here.'

* * *

Heat pricked at the back of Emma's eyes as she came downstairs. A bride usually carried flowers and a prayer book, but Emma's hands were otherwise occupied. Harry held one and Georgie the other. Harry carried the prayer book and Georgie clutched a posy of flowers.

'We practised with Mr Barclay and Bentham and Mrs Bentham,' Harry had informed her. 'When the priest asks, "Who gives this woman?" we have to say, "We do." Georgie puts your hand in Uncle Hunt's and I hand you the prayer book.'

'I keep holding the flowers,' Georgie said, 'because Mr Barclay said you wouldn't have enough hands.'

Neither child appeared to be in the least nervous. Which was a very good thing, because her own knees were shaking. The first time she had been married she had not been nervous at all. The only people present had been herself, Peter, his great-aunt, the groomsman and a very disapproving clergyman. The absolute legal minimum for a valid marriage.

This time the hum of chatter swelling through the open drawing-room door told her that the congregation was markedly larger and her stomach turned somersaults at the enormity of what she was doing. She was contracting—that was the only word for it—a marriage for financial gain and mutual convenience and need. She needed her children safe: he needed an heir.

'Ready, Mama?'

She managed a smile for Georgie, who beamed in utter confidence.

'You look like a princess, Mama.' Georgie sighed happily. '*Just* like Cinderella.'

'Thank you, sweetheart.'

Tears threatened again. Georgie's whole idea of marriage was what happened at the end of Cinderella. Wicked stepmother vanquished, the slipper safely on Cinderella's dainty foot and a happily-ever-after to follow.

At thirty-two, Emma knew it was not that simple.

There could be happiness, yes. Happiness together, even joy. But even she and Peter had not always been happy. There had been worry. About money, the children, sometimes the fear that the other might regret their choice. But they had been happy together. Happy, even joyful, to *be* together. Neither had ever regretted their choice. Because they had loved. Deeply and to the end. That and the children left no room for regret. *'No regrets, Emm,'* had been Peter's last words before he left her.

But this marriage was different. Love did not enter into it. This marriage was about duty. For herself and for Hunt. She had to remember that, and that her children, their happiness and safety, and Hunt's heirs must be at the core of her marriage.

But Georgie still believed in the innocence of fairy tales.

Emma blinked back the tears. She smiled at

Harry, so solemn and grown-up in his breeches, stockings and brown-velvet coat. 'Let's not keep your Uncle Hunt waiting.'

The sudden hush told Hunt that it was time. He turned and wondered if his heart had stopped. Certainly his breath caught. She stood just inside the door, the children on either side. Gone was the shabby, threadbare grey that had leached all colour from her face. Instead she shimmered in lace-trimmed amber silk. Her dark hair was uncovered and arranged so that soft curls framed her face. The pearls he had given her yesterday glowed at her throat and ears.

Their eyes met, hers shy, questioning. Now his heart really did stop. Would she regret this? Then she was moving, tugged along, it seemed, by Harry and Georgie, and he could see the laughter in her eyes. He nearly laughed aloud in response. Apparently those two had no qualms. And Emma was smiling now, all shyness gone, as she came to him down the length of the room and the guests watched her progress. Only the faintest blush betrayed her awareness of their scrutiny. Her chin was high and he knew a sudden fear, as she came to him so confidently. What if he had miscalculated and his strategy to confound Keswick misfired into a scandal?

Letty and Caroline sat at the front with their husbands, gracious smiles pinned in place. The pair of them had concluded that open disapproval would only cause gossip, according to Letty when she had spoken to him earlier. He had politely pointed out that *any* disapproval, open or private, would cause a family breach. Letty's mouth had thinned, but she had accepted the rebuke.

But if he'd got it wrong with Keswick...

Across from his sisters, Louisa Dersingham was all sweet smiles and a lace-edged handkerchief that she dabbed to her eyes when she thought anyone was watching. Dersingham's face was utterly rigid. More than one puzzled glance had been cast at him by guests obviously wondering who was going to give the bride away.

Then Emma stood beside him with the children. Harry, solemn and serious with responsibility, and little Georgie radiant.

Feigning a confidence he was far from feeling, he bent to Emma and spoke very softly. 'Trust me. Keswick has arrived. I have given instructions for him to be shown in here.'

Only the swift intake of breath betrayed her. Wide, questioning eyes met his.

'Trust me,' Hunt repeated, praying she was right to do so. 'He won't dare.'

'Giles, dear boy?'

He glanced at his cousin, waiting to marry them. 'A moment, David. A late arrival.'

David nodded obligingly. 'Of course.'

A moment later the drawing-room door opened and Barclay ushered in Keswick, Lord Martin Lacy and a small spare man Hunt recognised as the magistrate Sir Hector Sloane. Keswick's jaw dropped as he stalked in, leaning heavily on his cane, and realised the room was full. Lord Martin's startled gaze fell on Hunt and Emma and his expression froze. Swiftly he bent to his father, whispered something. Keswick's eyes bulged.

Hunt took a step forward. 'Welcome, your Grace, Lord Martin, Sir Hector. Please, be seated.' He waited—an instant that stretched into an eternity—praying it wasn't about to blow up in his face. Keswick's mouth opened and Hunt held his breath.

If Keswick simply walked out the scandal would be cataclysmic. If he made a scene... Lord Martin muttered in his father's ear.

Keswick's mouth shut like a trap and he stalked to the seat a footman was holding for him. His son and Sir Hector sat down to either side.

Releasing his breath, Hunt turned back to David. 'We're ready.'

David smiled at them, settled his preaching bands, and began. 'Dearly beloved...'

Only rarely did Hunt really listen to a clergyman enumerate the reasons for marriage, starting with procreation and advising the parties to be reverent, discreet and sober about it.

According to David they were marrying for all the right reasons. And it *felt* right, although he hoped the wedding night would not be particularly reverent. Sober, yes, but not reverent.

And then the question: 'Who gives this woman to be married to this man?'

'We do.'

The young voices rang out, accompanied by a startled murmur from the assembled guests.

Georgie placed Emma's hand in Hunt's and Harry handed her the prayer book. He took his sister's hand and they stepped back to stand with Lucy and Fitch in the front row of chairs. His throat tight, Hunt closed his fingers over Emma's, felt her tremble. All the right reasons, he reminded himself, as he turned to smile down at her, and he prayed that the ceremony would give Keswick time to come to his senses.

Emma kept her chin high and her smile gracious, as Hunt led her through to the music room to receive their guests. One by one they filed past and Hunt presented her. Bentham had already whisked the children back to the nursery, promising that there was a special meal up there and that it would be all boring speeches and adult chatter at the wedding breakfast.

Better, Hunt had murmured, if Keswick's heir and lost booty were not paraded under his nose for too long. She could only agree.

'A *private* word with you, Huntercombe.' Keswick sounded as though his back teeth were glued together. He glared at her, his face mottling.

'As many as you like, sir,' Hunt said calmly. 'After our other guests have left. Harborough!' He smiled at the peer behind Keswick. 'Good of you to come at such short notice.'

His breathing audible, Keswick moved on, making room for Lord Harborough and his lady who

were full of cheerful congratulations. Emma kept
her smile firmly in place as she greeted one after
another of Hunt's relations and close friends. And
then Lord Martin Lacy and Sir Hector Sloane…

'Ah, Huntercombe.' Sir Hector was perspiring.
'Happy occasion, what? Hope you don't think I intended…that is—' He wiped his brow.

Hunt smiled enigmatically. 'You're very welcome, Sloane. Emma, my dear, Sir Hector Sloane.'

Emma smiled the charming social smile she
had perfected over a decade before and pretended
that Sir Hector didn't know that *she* knew he'd
come with Keswick and Lord Martin to take custody of her children. Instead she reminded herself
that, as Hunt's wife, she outranked every other
woman in the room, including her own mother,
and most of the gentlemen, including her erstwhile
brother-in-law and the unfortunate magistrate.

After a wedding breakfast that gave no indica-
tion the marriage had been conducted with rather
less than twenty-four hours' notice, the guests
began to take their leave. Louisa took a sweetly
tearful, very public farewell of her daughter.

'A mother's heart, you know,' she said in lowered tones that somehow carried to everyone. 'So
glad, dearest, to see you so well settled.'

Emma's dignified smile held. 'Thank you,
Mother.'

Louisa sailed from the room, Dersingham bob-
bing in her wake, on a positive wave of social sen-
timent and approval.

With their departure the laggards began to take their leave. Emma saw Hunt stroll over and speak very quietly to Lord Martin, who for the past two hours had been the perfect wedding guest, laughing and smiling with the best of them, although giving his hosts a wide berth. Lord Martin's eyes narrowed, but he nodded and walked to where his father and Sir Hector stood chatting to Lord Cambourne and Mr Fox.

Emma returned polite platitudes to Lady Fortescue as she watched Keswick and his companions take a punctilious farewell of Hunt.

A few moments later the last guests were gone and Emma let out a shuddering sigh. Even Keswick had left without a fuss and they were alone. Except for the children and a houseful of servants.

'Alone for a moment.' Hunt picked up a glass and poured champagne into it. 'Here. Have this. I think a little fortification is in order.'

Something about the tone of his voice had Emma's eyes snapping to his as she accepted the champagne. 'Is something wrong?'

His mouth hardened as he poured a glass for himself. 'Keswick, Lacy and Sloane are in the library. No.' He touched her wrist lightly as she made to set the glass down. 'Finish it.'

'But, surely we should—'

'Make them wait.' A faint smile curved his mouth. 'Strategy. Making them wait at our convenience is to our advantage. Sloane is deeply uncomfortable anyway. Give him time to stew a little more.'

He touched his glass to hers. 'It will be all right, Emma. Trust me. By attending our wedding Keswick overplayed his hand. He can hardly turn around now and claim either of us to be an unfit guardian.'

Keswick stood scowling by the fire with Lord Martin and Sir Hector Sloane. The scowl deepened as Hunt and Emma entered, and the moment the door closed he started forward.

'Huntercombe, whatever folly you have embarked upon, I demand that my heir be—'

'Your *heir*? Not your grandson?'

Keswick spluttered. 'What nonsense is—?'

'You are not in a position to demand anything, Keswick.' Hunt kept his voice utterly calm, fiercely aware of Emma's hand gripping on his arm. Even though he had just married her for an heir, no child should simply be *the heir*. Or the spare. 'Naturally as Emma's erstwhile father-in-law you are a welcome guest, as are Lord Martin and Sloane.'

Keswick snorted. 'Poppycock! I don't know how she hoodwinked you into offering marriage, but my heir needs a proper education and guardian! While as for the girl—'

Hunt raised his brows. 'Again, your *heir*. And are you suggesting that I am an *im*proper guardian?' Sloane, Hunt noted, had paled. He continued, 'Or that I cannot see that Harry—yes, he does have a name, Keswick—is educated and trained to his position? You *are* aware that my marriage

to Harry and Georgie's mother makes me their
guardian-in-law?'

Sir Hector cleared his throat. 'As to that—'

'And surely no one,' Hunt continued as if Sloane
had not spoken, 'is suggesting that the Marchioness of Huntercombe—' his hand covered Emma's, felt it tremble '—is an unfit mother?'

The silence thickened and Lord Martin's mouth
flattened.

After a blistering moment, Hunt nodded.
'Good. Because I would have no hesitation in my
response.'

Emma's fingers tightened on his arm and Lord
Martin scowled.

'Now, Huntercombe, I am sure no one means
anything of the sort.' Sir Hector looked as though
he wished himself elsewhere. 'But as Lord Peter's
father, his Grace would be the natural guardian,
so *your* claim to be guardian by right of marriage
to the mother is—'

'In addition to Lord Peter's will naming Lady
Emma as sole guardian and specifically exclud-
ing his father,' Hunt said, his voice icing over,
'Keswick forfeited his so-called *rights* when he
repudiated his grandchildren at the time of Lord
Peter's death.' He sent Keswick a cold look. 'Perhaps, Sloane, you might like to read the letter Keswick sent then? I assume you know the contents,
Keswick, since the original bears your signature
and seal.'

Keswick scowled. 'That's beside the point. The
boy is now my heir and—'

'I'd be interested to see it.' Lord Martin ignored his sire's mutterings and held Hunt's gaze with his own. 'Very interested.'

Hunt inclined his head. 'Of course, Lacy.' He stalked over to his desk. 'I had my secretary make a copy. My solicitor has the original in his keeping and is arranging for notarised copies to be made.'

Lord Martin snorted. 'Careful, aren't you?'

Hunt drew the copy from his desk drawer. 'Extremely. Read it. Then ask yourself what the effect would be if it were read out in court. Or if one of those copies somehow found its way into someone else's hands.'

Keswick's eyes bulged at the implied threat as Lord Martin took the single sheet and scanned it. Slowly he looked up at his father. 'Do you remember what is in this, sir?'

Keswick shrugged in apparent unconcern, but his gaze shifted under the hard stare of his son. 'I don't recall exactly. It was years ago, for God's sake!'

Lord Martin handed the letter back to Hunt. 'Illuminating. I'll bid you good day, Huntercombe.' His gaze flicked to Emma and he executed a stiff bow. 'Ma'am. Accept my felicitations.'

'Where the devil do you think you're going?' Keswick demanded as his son walked towards the door.

'I have another engagement, sir. And after reading that I've nothing more to say to Huntercombe beyond congratulations.' He shot the Duke a scathing glance. 'I suggest you have a look at that letter if you can't recall its contents. Believe me, you don't want it read out in court. Or anywhere else.'

He nodded to Hunt, bowed to Emma and left, closing the door behind him.

Hunt met Keswick's furious glare. 'Do you need to refresh your memory?'

Keswick clenched his fists. 'Come now, Huntercombe. Be reasonable. Bygones should be bygones. The boy is now my heir; that changes things materially.'

'Of course, Keswick.' Hunt glanced at the letter. 'But it won't change the fact that four years ago you informed your son's widow that she and her *spawn* were welcome to end in the gutter where they belonged.'

'I say, Huntercombe!' Sir Hector looked scandalised. 'That's a little strong, don't you think?'

Hunt held out the letter. 'Not my words, Sloane. Read it for yourself and tell me if you think the man who could write that about his grandchildren, after cancelling their father's annuity, is a suitable guardian.' He glanced at Keswick. 'I'll have no hesitation in making the contents of this letter public, Keswick, if you attempt to wrest custody of the children from me.'

Sloane took the letter, frowned as he read it.

Emma held her breath. Hunt had possession of the children now, but if Keswick chose to fight he still had a claim that a court would be bound at the very least to consider. How much did he care about public opinion?

Sloane shook his head. 'While it *could* be argued that this letter does not waive your claim, Keswick, I couldn't advise you to pursue it. Your only remaining argument, now that Lady Emma has married Huntercombe, is that the boy is your heir. Huntercombe's own position negates that. The lad can clearly be trained to his position by his stepfather. It might be different had you taken some interest in the children before this, but as it is—' He shook his head. 'Unless you wish to question Huntercombe's moral fitness or his wife's moral fitness—' He cleared his throat. 'In which case *very* clear evidence would be required.'

There was a moment's shattering silence. Then Keswick turned on his heel and stalked out. Hunt heard the careful breath Emma released.

Sir Hector gulped. 'I think that concludes the matter, Huntercombe.'

Fierce exaltation shook him. He'd done it. He hadn't failed her. 'Thank you, Sloane.' Hunt kept his voice easy, as though a minor point of ownership had been settled. 'One thing—are you acquainted with Lord Pickford?' Best to get everything clear.

Sloane went very red. 'We've met.'

'I thought you might have,' Hunt said. 'An acquaintance of Keswick's, I believe. Perhaps you would convey to him anything from this meeting that you consider pertinent to his, shall we say, continued good health?'

Sloane wiped his brow. 'I could do that.'

'Thank you.' Hunt strolled to the door. 'I could deliver the message myself, but I feel it would not be at all conducive to Pickford's continued survival, I mean health, for me to speak with him. Permit me to show you out.' After which he would have to find something to take his mind off the temptation to sweep his bride off to bed, lock the door and ignore the existence of the entire world for at least twenty-four hours.

Chapter Eleven

Hunt wondered, as the children raced in the park with Fergus, just how many men spent their wedding day teaching a ten-year-old boy to play chess. Not to mention playing backgammon with a six-year-old girl. And then took them for a walk in the park. Shouts and shrieks of delight rang in the frosty air, interspersed with Fergus's barks as the ball flew.

However, a man had to do something while waiting for the clock to proclaim it a decent hour to take his bride to bed. Not that the clock's lack of progress would have stopped him doing precisely that…but Georgie and Harry needed to spend time with their mother, they needed to know him. And he didn't feel at all equal to the task of banishing them to the nursery and the care of servants just so he could bed their mother. But beyond all the practicalities of the situation, he was enjoying himself in a way that he had forced himself to forget.

'They are having such a good time,' Emma said. 'Thank you.'

He raised his brows. 'For taking a walk in the park? What else might we have done to pass the time with them?'

She flushed. It was a pretty flush, he noted. The wind had whipped colour into her cheeks anyway and he found himself wondering just how far the flush might extend. There was something to be said after all for anticipation. If only he wasn't so nervous about the whole business…

'I thought you might have said that the proper place for them was the nursery and—'

She stopped and he wondered if the flush had crept a little lower. 'It occurred to me,' he admitted. Anticipation could be wearing on a man's nerves. Too much time to think about everything a fellow could get wrong…

Emma's flush deepened to burning crimson and he laughed despite the nagging sensation in his stomach. Ignoring the dictates of propriety, he put his arm around her shoulder, drew her close.

'Hunt!'

'We're married.' He wanted to be a great deal more married.

'Yes, but we're in the *park*!'

'So we are.' He kept his arm precisely where it was and consigned the park, and all the world, to Hades. How long could the children run? Fergus would run until the ball wore out, but surely the children would tire?

Eventually Emma called them in and much to Hunt's surprise they came without protest.

Georgie, in fact, had an air of suppressed excitement. As Hunt drew his handkerchief from his pocket to wrap the cricket ball, she announced, 'We have a present for you, Uncle Hunt.'

He stared. 'A present?'

'Yes,' Harry said. 'It was my idea, but Georgie made it.'

'Because *boys* can't sew!' Georgie invested this with a level of superiority that would have befitted a duchess.

'We *could*!' Harry's indignation bubbled. 'We just don't. Because it's a *girl* thing.'

Hunt cleared his throat. 'My valet, John, can sew. He sews my buttons on.'

'Yes,' Georgie said. 'Because he helped me with this yesterday.' She drew a little crimson bundle from her muff and offered it. 'Mrs Bentham gave me the brocade.'

It was a bag made, he realised as he took it, from the same brocade as the drawing-room curtains. A golden-tasselled drawstring was provided. Hunt assumed the drawing-room curtains were intact since John and Mrs Bentham had been involved…

'It's for Fergus's ball,' Harry said with a grin.

Hunt stared at the bag—something lodged in his throat. He cleared it again. 'Well.' He struggled for words. For thoughts. And cleared his throat again. Over the expectant faces of the children he met Emma's gaze. She looked as surprised as he felt. He examined the bag carefully. Rather lumpy seams, anything but straight, and the bag had a decided list to one side. He opened it, dropped the ball in and pulled the drawstring tight. Well.

'Do you know, that is the second-nicest gift you two have given to me.'

Harry blinked. 'What was the nicest?'

Hunt smiled. 'Your mother. Thank you.' He tucked the bag into his pocket. 'John must be delighted with you two.'

'He did think it was a good idea,' Georgie said. 'I was going to make it a big one you could just carry, but he thought you'd like this more.'

Emma made a very odd sound and, as he met his bride's laughing eyes over the children's heads, Hunt made a mental note to tip John generously for saving him from something perilously close to a lady's reticule.

It ought to be easier the second time one married. Emma stared at the enormous bed with its delicate blue hangings and swallowed. She had slept in that bed the last two nights, Georgie curled beside her like a kitten, and been perfectly comfortable. She had not been thinking of it as her marriage bed. Now she was.

She swallowed again. There was absolutely nothing to be nervous about.

Oh, wasn't there?

Then why had an entire flight of butterflies taken up residence in her stomach?

Because she had absolutely no idea what to do. That was why. All those butterflies had moved in to take up the space left by her lamentable ignorance.

She knew well enough what was going to happen in the bed. But how would he expect her to behave? As her mother had told her the night before her aborted marriage to Sir Augustus?

Lie quietly and don't make a fuss.

She shoved the thought away. Her wedding night with Peter had not been at all like that, but she could not, must not, think of that now. Should she be in bed waiting? But what did she *do*? Just lie there? She could read, but should she read in bed, or by the fire? There was an Argand reading lamp over on the table there. But if she wasn't waiting dutifully in bed, would he think he was disturbing her? That she hadn't expected him? Or that she didn't want him?

For heaven's sake! She was more nervous now than when she had been about to lose her virginity on her first wedding night. Then she had been a little shy, but eager. Oh, God, she had been so eager. So wildly and desperately in love. And Peter had loved her as deeply. Had wanted *her*.

This was different.

She was eager now, too. But Hunt had not wanted a wife. Just an heir. And even if those kisses suggested that he desired her, she was *older*. What if she disappointed him? She was no longer a girl in the first blush of youth. She was *thirty-two*. Approaching middle age and she had borne two children.

It didn't matter how many times she reminded herself that Hunt had deliberately decided against taking a younger bride. His reasons had been perfectly rational and logical. That didn't mean they had a great deal to do with his personal preferences. Although he had expressed concern about the age gap between them...he would have been even more concerned about that with a girl of eighteen or nineteen. And she still hadn't decided whether or not she should wait in bed for him.

She let out a breath on a half-laugh. This was idiocy. Before she worried about where he would find her, she needed to get ready for bed and with these clothes she needed help undressing. Crossing to the dressing table, Emma tugged on the bell rope there to summon her maid.

Hunt, still fully dressed, sat by the fire in his bedchamber sipping brandy and wondering whether or not he should wear a nightshirt as well as his robe. Assuming he wore a nightshirt, should he keep it on during the entire...procedure? And when had he ever thought of it as a *procedure*? Let alone worried about the etiquette involved. When a man started worrying about the etiquette involved in bedding his wife, he knew he was in trouble. *Etiquette* and *bed*—two words he didn't think he'd ever framed in the same thought before. But how the devil *did* you go about taking a woman to bed when you hardly knew her? He'd done precisely that in his youth, of course, long before Anne. He'd been to several of the brothels in St James's that catered to gentlemen. You made polite conversation in one of the saloons, escorted the girl upstairs to a private room, removed any article of clothing you thought might be in the way—or instructed the girl to do so—and got down to business. But this was different. Emma was not a woman he had bought for the night.

She was his *wife*. His wife and his Marchioness—his convenient bride. It was even convenient that he desired her. It would be beyond *in*convenient if he didn't desire her. Desiring her didn't make him a randy old goat. He was supposed to desire her. He *wasn't* supposed to want to rush in there and spend the entire night making love to her. Or actually sleeping with her. Definitely not that, no matter how much he wanted that intimacy again. No. Pleasure her, bed her and retire to his own bed.

With a curse he set the empty glass down, rose and strode across the bedchamber into his dressing room. Before he did anything else he needed to get out of his clothes. His valet rose from a chair, setting aside the book he'd been reading.

'Evening, my lord. I understand her ladyship sent for her maid a few minutes ago.'

Hunt eyed John suspiciously. Was he being given a *hint*? That he was running late? And was that *amusement* in John's voice? He'd always suspected the man could read his mind. Stripping off his cravat, Hunt decided that he really didn't want to know.

Half an hour later, he was washed, shaved and in his nightshirt—better to err on the side of caution—and robe.

'I'll ring when I want you in the morning, John.'

The valet, already at the door into the hallway, nodded. 'Yes, sir. Goodnight, sir.'

A moment later Hunt was staring at the door that led from his suite into the Marchioness's rooms and wondering what they looked like now. He had not entered the Marchioness's rooms in years. Not even last year after ordering their refurbishment.

He set his hand to the doorknob, muttered a curse and made himself knock. If he walked in and her maid was helping her undress it would be embarrassing all round.

'Come in!'

He took a deep breath and pushed the door open.

Candlelight and lamplight danced and glowed. A fire crackled merrily, welcoming. The room might have been a different space. Gone were the deep pinks, the delicate floral wallpaper and the furniture he remembered. Instead the walls were a pale eggshell blue, the classical mouldings a soft, gilt-edged white. Bed hangings and covers matched the walls and his wife, clad only in a nightgown, sat at the dressing table brushing her hair. His mouth dried.

She had those gleaming, sable tresses pulled forward over one shoulder, her head tilted to one side as she pulled the brush through again and again in a steady, beguiling rhythm. The intimacy left him speechless.

Such a simple act, but one no other man would ever see as long as he lived. He hoped. With a shock, he realised that they had never discussed fidelity. He had offered a marriage of convenience as was usual for their class. That did not necessarily entail fidelity, on either side...

Her eyes met his in the looking glass. 'Good evening, sir.'

His gaze flickered to the maid, folding clothes, tidying up. 'My dear.' Did she expect, or want, the usual arrangement? Fidelity until she had provided an heir and a spare? And if she did, could he accept that? He had not, could not, offer love. What if she found it elsewhere? Did he have the right to demand that she forgo something he would not give?

Stupid question. As her husband he had every right. But he had never been very comfortable with the idea of demanding obedience as though his wife were of no more account than a favourite mare.

Emma glanced at the maid. 'Please douse the lamps as you leave, Maggie. I'll ring in the morning.'

The maid dropped a curtsy, attended to the lamps and left.

They were alone and he was adrift, as uncertain of himself as a green youth with his first woman. And she was watching him in the glass, the brush stilled now, almost wary. As if she watched one of the lions at the Tower, expecting it to pounce.

Because she doesn't know you, idiot!

And with the realisation, his own knot of nerves unravelled. She was as uncertain as he. As unsure of how to go on.

He let out a breath, smiled. 'Are the rooms to your liking?' He walked across, closing the space between them, and took the brush from her grasp. 'May I?' Was that *his* voice? Husky, aching?

'Yes. Yes, please.' And hers. Soft, yet steady. Her eyes on his in the glass, the wariness melting from them. He wanted more to melt. He wanted to be causing the melting…

Dragging in a breath, he sought for something, anything, to say. 'Ah, these rooms were completely refurbished last year.' He brought the heavy, dark mass of her hair behind her to tumble down her back, alive, rippling. He drew the brush through, felt the cool silk caress his fingers and hardened. He tried to remember what he'd been saying. Thinking. The rooms. Refurbishment. 'If you wish to change anything—'

'No. It's lovely. Thank you.'

Again and again he drew the brush through the shining length. 'One hundred strokes?' And immediately regretted the question. It brought quite another image to mind and he hardened even more.

A quick intake of breath. 'I... I always lose count.'

He swallowed. The fragrance of soap and warm, sweet woman filled him. God help him, but he'd be lucky to count to five right now. He brushed steadily, aware of tension melting from her as his own tension rose with need and...lust. Lust. In German the word meant *joy*. He was going to be joyful with her. There was nothing wrong with joy. But did *she* want to be joyful? With him?

'The children are comfortable?'

'Yes. Thank you.'

For an experienced man, and he admitted he was, he was ridiculously close to floundering.

In the glass her eyes were closed, unreadable... but, that slight smile, the softness to her lips and... his breath caught, his cock leapt...under the linen, had her nipples peaked? Oh, surely... He needed to know. She had been rushed into marriage. There had been no choice about that. But he did not need to rush her into bed if she wanted more time. No matter how much his body insisted otherwise.

Gritting his teeth, he stopped brushing, leaned forward to set the brush down and felt the warmth of her body. He stepped back and every instinct howled a protest.

'Emma?'

Her eyes opened, dreamy, full of mystery, and she rose, turning to him, her linen-veiled breasts brushing against him. Madness beckoned, burning through him...

'Yes.'

And there it was. More than a simple response to her name, that single word held consent. Yet still he hesitated. Did she consent because she believed she had no choice? Because she believed it was expected of her? What if—

She smiled and walked to the bed, held out her hand in an invitation no sentient, breathing man could mistake. All the *what-ifs* drained out of him. He went to her, his eyes never leaving hers, held by the siren's call in their blue, blue depths. He stopped a foot away, controlling the urge to take her in his arms and tumble her to the bed. His body was already on fire, beyond ready. His brain, what little of it still functioned, held him back.

It had been a long time for her. *Wait. Don't rush this.*

He reached for her, setting his hands to either side of her waist, feeling the warm, supple curve through a layer of linen. He wanted skin. Ached to have them both naked. Hot skin to hot skin. But if he did that…he swallowed. *Slow.* He held her gently, almost chastely, brushed his mouth to her temple, her cheek…breathed her fragrance, soap and woman. Emma.

She slipped her arms around his neck, rose on tiptoe and kissed him full on the mouth. Warm, willing. Welcome incarnate. His control broke, his mouth took hers and heat consumed him, incinerating his good intentions. Her mouth, hot and lush, lured him in, promise and demand inextricably entwined. Her body, all yielding curves, pressed to him as time and the kiss spun out on a web of gilded light. And beneath it all the punch, the shock of lust burning through him, igniting every nerve and vein so that he burned as he had never thought to burn again.

She had meant to be restrained. Not cold, but not this raging inferno that wanted everything and more. Now. At once. She had known she was hungry. She hadn't realised that she was starving. Starving for his touch, his kiss. His body. No matter that she still wore her nightgown, that he wore both nightshirt and robe. His heat, her own heat, still burned.

Everything in her centred on the raging need within. On his fingers working at the buttons of her nightgown, shaking, tugging to slip button after button until it hung open. Her breath came in on a shaken cry as he slid one hand in to cup her breast. Wicked, knowing fingers stole her breath and all thought.

Silk. Satin. Her gasp of pleasure fired him. Such a sweet weight, perfect and ripe in his hand. With a groan he passed his thumb over the peaked nipple, did it again just to hear her sob, feel her body arch for more. And through it all the kiss. Their mouths fused and mated, his tongue dancing with hers in a rhythm that seared his veins. Her arms about him, her body moulded to his in flagrant invitation. His dressing gown hit the floor and he was on the bed with her half beneath him, still in their night rail. It didn't matter. Nothing mattered except this hot, fierce need that scorched everything in its path.

Ravenous as he was, she was with him, her hands as greedy as his, her mouth as wild as he took a handful of linen and shoved her nightgown to her waist. Lost in the maelstrom, he found the silken curve of a rounded thigh and stroked. Warm, parting eagerly at his touch, begging for more, for everything. Something tore as he tugged her nightgown free of one shoulder, baring her breast to his hungry gaze. He lowered his mouth to it, licked, teased, as she gasped and sobbed, and finally drew it deep into his mouth. Her body arched up on a cry of pleasure as he suckled and her knee came up to caress his flank, opening her utterly to him, her hips lifting to him, answering the demand of his mouth at her breast.

Reaching between her parted thighs, he discovered her wet, ready. This. Just this. She was so soft, and warm, and welcoming. He stroked the slick entrance, felt the quake that shook her and the last burning link of his control snapped. He rose over her, pressing her thighs wider as he guided himself to her. And he was there, pushing inside where she was so wet and tight.

She cried out and he fought to slow down, to wait for her, but it was already too late and he moved in her in hard, deep strokes, again and again. Release crashed through him and he hung over her shaking in pleasure, even as he registered the coiled tension in Emma.

'Damn.' He let himself down on her damp,

trembling body. Beneath him, Emma stiffened and he realised he'd spoken aloud. If he'd had sufficient strength left he'd have kicked himself. In a moment…when he'd caught his breath…he pressed a kiss to Emma's temple, breathed the fragrance of heated, aroused woman, as carefully he disengaged from her body, her tense, frustrated, disappointed body…he could still satisfy her…he eased away from her, sank into the mattress and drew her close. He wasn't twenty any more…he needed a moment, then he would see to her pleasure and return to his own bed… His own bed was the last thing he wanted. She felt so utterly right in his arms, but it would be safer, more sensible. In a moment…

Emma lay in her husband's arms, felt the warm, heavy limbs relax as his breathing slowed, steadied…into sleep.

She let out a shuddering sigh. *Damn?* What did that mean? *Damn*, they'd had sex? *Damn*, he hadn't enjoyed it? Damn, *she* had been too eager, too wanton, too…*something*? She burned, ached with need, with longing, and he was asleep. Slowly the tension seeped from her, leaving her restless and wistful. She wriggled, wondering if she ought to disentangle herself, but the heavy arm over her waist tightened and he turned more fully to her. Despite the…what? Disappointment? Frustration? All of that. Despite it, the intimacy of the sleeping gesture disarmed her and she snuggled closer.

* * *

Hunt woke with a sense of utter well-being, warm and comfortable…a little more of his mind surfaced. No, not comfortable precisely—he had a hell of an erection. Fortunately he had a warm bundle of feminine curves pressed against him.

Emma. His wife. Memory asserted itself and he groaned. He'd rushed her, completely failed to satisfy her and fallen asleep.

He hadn't meant to sleep with her.

At least he hadn't dreamed. Perhaps he hadn't slept for long…

Six soft chimes dispelled that hope. She had been willing, eager and generous. He couldn't say the same for himself. Willing? Eager? Hell, yes. Generous? She must think him a complete oaf. She'd satisfied him beyond all measure and he'd fallen asleep without returning the favour.

He grimaced. She'd seemed stunned after-wards, despite her wild response. This time he wasn't going to have at her like a randy school-boy with his first woman. He was going to take his time, reassure her that her husband had *some* control and finesse in bed. That he was capable of pleasing a woman *before* he slaked his own greedy lust.

He shouldn't have slept with her at all, but since he had he rolled over, gathering his sleeping wife close. She gave a contented sigh and wriggled even closer. His heart swelled as he feathered kisses over her temple, her cheek, found the corner of that fascinating mouth…through the linen, female curves warmed under his hand. Hip, waist, and the silken weight of a breast. Pity it was dark, but he had no intention of leaving off to get up and light a candle. Carefully he unbuttoned her night-gown, pushed it aside and found soft skin, fluid and delicate.

Slowly. Slowly.

Sleek and pliant in sleep, she responded, skin heating, becoming damp as he caressed and kissed his way down her throat. Hungry, he kissed the upper slope of one breast, found the nipple and sucked gently. Felt her pleasured sigh as she arched up to him and wondered if he could bring her to pleasure before she woke…

'Mmm.'

Tenderness consumed him at the sleep-drowned murmur. She would be awake before he'd finished…

'Mmm.'

Lord, she tasted…he was going to discover *exactly* how she tasted… He reached for her nightgown, easing it up the slender legs—

'Mama? Is it time to get up?'

Every fibre froze rigid in horror. *'Georgie?'*

There was a shocked silence, followed by the rustle of sheets. In the dim light he saw a small figure sit up. 'Yes. Why are *you* here, Uncle Hunt?' The child's voice held a world of indignation. 'This is *Mama's* bed.'

Between them—and thank God she was!—Emma stiffened. 'Georgie?'

'Yes, Mama. Why is Uncle Hunt here?'

'Because I married your mama yesterday, Georgie,' Hunt said. 'One of the privileges of that is that *I* get to share your mama's bed. Off you go. Back to your own bed, please.'

For God's sake! What if the child hadn't spoken? Heat scorched his cheeks with the knowledge of what he'd been about to do.

'But I always—'

'Your own bed, Georgie.' He kept his voice quiet.

'Hunt—'

'I slept here the other nights!' Georgie's voice wobbled. 'And I've lost Anna Maria. Mama—'

'That was because your rooms weren't ready,' he said. 'Off you go!' Who on earth was Anna Maria?

Emma sat up. 'Anna Maria? Oh, Georgie!' Emma's voice softened. 'Hunt, she doesn't understand. She—'

'She will now,' he said firmly, interrupting Emma's low-voiced protest. Apart from anything else, it wasn't safe for the child to wander around unsupervised. What if she fell down the stairs? 'She needs to know there are rules here. *Now*, Georgie.'

'But I might not find my way back to my room!'

'You found your way here,' he said inexorably. 'And if you can't, the servants are up now. One of them will see you back. Run along.'

There was a muffled thump as the child slid from the bed. His eyes fully adjusted to the dim light from the coals in the fireplace, he saw his stepdaughter glaring at him.

'It's not fair!'

'Georgie, you need to go now. I'll come up after breakfast.'

Emma's quiet voice seemed to do the trick. The child caught her breath. 'But I was lonely without Anna Maria, Mama.'

'I know, sweetheart. She'll turn up. Go now.'

As the door closed, Emma turned to him. 'Hunt, there was no need for you to interfere. I am more than capable of managing my own child. She didn't understand at all!'

Interfere? 'I know she didn't,' he said grimly. 'Have you considered what you might have had to explain if we hadn't realised she was there?'

'Yes, but—'

'Emma, she needs to stay in the nursery, in her own room. Just because she slept here the first two nights—'

'It's not just that.' Emma's voice was stiff with something. 'She has always slept with me.'

'Always?'

She shrugged, threw back the covers and got up. 'Yes. There *were* only two rooms upstairs in Chelsea. Harry had one, Georgie and I shared the other. Before Peter died we had a larger place, but even there she was in a crib in our room.'

Embarrassment. That was the edge in her voice. He let out a breath. He'd never been upstairs in her house. Hadn't realised the small size meant there could only be two rooms up there. Hadn't thought, more like. He'd never considered all the ramifications of the poverty to which she'd been reduced. But that didn't change the situation here.

'Emma, she can't wander around the house at night.'

'*I* know that,' she said. 'But *she* doesn't understand it!'

'She ought to now,' he said.

She stared at him. 'You think it's that easy? You just tell a child that everything about her life has changed and…that's it? They magically do exactly what you want?'

He stiffened. 'Certainly. If they have been properly—' He broke off too late. *If they have been properly brought up.*

Emma swept up her dressing gown from the floor, flung it on. 'I'll ring for my maid now. Good morning, my lord.'

'Emma—'

The dressing-room door closed behind her.

Hunt pushed back the covers with a curse.

Who had known that being a stepfather was this complicated? So far he was making a complete muddle of everything. Well, there was one thing he *could* do and get right. They still had to tell Harry that he was Keswick's heir.

Chapter Twelve

Harry stared from Emma to Hunt. 'A *duke*?'

Hunt could only guess at the boy's feelings. His own experience had been very different. He had been born with the courtesy title of Earl of Tremaine and had been raised to succeed his father. He had grown up with all the servants calling him *my lord* and very few people, apart from his sisters and Anne, had ever used his Christian name. Even his father had called him Tremaine. His mother had mostly followed suit. He had become Huntercombe at thirty on his father's death. There had been no shock, no moment of revelation, no turning upside down of his world. Just a steady progression and certainty.

'Sir,' Harry appealed to him. 'Do I have to?'

'Harry, dear—'

'Yes,' Hunt said firmly.

Harry swallowed. 'But—'

'If your father had lived, *he* would be the next Duke,' Hunt said. 'Granted it is an enormous responsibility, but I think your father would have been more than capable and, since you are his son—' He left the rest for Harry to work out.

The boy was silent for a moment. 'But won't I have to live with my—the Duke?'

'No,' Emma said very firmly. 'You don't.'

Harry looked at Hunt. 'I don't?'

Hunt shook his head. 'No. Your mother and I discussed the matter with your grandfather yesterday. You will remain with us and visit his estates with us from time to time. When you are older you may like to go by yourself. I can teach you much of what you will need to know about running estates generally. Later we can think about the specifics of Keswick's estates.'

'You'll help me, then, sir?' Harry sounded slightly less panicked.

'Yes, of course.'

'And I'm Thirlbeck now? A viscount?'

'A courtesy title,' Hunt said.

'Does Georgie have to call me *my lord*?'

Hunt bit back a laugh at the hopeful tone. 'Don't count on it. And perhaps for now you may like to leave it at *Master Harry* for the servants.' The boy had quite enough adjustments ahead of him.

'Yes, please.' Harry flushed. 'I just thought— never mind.'

Hunt kept a straight face. Not unexpected that Harry, despite his shock, had been able to see at least one advantage in his new status.

Harry looked at his mother. 'Should I go to see my grandfather? Do I have another grandmother?'

'Yes, you should. And, yes, you do.' Emma's smile looked as though it had been glued in place. 'As well as an uncle, Lord Martin—the tall gentleman with your grandfather yesterday. And several aunts.'

'Oh.' Harry bit his lip. 'When I saw him—Lord Martin—yesterday, just for a moment I thought it was Papa.' He looked at Hunt. 'Cannot *he* be Duke?'

'No, Harry,' Hunt said. 'It has to be you.'

'But I don't have to live with the Duke.'

'No.' That, Hunt realised, was the boy's greatest fear.

Harry was silent for a moment. Then, 'What if Mama hadn't married you?'

Hunt hesitated, glanced at Emma who had paled. Lord, the boy was quick.

'He was going to take me, wasn't he? And Georgie?'

'Yes.' He heard Emma's gasp, but if the boy had realised there was no point lying. The important thing was to reassure him that he was safe. 'The Duke was anxious that you should learn about the job you will have to do. He did not know that I had already asked your mother to marry me.'

Harry scowled. 'I still don't like him. He was unkind to Mama.'

Hunt cleared his throat. 'You don't have to like him, Harry. But you do need to show him proper respect. It is what your father would expect of you.'

'But if he's horrid to Mama, Papa would expect—'

'That you explain politely that your mother *is* your mother and is to be respected,' Hunt said calmly. He suspected that as long as Harry was scrupulously polite about it, Keswick would be obliged to choke it down. It might even engender a respect for the boy. Keswick was stubborn and opinionated, and he'd been blindly so about Lord Peter's marriage, but he was not a fool.

'Will you tell Georgie, Uncle Hunt?' Harry asked.

'No,' Emma said. 'I think it might be better coming from me.' Her eyes met Hunt's in direct challenge.

Hunt concurred silently. Right now he wasn't entirely sure that he could face his stepdaughter without blushing.

Georgie went straight to the issue of most concern to herself.

'Do I have to call Harry *my lord*?'

Emma squashed the urge to laugh. 'No.'

Georgie relaxed in Emma's lap. 'Good. Is he awfully rich? Richer than Uncle Hunt?'

'No. Harry isn't rich. Your grandfather is very well off, but it's not considered polite to ask.'

'Does Harry have to live with him?'

'No.'

Georgie nodded. 'Can I sleep in your room tonight, Mama?'

Emma braced herself. At least she didn't have to

open that conversation. She was going to be firm. Kind, but firm. 'No. You can't.' Somehow she had to ensure that Georgie began to understand the changes that had come into their lives. And then she had to make sure Hunt understood that the children, especially Georgie, would need time to adjust and learn how to go on in their new lives.

'I don't see why not.' Georgie's lower lip wobbled. 'Uncle Hunt can. And the bed is simply *huge*.'

'Don't be a silly baby, Georgie.' Harry, curled up reading in a chair by the fire, looked up. 'Mama has to share a bed with Uncle Hunt now.'

Georgie's scowled. 'Why? She's *our* mama. Why can Uncle Hunt sleep with her?'

Harry rolled his eyes. 'Because that's what married people *do*. Papa and Mama always slept together in the other house.'

Emma blinked. Of course—Harry was old enough to remember that.

'It's to do with having babies,' Harry added, without much interest since he was looking at his book again. If there was any air left in the world, it certainly wasn't in Emma's lungs. Her cheeks burned.

'Babies?' Georgie looked even less impressed. 'Mama isn't going to have babies.'

Harry gave her a superior look. 'Yes, she will. That's what happens when ladies get married. Besides, Uncle Hunt needs to have babies. I heard the maids talking about him needing to have a son to be Lord Tremaine like I'm Lord Thirlbeck.'

Emma had the sensation of having been dropped into a maze without any exits.

'Are you having a baby, Mama?' Georgie demanded.

'Not right—' Emma hesitated. It was altogether possible that she was. 'I don't know.'

'But you don't *want* one, do you?' Georgie tugged at Emma's sleeve.

Emma met her wide-eyed gaze. Harry had set his book aside, was watching her interestedly. 'Yes,' she said gently. 'I do. Very much.' It was the truth. She wanted more children. Hunt's children. Although it seemed he didn't think too much of her ability as a mother after this morning.

'But you've got *us*!' Georgie wailed. 'Why do you have to have a baby?'

Emma remembered exactly how pleased a four-year-old Harry had *not* been over the prospect of a little brother or sister. 'What about Uncle Hunt?'

Georgie shook her head. 'He can share us. Harry can be Lord Tremaine *and* Lord Thirl-thingy.'

'It doesn't work like that, Georgie,' Emma said.

Georgie's lower lip stuck out. 'We could go back to Chelsea. Uncle Hunt could just visit sometimes.'

'No, Georgie. It doesn't work like that either. Tell me, have you found Anna Maria yet?' Anna Maria was Georgie's favourite doll, tattered and beloved beyond all other possessions.

'No. Bessie says she must be here somewhere.'

Georgie's eyes filled. 'But we looked everywhere! I think she's gone back to Chelsea.'

'Oh, Georgie. Anna Maria wouldn't run away from you.'

'She might. If she didn't like it here. If people were horrid and didn't let her sleep in my bed.'

Emma hugged her. 'Maybe she forgot to get in the carriage. If she doesn't turn up we'll go and fetch her.'

Harry rolled his eyes. 'It's just a silly doll, Georgie. And there are dolls here. Bessie found you a better one last night.'

'I want Anna Maria!'

'Mama? Did other children live here once?' Harry asked.

She looked at him. 'Yes. Why?'

He held up the book. 'Well, this. And the doll Bessie gave Georgie. Mark, the footman who helps look after us, and Bessie unpacked lots of books and toys from the attic. There's a whole *army* of toy soldiers. But Uncle Hunt said he didn't have any children.'

Emma took a careful breath. 'Uncle Hunt's children died, Harry.'

Hunt froze, his hand on the door knob, as memories poured through him in an agonising flood, sweeping away the eleven years since he had visited these rooms. Simon, Lionel and Gerald, sprawled on the floor with those toy soldiers massed ready for battle. Marianne curled in a chair, dressing one of her dolls for a ball. The smell of clothes drying by the nursery fire and Anne's quiet voice reading. Unlike many of their set, Anne had enjoyed spending time with the children. So had he.

Other children lived. Why had his died?

'Died?' Georgie sounded horrified and his stomach churned, remembering the small white coffins, the knowledge seeping into him that the nightmare was real, that he wasn't going to wake up.

'Yes. They and their mama were very sick.'

'And they *all* died?'

Hunt clenched his fists. He'd pounded on the walls of that room in his early rage and despair at the emptiness where once there had been so much life, so much potential and so much joy. And now there was life, potential, even joy again and he wanted only to turn back the clock, reverse time and undo death…

'But what if *you* get sick, Mama?'

The sudden fear in Georgie's voice jerked him back. Perhaps Emma had been right this morning. She was just a little girl and—

'Then Uncle Hunt would look after you.' Calm, confident. Emma made it sound as though anything else were unthinkable. Was it? It had seemed so simple when he decided that a widow with children would suit his purpose. It had still seemed simple when he met her. So reasonable, logical that they should marry, the contract benefiting both of them and the children.

He had not thought of Harry and Georgie as

children. As *his* children, which, according to law, they now were. He was obliged to be a father to them, when hearing and seeing them in these rooms that his children had lived in ripped open wounds he'd thought healed. They were not. Perhaps they were not meant to heal. That did not absolve him of the duty he had accepted in regard to these children and any that Emma might give him.

He leaned against the wall beside the door, unable to walk through it. This was what came of rushing into marriage without giving anyone, himself included, time to adjust or to plan for the change. No nursery staff meant that Emma was still needed hands-on with the children. And given Georgie's excursion this morning, the children needed time and space to adjust. And Emma was very like Anne in that she enjoyed her children, liked being with them.

He let out a breath. If he had wanted the other sort of wife, then he should have married Amelia Trumble.

And what if something *did* happen to Emma? Something he couldn't protect her from? Or worse, something he caused. Like childbirth.

She *didn't* need another child, although she had told Georgie and Harry that she wanted one.

Talk about topsy-turvy; right at this moment he wasn't sure that he wanted one, although he *needed* an heir.

Harry and Georgie had already lost their father. How could he face them if he were responsible for

Emma's death? What if he failed *them*, as he had failed Gerald and his own children?

Quietly, he went back downstairs. He'd send a footman up to ask Emma to bring the children down when they were ready for a walk. It would be best if he kept the relationship more formal. Not emotionally intimate. Friendly, polite, kind. It would be enough.

Chapter Thirteen

Since the sky held a very real threat of rain, Emma suggested that they restrict the walk to the square. Georgie had a slight sniffle, but Emma refrained from saying anything about that or Georgie's tendency to catch cold, not wishing to spark a rebellion on Georgie's part or give Harry any reason to tease. Harry was inclined to think the square very poor sport, but he subsided at a pointed look from Hunt.

Emma winced mentally at the ease with which Hunt quelled Harry's grumbles. She had been an idiot this morning. Hunt had been perfectly right to tell Georgie to leave. She had already spoken to Bessie about having a maid sleep in the same room as Georgie. And perhaps she might make sure the door from the corridor to her own room was locked at night. Then if Georgie did come down the worst she could do was knock. Or kick the door panels, Emma admitted to herself as she watched her daughter take her turn at throwing the ball and argue that she ought to have *two* turns because she couldn't throw it as far, so it really wasn't fair…

Hunt was nipping that in the bud before Harry could, when Emma saw two familiar figures entering the square. The Countess of Cambourne was warmly and stylishly dressed in a deep blue pelisse with a white-velvet muff and a very pretty bonnet. She came across the wintery grass with a shy smile, accompanied by her brother.

'Good morning. James is sequestered in his library, but he saw you out here and sent a message up to me. Do you mind our joining you?'

'I'm delighted.' Emma smiled at the younger woman. Despite the difference in their ages, this was someone she could be friends with.

Fergus charged up, tail whirling, and dropped his ball at Lady Cambourne's feet.

The Countess laughed. 'Thank you, Fergus, but I think it is Harry's turn.'

Harry, hard on the dog's heels, promptly picked up the ball and bowed to the Countess. 'Good morning, ma'am.' He looked shyly at Fitch, who put out his hand with a gruff mutter and the two boys shook hands with excruciating formality.

'Good morning, Harry.' Lady Cambourne glanced at her brother. 'Fitch, make your bow to Lady Huntercombe.'

The boy bowed, with a charming, lopsided smile. 'Good morning, ma'am.'

Emma smiled at him. 'How nice to see you again, Fitch. Are you going to join Harry and the others?'

He looked questioningly at his sister, who smiled. 'Off you go. You can't possibly imagine that I need your escort in the middle of Grosvenor Square whatever James says.'

She turned back to Emma as the boys rushed off with the dog. 'Harry is very like you.'

'He is,' Emma said, 'Thank you for bringing your brother. I'm glad for Harry and Georgie to make a new friend.'

Lady Cambourne's smile lit her face. 'Fitch has not said much, but I think he was quite eager to meet Harry again. He's rather overwhelmed by most of the boys that he meets.'

Emma couldn't imagine why. The boy seemed very much in command of himself. 'Shall we walk?'

As they did so it became apparent to Emma that her companion, despite her charm and rank, was as uncertain of her welcome in society as Emma herself. Despite this there was a sweetness about the Countess that appealed to Emma. Her approval of Hunt's marriage was touching.

'He was so kind last year when I married Cambourne. It is lovely to see him happy with you.'

Was he happy? She hoped so.

With the boys thoroughly occupied, Hunt went to join the ladies, Georgie at his side. An unexpected fit of shyness had assailed her with Fitch's appearance. She hurried to Emma and clutched her hand, gazing up at Lucy as if she wasn't quite sure she liked her. Hunt eyed her narrowly, but said nothing.

'Lucy.' He doffed his hat, bowing to Lucy. 'James is well? And you?'

Lucy's smile lit her eyes and, not for the first time, Hunt saw exactly what had attracted his friend. He had been inclined to disapprove of James's choice at first, but the more he saw of Lucy the more he liked her. And this morning she positively glowed.

'Yes, he's well. And I am very well, too.'

'From what James said the other day I thought you might have left town already.'

She nodded. 'We're returning to Chiswick to-morrow.' She turned to Emma. 'Cambourne has a house there. He needs to be here for Parliament, but he thinks it is better for Fitch to be out there.' Her shy smile beamed. 'And he says the air is better for me. So he is going to ride back and forth. We only came in because I had a little shopping to do.' And for some reason she blushed.

Hunt hid a smile. James had been perfectly happy for Lucy to be in town for Parliament last November and for the spring session this year. He could think of one reason as to why the Countess might be glowing and why a loving husband might think the fresher air of Chiswick better for his young wife. A pang went through him. Would *he* soon be thinking that fresh country air would be better for Emma?

Lucy glanced to where Fitch and Harry were throwing the ball back and forth, with Fergus rushing between them. 'We were going to leave yesterday, but we wouldn't have missed your wedding for any consideration. Will you be staying very long in town?'

Emma glanced at Hunt. 'Huntercombe needs to be here for Parliament. And I need to shop.' She gestured to her walking gown with a grimace. 'As you may see. We barely scratched the surface the other day.'

Hunt suppressed a growl. Although neat, the gown was years out of fashion and had all the look of genteel poverty. Another thing to lay at Keswick's door—Emma had been given no time to outfit herself before they married. Letty and Caroline had been more than vocal on the subject yesterday although Emma's wedding dress had been all that it should be.

Lucy smiled. 'I thought you would have a great deal of shopping to do. I did, too, last year. Would you like to come with me again this afternoon? I have a few more things to order before we leave tomorrow and it's always nicer to shop with a friend.' She flushed. 'If you don't think I am being forward?'

'Oh, that would be—'

'You can't, Mama.' Georgie's objection cut across Emma's reply. 'You have to take me to Chelsea to find Anna Maria.'

'Georgie!' The glare Emma shot at the child

would have made a charging bull reconsider, but Georgie glared right back.

Hunt opened his mouth to back Emma up and closed it. Emma had not appreciated what she had called interference this morning. Granted he had not intended it that way, but he needed to step carefully here.

'That was extraordinarily rude, Georgie. Apologise, please.'

Georgie scowled. 'Well, you did say we could go and I asked first!'

Emma took an audible breath. 'I did not say *when* we would go. We can do that tomorrow. Lady Cambourne is leaving London tomorrow, so—'

'But I want to go *now*, Mama! You promised!'

Again Hunt bit his tongue.

'Georgie, I said we'd go and look for Anna Maria *when* we were sure she was not here. We will go tomorrow. In the meantime you may have a good look with Bessie to make sure she is not here hiding from you.'

'But, Mama—'

'No, Georgie. I am going out with Lady Cambourne.'

Georgie stopped dead, tugging her hand free of Emma's and stamping her foot. 'Then one of the servants can take me!'

That did it. Hunt's restraint snapped. 'No.' He bent his sternest look on his stepdaughter. 'The servants have enough work to do. Your mama has said she will take you tomorrow, but even that will depend on how well you can behave yourself.'

'Mama said!'

'Hunt—'

'Your mama said *no*. And now, *I* have said it as well.' He would not stand back and let Emma bear the brunt alone when the child was having a tantrum in the square. 'You will apologise to Lady Cambourne for rudeness at once.'

'Won't!' Another stamp of a small foot.

'Very well.' Hunt scooped the child up under his arm and, ignoring the shrieks and struggles, headed for the gate out of the square.

'Hunt!' Emma was at his side, breathless. 'What are you doing?'

'Taking her home. You stay with Lucy and the boys.'

By the time Hunt reached the nursery Georgie's fury had subsided to angry sobs. He opened the door, stalked in and deposited her on her bottom in the middle of the floor.

'Miss Georgie!' Bessie hurried out of the next room and fixed the child with a glare. 'Have you been naughty?'

'Mama promised!'

'Listen to me, Georgie.' Hunt's tone had the child turning to him. 'If you were a boy I'd spank you for a performance like that. But you aren't. You will go to bed now and stay there until your mother returns from her shopping when you may apologise to her for your rudeness. Also, when

Harry and I walk Fergus tomorrow morning, you will write an apology to the Countess.'

Expression mutinous, Georgie opened her mouth, but Hunt forestalled her. 'Until both apologies are made there will be no walks with Fergus and your mama will not take you to find your doll. Bed. *Now*.'

Georgie's jaw dropped and she seemed to regain control of herself. Hunt raised his brows…

'But I didn't *mean* to be rude, Uncle Hunt.' A wheedling tone, the merest hint of a quivering lip and brimming eyes. Hunt remembered another small girl, pulled up for rudeness, trying exactly the same ploy with him. And gave Georgie exactly the same answer.

'Yes, you did. Bed.'

For a moment Georgie stared at him. Then, incipient tears miraculously dried and replaced with a ferocious scowl, she obeyed. The bedroom door banged behind her.

Hunt turned to Bessie. 'See she stays there.'

'Yes, m'lord.'

Hunt found Emma in her dressing room, half in and half out of a pelisse. Good. She was going with Lucy. He had been half-afraid she would not and that even if Georgie did not get her own way, she would win by default in stopping Emma going out.

She swung around, her face pale. 'Did you spank her?'

He blinked. 'Of course not! I sent her to bed to contemplate her sins.' The distress in her face stabbed at him and he went to her, caught her hands in his. 'Emma, she's a little girl, of course I didn't spank her. Although I did tell her I would have if she'd been a boy. She just needed to know that she couldn't give orders like that and expect you to give in.'

Emma's hands trembled in his. 'You must think me an appalling mother if you thought I would have given in.'

Ah. So that was it. And he'd nearly said something this morning about children being obedient if properly raised. A foolish thing to say. Children, well raised or otherwise, were all capable of disobedience.

He drew her close, raised her hands to his lips. 'No, sweetheart. I don't think any such thing. And I did *not* think you would give in to her. But I couldn't stand back while she was rude to you. That would let her think I didn't mind. And don't you think it will be easier for you if she understands that there are two of us now?'

A smile quivered on her lips. 'Much easier. You were right to send her away this morning. I am sorry I—'

'And you were right to remind me that she is only a child and that this is all very new and strange for her.' He bent, brushed his mouth over hers. 'Don't worry too much, Emma. You don't have to do it all any more. She will be ready to apologise by the time you come home. Then tomorrow while Harry and I walk Fergus, she is going to write an apology to Lucy. Where is Harry, by the way?'

Emma let out a breath. 'He went with Fitch. Lucy suggested it. She's waiting in the drawing room. So you think I should go out?'

'From Georgie's perspective, yes,' he said. 'From my own point of view—' He lowered his mouth to hers, nipped at that lush bottom lip and soothed it with his tongue. His whole body hardened. 'I'd much rather you stayed home. I was going to make you an apology this morning when we were interrupted.'

'An apology?'

'Mmm.' He drew her into his arms, feathered kisses over her temple, down the silken curve of her cheek and jaw to the dancing pulse in her throat. 'For my clumsiness last night. I warn you now, it's likely to be a very lengthy apology. This time I won't let you rush me.'

'Oh.' A small, wicked smile curved her mouth. 'That sort of apology. Will you write it out in your best handwriting?'

He grinned. 'Minx. Barclay's hand is much better than mine and I'm certainly not going to dictate this to him.'

Lucy wriggled on the seat as the carriage pulled away from the curb.

'Is something wrong?' Emma asked.

The Countess turned slightly to look down at the back of the seat. 'I'm sitting on something… ah!' She pulled at something caught down between the squabs and the seat. 'Look!'

'Well, for goodness sake!' Emma stared at the bedraggled doll. 'That's Anna Maria.'

'I thought it might be.' Lucy considered the doll. 'Do you want to take her up to Georgie now?'

Emma hesitated. It would only take a moment, but— 'No. Hunt was right to send her to bed, and if she gets Anna Maria back now it would be like a reward for naughtiness. She may have Anna Maria tomorrow. *After* she has written her apology to you.'

She sat the doll between them. 'Anna Maria can come shopping with us instead.'

Lucy smiled. 'I hope I am going to be as good a mama as you are.' Her hand went unconsciously to her stomach.

Emma looked at her with a questioning smile and Lucy blushed, nodding. 'Congratulations. Is Lord Cambourne pleased?'

'Oh, yes,' Lucy said. 'That is why we're going out to Chiswick. And it's better for my brother out there.' Her smile flashed. 'Believe me, Georgie isn't the only one who can set a household by the ears!'

Georgie scrambled into bed without getting undressed. She didn't *care* if her clothes got crumpled from being in bed. It wasn't fair! She hadn't really meant to be rude. At least, she *had*, but not to Lady Cambourne. And it wasn't Uncle Hunt's business anyway, was it? A very inconvenient little voice whispered that maybe it *was* Uncle Hunt's business now, but she ignored that. It *still* wasn't fair. Now she had to stay in stupid bed for *hours*. She had been shopping with Mama and Lady Cambourne on the day before the wedding and it had taken *ages*. And simply anything might happen to poor Anna Maria all alone out at Chelsea. What if someone stole her?

The door opened and Bessie looked in. 'Good. You're in bed. Now you think about what his lordship said like a good girl. All that fuss over a doll! Why, I wouldn't be surprised if her ladyship didn't take you tomorrow neither!'

Georgie's lip quivered and she dived under the bedclothes to hide the rush of tears. It wasn't fair! She heard the door close and emerged cautiously. She really had been naughty. So perhaps Mama *wouldn't* take her tomorrow and Anna Maria might be lost for ever... But it wasn't *that* far to Chelsea. They had walked to Hatchard's every week...

Two hours after sending Georgie to bed, Hunt leaned back in his desk chair. 'You're happy with that, William?' He hated making Parliamentary speeches, but he must say something about the war with France. He was very much afraid they were in for a long and costly struggle. No matter what his friend Fox thought, Bonaparte's ambitions worried him.

Barclay nodded. 'Yes, sir. Very clear and to the point. I believe it strikes just the right note.'

'I'm relieved to hear it,' Hunt said. The whole time he'd been dictating the speech, he'd been thinking about dictating a certain apology. He wasn't quite sure how his secretary might have reacted if any of *that* had slipped out.

Barclay set his pen back in its holder. 'Will there be anything else, sir?'

Hunt frowned at his diary, scanning the next couple of days. One appointment leaped out at him. 'Yes. That engagement with Kendall for to-morrow morning—'

He broke off as the door swung open and Harry burst in. 'Uncle Hunt!' He charged across the room, nearly tripping over the Turkey carpet. Fergus leapt from the hearth and trotted to meet him.

Hunt rose. A father figure, yes. A kindly one. But there were limits and his stepchildren were trying them severely today. 'Harry—'

'Sir!' Harry slid to a halt in front of the desk, breathless and scarlet, not even glancing at the dog. 'I'm awfully sorry, but we've lost Georgie!'

Chapter Fourteen

Hunt, with Barclay, Bentham, Harry and a terrified Bessie, stared at the side door used by the servants and deliveries.

'How the devil did she even *know* about this door?' he demanded.

Harry looked ashamed. 'We were playing hide and seek yesterday. Exploring, you know, after the wedding. And we wondered where it led…' He trailed off, very red, then continued. 'But we only peeped out, I promise.'

Hunt cleared his throat. 'Very well. You opened it then. But it's usually bolted. Top *and* bottom. You might have reached the top bolt, but how did she reach it?' It wasn't bolted at all right now.

Bentham spoke. 'As to that, my lord, the top bolt is only shot at night now.' He looked upset. 'During the day…well, it's been a long time since there were children in the house.'

Hunt grimaced. Over the years since his own children's deaths, some of the protocols observed to keep *them* out of mischief would have been relaxed. Like this door.

He put that aside. Georgie's whereabouts were more important and the door would be bolted from now on without him saying a word. 'So where the hell has she gone?'

'Sir?'

He looked at Harry. 'Yes?'

'She might have gone to find Anna Maria.'

Hunt felt his jaw drop. 'What? Her *doll*? You think she's gone—*walked*—to Chelsea for a *doll*?'

Harry looked embarrassed. 'I know it's just a doll, sir. But Georgie, well, she sort of thinks she's real. She talks to her all the time and makes up stories about her.'

Marianne had been much the same. Hunt looked at Bentham. 'The house has been searched?'

'Top to bottom, my lord.'

Bessie's face worked. 'Yes, me lord. The maids, couple of footmen, not to say Mr Bentham and Mrs Bentham. Checked everywhere they did, knowing the house better nor what I do. She's not here.'

'How long has she been missing? Do we know that?'

Bessie looked ready to cry. 'Mebbe two hours. I looked in on her and spoke to her right after you sent her to bed. Then I went to see Mrs Bentham about the children's supper, but I looked in when I came back up and I thought she were there, asleep right down under the blankets, so I left her be. Not fifteen minutes it wasn't. And I was in the nursery after that till Master Harry came home.'

'She'd taken the pillows from my bed, sir,' Harry said. 'She'd stuffed them under her bed-clothes to look like she was still there. I saw they weren't on my bed and asked Bessie where they were.' He added loyally, 'It wasn't Bessie's fault.'

Hunt swore mentally and forced himself to think past the rising worry. All very well to sus-pect the child had gone off to Chelsea. He had to be sure. 'Harry. Run up to the nursery. Bring down something of Georgie's. An article of cloth-ing. Something she wears next to her skin.' He glanced at his secretary. 'William—'

Barclay nodded. 'Yes, sir.'

Five minutes later, Hunt offered Fergus the glove Harry had brought down, led him out the open door and said, 'Find!'

The dog sniffed the glove, put his nose to the ground and snuffed around eagerly, casting back and forth. After a moment he gave a sharp bark and looked back at Hunt who held his leash.

'That would seem to settle it,' Hunt said grimly. 'William, the—'

'I ordered your curricle when I fetched Fergus, sir. Lady Huntercombe has the closed carriage. And the footmen and grooms are mostly out scour-ing the nearby streets, just in case.'

Hunt managed a smile. 'Thank you.'

'Can I come, sir?'

Hunt glanced at Harry, frowning. 'I don't think—'

'Might be a good idea, sir.' Barclay held Hunt's startled gaze. 'I told them to find a warm jacket for Harry, as well as something for Georgie, blankets and so forth.'

Hunt let out a breath. 'At least I'll have you under my eye.' He clicked his fingers at the dog. 'Fergus—go! Go find!'

The spaniel put his nose to the ground with a bark and headed towards the back of the house.

Hunt stopped him. 'Wait.' He looked back at Harry and Barclay. 'She was bright enough not to go towards the square where she might have been seen from the windows and stopped. Harry, tell whoever brings the curricle around to meet me on Mount Street. Whoever it is will have to be prepared to run with Fergus at first.'

Hunt reached Mount Street ahead of the curricle and praised the excited dog. He had no doubt Fergus had the scent now, but how long he could keep it if it came on to rain was anybody's guess. Or if too many other scents overlaid it.

The rattle of hooves and wheels alerted him as his matched chestnuts brought the curricle around the corner at a smart trot. His coachman, Masters, had the reins, Harry beside him. Masters drew the curricle to a halt.

'You'll take their heads for a moment, my lord?'

Hunt was already at the nearside gelding's head. He drew Georgie's glove from his pocket. 'Up to a run, Masters? You'll need to keep Fergus on the scent.'

Masters grinned as he jumped down. 'Oh, aye. That's why it's me, not one of the younger boys.' He took the leash and glove from Hunt and set his own hand to the nearside bridle. 'We'll find her, sir. Never fear.'

Hunt jumped into the curricle beside Harry. 'Warm enough?'

Harry nodded. 'Yes, sir. Has Fergus still got the…the scent?'

'Judging by the way he pulled at his leash, yes.' Hunt watched as Masters set Fergus again. The dog cast for a moment, then set off at a run, nose to the ground, along the rain-damp footpath, Masters running behind him.

'Hold tight, Harry.'

Fergus lost the scent just past Hyde Park Corner. He cast back and forth for several minutes in the rain with Hunt while Masters held the horses, but failed to pick it up again.

'What now, sir?' Masters asked.

Hunt looked at Harry. 'She knows the way from here, doesn't she?'

Harry nodded. 'Yes. If she got this far she'd go straight home. I mean, she'd go to Chelsea. We came this way all the time.'

Hunt stepped into the curricle. 'Then we go to Chelsea.' He clicked to Fergus. 'Up you come!' The dog leapt in and shook himself vigorously.

Hunt swore, remembered his company and said, 'Do not say that in front of your mother!'

Harry grinned. 'No, sir. Jem the groom said it when one of the chestnuts stepped on him before. He said the same thing—not to say it in front of Mama. Or you.'

Masters, jumping up behind, muttered something about Jem keeping his clumsy feet out of the way in future and his tongue in check.

They made good time, despite the rain, but there was no sign of Georgie and every mile the fear in Hunt's gut froze harder. Harry directed him along the route Emma had used most frequently. 'It's the shortest way, sir. She'd want to get there quickly.'

Hunt reminded himself that the child had got a two-hour start. More when he added in the time to bring the curricle around. But he'd hoped to catch her up, get her home before Emma returned. And now it was pouring. He concentrated on the horses, brought them around the last corner into Symons Street and—

'Bloody hell!' breathed Masters.

Harry let out a shocked cry and Hunt swallowed a curse.

Emma's house—the entire row of houses—lay in blackened ruins, a couple of chimneys still standing in the end houses.

'Take their—'

Masters was already at the horses' heads, throwing blankets over their steaming hides.

Hunt jumped down, realised Harry was right

behind him. 'No. Wait here.' Surely, surely this had not just happened. But if it had, if Georgie had been here—he swallowed, sick to his stomach. The boy mustn't see. But Harry let out a yell and sprinted past him.

'Mr Adams! Mr Adams! It's me, Harry Lacy! Have you seen Georgie?'

Emma's tea sat cold and abandoned beside her at the library window overlooking the square. She couldn't eat, had barely been able to sip her tea for the fear consuming her. If only she had taken Anna Maria inside! She could have put the doll away until tomorrow. But at least Georgie would have known the doll was safe. And now the child was lost. How long did it take to go to Chelsea and back in a curricle?

She sat, hands gripped in her lap, flinching every time a carriage of any sort entered the darkening, rain-swept square. The last of the footmen and grooms out searching had come back half an hour since without finding Georgie. The maids had searched the house from top to bottom again. More, Emma thought, to feel that they were doing something, so that *she* would be comforted that something was being done, than anything else. The moment William Barclay had told her what had happened, Emma had realised that Harry was right. Georgie had gone after Anna Maria and she'd had the wretched doll safe in the carriage all the time.

If anything had happened to Georgie…dark was closing in and it was still raining.

A carriage rattled around the corner and Emma looked up, hardly daring to hope…a curricle—she half-rose, hope slicing into her. It would stop too soon…or drive past.

It did neither. Instead it drew up in front of the house and the groom leapt down, ran to the horses' heads. But…there were only two figures in the curricle. The smaller one jumped down and in a rush of relief she recognised Harry. Fergus followed and then she saw the small, still, blanketed form cradled in Hunt's arms as he stepped down.

Even as she ran into the hall the footman had the door open and Fergus rushed in to shake himself liberally.

'Mama!' Harry followed. 'Our house burned down!'

Emma's throat closed and she could only stare at Hunt, terror choking her as he came into the hall.

Huge dark eyes in a pale, agonised face pierced him to the heart, as did the small frail weight in his arms.

'She's quite safe, Emma.' He turned a little so she could see the sleeping face of her daughter. 'The house burned down the night you left. She's just worn out from the walk and getting soaked to the skin.' He glanced at Harry. 'Not the best way to reassure your mother, Harry.'

'Oh.' Harry blinked. 'Sorry, Mama.'

'It's all right.' Amazing that her voice worked at all, let alone sounded calm. Everything in her trembled. 'Where was she?'

'Safe with Adams and his wife,' Hunt said. 'Harry, take Fergus to the kitchen, please, and rub him down by the fire. Mark?' He turned to the footman. 'Have hot water taken up to the nursery at once for Miss Georgie's bath.'

The footman bowed slightly. 'Mr Bentham's already arranging it, my lord.'

'Excellent.' He smiled at Emma reassuringly. 'I'll carry her up.'

'Mama?' The child stirred in his arms.

'She's right here, sweetheart.' His heart shook as Emma pushed back the blanket to touch the soft little cheek.

'I'm sorry, Mama. I shouldn't have gone.'

'No. You shouldn't.' There was no anger in Emma's voice and Hunt couldn't fault her for that. Not now. She would have been terrified to find the child missing. Time enough to discuss discipline later.

The small face crumpled. 'But Anna Maria must have been there and—'

'No.' Emma's mouth trembled. 'She wasn't. She was hiding in the carriage all the time. And now she's upstairs in your bed.'

An hour later Emma found Hunt in the library going through a pile of cards with his secretary. She just stood, watching him for a moment. The lamp on the desk lit the austere planes of his face, the strong line of his jaw, gleamed in the silver at his temple. He had changed out of his damp clothes for evening attire: a dark coat, snowy waistcoat and satin knee breeches.

She hesitated, wondering if she should go away. She was supposed to be a support to him and he had already spent his afternoon chasing after an errant stepdaughter. But Hunt looked up over his reading glasses and for a long moment their gazes met and held in the glow of the lamplight.

Barclay rose and left with a bow for Emma.

Hunt walked over to the fireplace, held a chair for her. 'Come and sit down. Would you care for a glass of wine? Tea?'

'I didn't mean to interrupt you,' she said.

'You didn't,' he said. 'Saved me would be closer to the mark.' He grimaced. 'Invitations. The news of our marriage is out and we've been invited everywhere. And I do mean everywhere. Is she all right?'

'Yes.' She tamped down the lingering fear that Georgie might have taken a chill. That the wetting and long, cold walk might have worsened the slight sniffle she'd had that morning. Like Peter... Emma knew to her cost how easily a slight cold combined with a wetting could lead to an inflammation of the lungs. 'She's tucked up in bed, sound asleep with Anna Maria.'

She reached him, but didn't sit down. 'Hunt, I'm so sorry. I should have realised, not gone out. It was—'

'Not your fault,' he said, taking her hands. 'She

was extraordinarily naughty, but you were quite
right to go out. Otherwise she would have known
that *she* had forced you to back down. It was sheer
bad luck that she knew a way to get out of the
house without being seen.'

'But if I'd taken the wretched doll up! Told her
she couldn't have it until tomorrow...'

He was silent for a moment, then drew her into
his arms. 'Hindsight is a cruel deception, Emma.
If only I had known! If I had known eleven years
ago, I would not have sent my wife and children
down to Cornwall a week early. If not for that we
would have heard about the outbreak of smallpox
in time and not gone at all. If I had known, you and
I would not be standing here, would we?'

She froze in his arms. 'Hunt.' She could barely
get the word out.

His arms tightened. 'But I did not know then
and nor could you have known this afternoon. Just
as I didn't think about that door. When my own
children were...here, it was always bolted, top and
bottom. But apparently, over the years, that has
been relaxed somewhat.'

'You couldn't have—'

'No. And nor could you have known.' He tipped
her face up to his and she met that steely gaze. 'We
can only make the choice that is right at the time.
Look what a mess Macbeth created thinking he
could control his future by committing a crime.'

She swallowed. What choice would Hunt make
now, though, if he could turn the clock back and
control the past? What choices would *she* make?

She no longer knew. Peter seemed so very far away, as if he were part of another life. This was her life now. With Hunt.

'I suppose you have a Folio edition of that?'

Some of the tension slid away as Hunt smiled. '*Macbeth?* I do. It's at Pentreath.'

'What about the house, Hunt?' Emma could not quite believe that it was gone. They had moved there just after Peter's death. Small and shabby though it was, it was the only home Georgie knew and even Harry had barely remembered the other house.

Hunt frowned. 'Yes. The house. It's odd. The whole row burned down.'

'Oh, poor Mr Adams!' Emma felt sick. 'Was anyone hurt? Do they know how it started?'

Hunt hesitated. 'No one was hurt. But, according to the neighbours, it spread from your house.'

Emma's stomach lurched. '*My* house? But *how*? Bessie and I put the kitchen fire out *and* the fire in the parlour. We were so careful!'

He nodded. 'I know. I saw you put them out. But Adams was certain. And your house—' He swallowed. 'Well, the houses to each side and the rest of the row were in ruins, but yours—it was razed.'

'*Razed?* But—' She dragged in breath. 'There's no point making excuses. I must have missed a coal somehow. And I didn't even tell Adams I was leaving! He'll be furious with me.'

Hunt reached out and gripped her hand. 'He was more relieved that you were alive and safe. His wife wept all over Harry and Georgie.'

'What?'

'Everyone assumed you had all been trapped and killed.' His eyes were grim. 'There was nothing left to show otherwise. No one realised you'd left.'

She couldn't speak. Could barely think. But she forced down the horror. 'I have to compensate him. It must have been my fault somehow.'

Hunt let out a breath. 'I told him you'd feel that way. He doesn't agree. He thinks some vagrant saw us all leaving and thought it would be a good time to break in. Apparently one of the neighbours saw a stranger hanging around earlier. He'd warned the fellow off several times before. And Adams said there was a stench of burning lamp oil. If that caught fire, well…'

Emma frowned. 'We always kept the lamp oil in the shed at the end of the garden—for just that reason. Bessie or I only ever brought enough in to fill the lamps. And I'm sure we locked up.' She hesitated. 'There *was* a strange man around. I used to see him when we were out. In fact…' she swallowed '…I thought he might be following *me*.'

Hunt's gaze narrowed. 'You never mentioned this.'

'No.' She'd been so reluctant to confide, to rely on anyone. 'It seemed so unlikely. But later, after Keswick came and it was clear he knew about your visits, I thought he'd probably paid to have me watched.'

Hunt raised his brows. 'Perhaps, although I can't see why he'd want to destroy your house. I'll write to Adams mentioning that you also noticed a stranger and I do know you locked up. He's refusing compensation, says that's what he pays the fire insurance for, but we'll see about that. Meanwhile, come and look at these blasted invitations that poor William has sorted into piles for us.'

For a moment she hesitated, but then accepted she could do nothing further about the house this moment. 'Piles? What sort of piles?'

Hunt grimaced. 'Must attend, *should* attend and snowing in Hades before we attend.'

Emma choked back a reluctant laugh as he drew her over to the desk. 'Are those Mr Barclay's words?'

Hunt chuckled. 'No. Mine. William is much more discreet. There is a ball tomorrow night in the "absolutely *should* attend" pile. The Westerfolds. You know them?'

She nodded. 'Yes.' The Duchess of Westerfold was close to her own age.

He smiled. 'Then I'll look forward to dancing with you. The minuet is mine.'

Despite her worry about the house, Emma's heart skipped several beats and heat rose in her cheeks. The minuet? Where they would dance together the whole time, gazing into one another's eyes? Oh, folly! She was already looking forward to it. She could write to Mr Adams tomorrow. Insist that he accept compensation…

'That's not the worst of it, though. You'd better look through these tomorrow.' Hunt sat down and handed her a thick stack of invitations. 'But

William kept this one separate. A category all of its own.' He held up a sheet of notepaper, his expression that of a man being loaded into a tumbril.

She blinked. It looked more like a letter, but was too far away to read. 'Who sent that?'

'Caro. For dinner. Tonight. I had actually accepted for myself some days ago. This is the revised edition to include you. And—' he smiled into her eyes '—before you dismiss me as completely frivolous, I promise you we'll see about compensating Adams whether he likes it or not.'

Apparently her husband could read minds. As she went upstairs to change, Emma reflected that might not always be convenient.

Waiting in the entrance hall for Emma, Hunt wished they didn't have to go out. He could quite see his sister's point about the importance of Emma being seen as soon as possible by society. Her letter commanding him to bring Emma to dine had been nothing if not blunt.

We must move quickly to make it clear that your choice of bride, however unexpected, has the Family's approval. We cannot allow gossip to take hold.

He had not moved in society for the past thirty years without understanding how it worked—the best defence against unwanted gossip was to create the gossip you *did* want. Taking Emma to dinner at Caro's for her first appearance in society was an opportunity he couldn't let slip. The little fact that the eager bridegroom would have preferred taking his bride to bed early and making a detailed and lengthy apology for the wedding night was not a sufficient excuse for declining Caro's invitation. Even if he did, he wouldn't put it past Caro or Letty to show up on his doorstep tomorrow to bring him to a sense of his iniquity. Nor would they hesitate to blame Emma.

Quite apart from that, going out tonight would take Emma's mind off the business of her house burning down. He didn't want her worrying that she had been somehow responsible or that she and the children might have died had they not moved out. Every time he thought about it, his gut churned. Thank God he'd insisted they come with him that night! Otherwise…he flinched away from the dreadful image of the destroyed house, the knowledge that they would have been lucky to get out if they'd been there.

Light footsteps sounded on the upper landing and his heart stuttered as Emma came down the steps towards him, glowing in cherry silk and the pearls he had given her. His breath and brain seized. The dark curls were piled high and plumes that matched the dress nodded gracefully. There wasn't enough air left in the world. All he could think about was peeling her out of the gown to discover what she was wearing underneath it, then dispensing with that and sliding his fingers into the glossy sable curls, scattering hairpins and plumes to perdition… He cursed Caro and her dinner party. Since when did a man have to take his bride out for dinner less than forty-eight hours after marrying her?

Emma descended the last few steps. 'Will I do?'

He could only nod as he took the cloak folded over her arm and slipped it around her shoulders. He had not until now been aware of just how scandalously low women's gowns were being worn. Now that he couldn't actually *see* the creamy upper breasts over that excuse for a bodice, he might find a few intelligent remarks to make. Except of course that she couldn't wear a cloak during dinner and, as a newly married husband, he'd be seated beside her. Which might be easier than sitting opposite…except he'd be watching the bastards who *were* seated opposite, and—

'You don't like it.'

He could have kicked himself, seeing the worried frown on her face. 'Yes, I do like it. Very much.' He steeled himself. 'I'm just thinking about how much every other man present is going to like it as well.'

'Oh.' She flushed. 'You don't think—'

'No. I don't,' he said, with a rueful smile. 'Most of my thinking apparatus just leaked out of my ears. Stop worrying, Emma. You look beautiful and elegant. Did you look in on Georgie? How is she?'

Emma bit her lip. 'She's asleep. Bessie said they woke her for supper, but she didn't want any.'

Hunt cocked his head to one side. 'Are you worried about her?' He didn't have to ask. He could see that she was.

'A…a little. She is probably just tired, but she does get dreadful colds. Like…like Peter did. And she was sniffling this morning, so—'

'Bentham.'

'My lord?'

'If Mistress Hull is concerned about Miss Georgie, send a footman around to Lady Caroline's immediately.'

'Hunt—'

'Certainly, my lord.'

Hunt offered Emma his arm and escorted her out to the waiting carriage.

'Hunt, I can't possibly tell your sister that—'

'I can.' Hunt handed her up into the carriage. He might have to forgo an early night with his new bride, but he refused to subject Emma to an evening of worrying about the child just to allay society's curiosity.

Lady Caroline stared at Hunt in outrage. 'You said *what*?' She kept her voice low. 'That you were to be summoned in the middle of dinner? Really! If you cannot manage your wife better than—'

'Caro.' Hunt spoke very quietly. 'Emma is worried about the child. I have tried to set her mind at ease. That is all.'

Caro gave a disdainful sniff. 'I see. Well, I hope Bentham knows his place better than to actually *send* such an unnecessary message. It would be most disruptive.' She fluttered her fan. 'However,

I am pleased to see that dear Emma is suitably dressed this evening. I offered my advice the other day, but she appeared to think it unnecessary.'

Hunt simply looked at his sister with raised brows. Had Caro really thought that Emma was incapable of dressing well without the benefit of her advice? 'I have every faith in Emma's taste. However, she went out with Lucy Cambourne today. I gave her *carte blanche* to spend whatever was necessary.'

Caro fluttered her fan. 'Is that connection wise? I mean, there were whispers last year about—'

'Since Cambourne is a close friend I am delighted that my Marchioness should be friendly with his Countess. On the other hand—' Hunt's glance flickered to where Emma was undergoing a baptism of fire in a circle headed by her erstwhile mother-in-law, the Duchess of Keswick. His mouth thinned. 'Was that necessary, Caro?'

She followed his gaze. 'What? Oh, the dear Duchess? Of course it was! I was fortunate that they were able to attend at short notice. Lady Keswick is extremely influential and she is very much upset to have been denied her grandchildren, you know. I cannot imagine why you are supporting Emma in this folly. So much easier if—'

'Caro? Mind your own business.' With Caroline it was necessary to go straight to the point. With the most charming smile he could muster he strolled away. A glance at Emma showed that she was managing the Duchess well enough, listening with pretty deference, keeping a polite smile in place as the Duchess held forth…

'Odd of Huntercombe to countenance such an arrangement. And after I had gone to such trouble finding a governess. Now, of course, I have no need of the creature, so it was all for naught.'

Hunt blinked. Had the Duchess, certain of Keswick's gaining custody of the children, already engaged a governess?

'Not at all, ma'am.' A touch of chill in Emma's tone, there. 'If you care to give the governess my direction, I shall be happy to interview her.'

Hunt had the impression that the Duchess's guns had been well and truly spiked with that suggestion. It sounded as though Keswick and his Duchess were passing off the attempt to grab the children as a well-meaning favour to Emma on the assumption that he would not wish to take on the responsibility for another man's children.

Satisfied that Emma could hold her own, Hunt strolled over to join his brother-in-law, Lord Fortescue.

Fort greeted him with a smile and offered a glass of wine. 'A toast to your bride, Hunt.' He lowered his voice. 'Must say, she's a great deal livelier than Amelia. Can't imagine what Letty and Caro were thinking!'

Chapter Fifteen

Hunt handed Emma up into the carriage at the end of the evening and she sat back against the squabs with a sigh. 'Letty is going to drive out with me tomorrow.'

He laughed and reached for her hand. 'Don't if you'd rather not.'

She turned her head and smiled. 'No. It's very kind of her, you know. I had simply forgotten what it is like.'

'Forgotten?'

'How careful one needs to be in society.' A wry smile curved her mouth. 'What with the Duchess trying to persuade me that it was only proper that the children ought to be with her while you and I enjoy a *short period of seclusion* and everyone wishing to know if I will recognise Mrs Fox—I was very circumspect about that. I had no idea what you might think, but I believe she is a friend of Lucy's, so—'

Hunt grimaced. 'Fox is Cambourne's godfather. Fox and I are friends, although we disagree on nearly everything political. And Elizabeth—' His old friend Fox, member of the Commons, had shocked society last year by announcing that he had married his long-time mistress, the courtesan Elizabeth Armistead, seven years earlier. 'I am fond of Elizabeth, myself.'

'Would I like her?'

Heresy to suggest that a well-bred, virtuous woman would like Elizabeth, but— 'I think so, yes.'

'Were you ever—?' She broke off. He didn't need to look to know she had probably turned scarlet. He knew what she had been going to ask: Had he and Elizabeth ever been lovers?

'Yes.'

'Oh. Would you prefer that I did not—?'

He shook his head. 'No. That would be utterly hypocritical, unless I also told you not to recognise several high-ranking ladies you will be hard put to ignore.' Now he did look at her. Her expression was quizzical. Honesty. It was vital in any marriage and he was offering Emma so little of himself, he could at least give her that. 'I haven't been a monk for the past five years, Emma. But Elizabeth was long ago. Before I met Anne.' A laugh escaped him. 'Before Elizabeth met and fell in love with Fox for that matter. After that, there was never anyone else for her.'

Her fingers tightened in his. 'Or for you after Anne?'

'Or for me. Until—' He really didn't want to talk about this, but honesty was a hard taskmaster. 'After a few years, well, I won't make excuses, but I needed, wanted—' Lord, how did you talk about this to your wife?

'A woman?'

He let out a rueful laugh. 'Yes. I want to say they weren't important, but that belittles them.'

'I think I understand,' she said softly.

'Do you?' He raised her gloved hand to his lips. He knew women had the same needs, but society was not as accepting of a woman's supposed sins as it was of a man's. A man could bed as many widows as he liked and be accounted a devil of a fine fellow. But let the merest whisper of gossip sully a widow's skirts and she was accounted 'fair game'. 'I will tell you this—when Gerald died last year and I realised that I had to marry again, I broke off the affair in which I was engaged. Since then I have not…that is, I thought it would not be fair to, well, to anyone.'

'You have been celibate? Until—'

'Yes.' Would she understand what he was telling her? That he would be faithful? This was not something they had discussed and fidelity was not necessarily expected in a marriage in their circles, but he did not know how to be anything else but faithful. Yet he had not stipulated it. If she did not choose to reciprocate…

There was a short silence and then Emma's hand tightened in his. 'Thank you, Hunt. I…thank you.'

Another silence followed, yet it did not feel uncomfortable. It was an easy silence, the silence of friends who have said all that was needful for complete understanding on a subject.

Emma glanced sideways at Hunt in the darkness of the carriage. Her hand remained in his, resting on the seat between them in the companionable silence. He was leaning back against the squabs, his eyes closed, yet she did not feel ignored. He was not being distant. Simply quiet.

It did not surprise her that eventually there had been other women for Hunt. But, her heart shook, the moment he knew he would have to marry again he had broken off a liaison. Not simply because he was actively looking for a wife and felt he owed his as-yet-unknown bride something, but because he had thought it would not be fair to the woman he had been involved with.

Oddly enough, that touched her more deeply than his implied faithfulness to herself. That and his refusal to say that the women he had been involved with in the past few years had not been important. He had not simply used them for a physical release, which most men considered a God-given right and despised them at the same time. He had given them respect. And he refused to be hypocritical about the notorious Elizabeth Armistead.

As the carriage drew up to the curb before Huntercombe House she wondered how she was supposed *not* to fall in love with a man whose code of honour was only equalled by his sheer kindness.

His eyes opened and he smiled at her, that smile that left her breathless and threatened to steal her heart. He leaned towards her and his mouth brushed over hers in aching promise.

'I've been thinking about that apology,' he murmured. 'Refining it.'

Her breath caught and his mouth drifted down, found the racing beat in her throat. Inside her everything melted. 'Hunt—'

He sat up as the door opened. 'Soon.' His voice, deep and soft, held a world of promise.

The footman let down the steps and Hunt got out to hand her down. His gloved hand closed about hers, firm and possessive.

Bentham greeted them in the hall. 'Good evening, my lord. My lady.' He bowed deeply to Emma. 'Mistress Hull would appreciate it if you could go straight up to the nursery, my lady. She is concerned about Miss Georgie.'

Emma's stomach turned to icy lead. 'Concerned?'

Hunt, stripping off his gloves to hand to the footman, turned and stared. 'I believe I left instructions that a message was to be sent if there was any reason for concern, Bentham.'

Emma was already running up the stairs, Bentham's response floated after her.

'Your pardon, my lord. I sent Robert around.

He came back saying that he had given his message. I've no reason to doubt him.'

Dimly she heard Hunt asking to speak to Robert immediately, but she kept going. All that mattered was Georgie.

Emma stared down at Georgie in fear. The child's face was flushed and damp and she tossed restlessly in her sleep. This morning the sniffle had been slight, the cough not too worrisome. Nor had the child had a fever.

'How long has she been like this, Bessie?'

'Getting worse all evening, my lady.' The maid twisted her hands together. 'Mrs Bentham came up and between us we got Miss Georgie to take some willow-bark tea with honey. But—' The woman's eyes were huge. 'She was that upset you weren't here. She got off to sleep an hour ago. Wondered if we should give her a little laudanum, but Mrs Bentham thought better not without your say so and she drifted off in the end.'

Emma nodded. Somehow the message had gone astray. And Georgie, her baby, sick and fretting for her. 'Never mind. I'm here now.'

'Mama?'

Emma looked down, summoning a smile. 'Yes, sweetheart. Feeling better?'

'No. Can you stay a bit?'

'Of course.' She sat down and took the small, hot hand in hers. She should never have left the child this afternoon or this evening. Memory reared up. Peter coming home feeling low with a slight cough and a sore throat. Ten days later—she forced the memory back, tamped down the fear.

'Shall I read to you?'

'Yes.' A fit of coughing racked the child. When it eased and Georgie was breathing more easily, she leaned against Emma's shoulder. 'I'm sorry I was so naughty, Mama. Is Uncle Hunt very cross?'

Emma hugged her gently. 'It's all right, sweetheart. You can apologise to him later.'

'I did that on the way home.' She frowned a little. 'He said that he had to mind his horses and we'd talk about it later. Is it later yet?'

'Not quite yet. What shall I read to you?'

'Something nice, Mama. *Beauty and the Beast?* In English?'

Emma picked up the book from beside the bed. 'Very well. In English as a special favour.'

Hunt dismissed his valet after he had been helped out of his evening coat and shrugged himself into his dressing gown. He doubted that Emma was in her room yet, if she came down from the nursery at all.

A light tap at the door between their rooms made his heart leap. He strode over and jerked it open.

'Emma.' He reached for her…then let his arms drop.

She wore one of her old gowns, her hair caught up in a simple twist. He noticed those things in passing. What held him back was the fear in her eyes. 'What's wrong?'

The breath she took was audible. 'I have to go back up to her, Hunt. I just came down to change.'

His stomach twisted. 'Is she very ill?'

'I don't know. She has a fever and her breathing is bad, but she is asleep now so I came down to change.' She managed a wobbly smile. 'She always gets dreadful colds, but—'

'Should I send for the doctor?'

'In the morning. But I… I can't stay. I'm sorry.'

'I know.' He nodded and kissed her gently. 'Go back to her then.'

Her hand came up, fingertips tracing his jaw. The light touch tore at him, moved him unbearably.

'Thank you.'

The door closed behind her and Hunt leaned back against the wall beside it. Fear gnawed at him. A cold contracted after a wetting was not smallpox, but a child's life was so fragile. He would send for a doctor first thing. The doctor who had attended upon his own children in London had died, but no doubt Letty or Caro would know of one.

Doctor Thompson smiled reassuringly at Hunt over his sherry. 'Nothing to worry about, my lord.' He sipped appreciatively. 'Ah! Very fine, indeed. The merest sniffle and a little congestion. I fear her ladyship's natural maternal concern has misled her. I dare say the child will be up and about in a day or so. On no account should she be overindulged. Ladies, being tender-hearted, as one would wish, are inclined to make much of little.'

Hunt blinked. 'Oh. Then Lady Huntercombe should feel no concern about leaving the child for a few hours tonight?'

Thompson waved the suggestion away. 'Goodness me, no! Her ladyship need not concern herself in the least.'

Hunt breathed a sigh of relief. 'Well, thank you, Thompson. I'll see you out.'

He would be able to dance with Emma after all. All the way up to the nursery corridor Hunt dwelt on this prospect, imagining the delight of dancing the minuet with Emma, taking her through the stately steps, his gaze on her and only her…and afterwards they would come home together, go to bed together…she wouldn't need her maid and he'd tell John not to bother waiting up…

He met Emma in the corridor just outside the nursery. She was still in the old gown she had put on last night. 'Are you off to change? You're driving out with Letty, are you not?'

She shook her head. 'No. Just stretching my legs for a moment. I've sent an apology around to Letty. Hunt, can you—?'

'I saw Thompson.' His relief still bubbled through him. 'Excellent news. The Westerfold ball is—'

'Hunt, I can't possibly leave her.'

He stared. 'The doctor said—'

'Thompson is an idiot,' she said. 'Positively mediaeval! He spoke of the four humours as if he referred to modern medical knowledge! I'm surprised he didn't recommend I put a toad on Georgie's wrist to draw out the fever, and if Letty and Caroline had him to attend on their children it's a wonder any survived.'

'Emma, are you sure—?'

'Yes.' Her eyes narrowed to fiery blue chips. 'And the message Bentham sent last night? I sent Robert back with a note asking Caroline what happened. She replied she had not wished to have her dinner party ruined!'

He might have known it. Poor Robert had insisted that he had delivered the message—an urgent request for Emma to come home. Still… 'Emma, if it *is* just a cold—'

'I am sure the Westerfold ball is important, but my husband—that is, Georgie's father—died of *just a cold*. You will excuse me, my lord. Please convey my regrets to the Duchess.' She slipped back into the nursery and closed the door in his face with a decided click.

Hunt stared at the door and let out a muttered curse. Did she really think he was worried about the importance of a ball? But he did want to dance with her, damn it!

In the end he sent his regrets for the dinner they had been invited to attend, but went to the Westerfold ball for an hour by himself. Long enough to make an appearance and quell any incipient gossip. Letty had sent a furious note about Emma's decision not to go out with her.

> *I had assured people that she would be with me this afternoon, that she is perfectly respectable and that we are delighted with the connection. For her not to be seen will cause gossip. You must insist that she attends the Westerfold ball this evening...*

And more in a similar vein. But he didn't have that sort of marriage with Emma and nor did he want it. He had struck a bargain with her. She had married him to protect her children from Keswick, not for him to assume authority over them, let alone over her.

By the time a dozen people had twitted him on his bride's absence, he was irritated and defensive. Was he supposed to have exercised his husbandly authority and insisted that she accompany him? Nobody had said so outright, but Letty had come perilously close...

'My dear Giles, it is very bad for a child to be coddled by anyone, let alone the mother. Sitting with a sick child is a task for a servant, not a lady. Never mind, I am sure you will guide her aright in the future.'

She had changed the subject and then sailed regally away before he could tell her to go to hell. Guide Emma aright? She was more than capable of guiding herself. A sick child was far more important than a ball. What the devil would they say later if Emma *had* attended the ball and Georgie was seriously ill and died?

And he had suggested that it was *just a cold…*

'My husband died of "just a cold"…'

He was a fool. His own family might have died of smallpox, but Emma knew, none better, how what began as a minor illness could turn out to be nothing of the sort.

'Your lady is not with you tonight, Huntercombe?'

Recognising the mocking voice, he turned. Lord Martin stood before him, a perfectly unremarkable young lady on his arm. To his surprise the girl met his gaze squarely, no simpering or coyness apparent, and the smoky eyes tugged at a memory. Hunt frowned slightly. He had seen this girl somewhere before. Wondering, he bowed slightly to Lord Martin. 'Good evening, Lacy. One of the children is unwell.'

Lord Martin stared. 'She is sitting with a sick child?'

Hunt returned the startled gaze coldly. 'Yes. Mothers do that, you know.'

The young lady smiled. 'My own mother used to sit with me when I was ill.'

Lord Martin shot her a wry glance. 'Did she? I can't say that mine ever did.'

Hunt smiled at the young lady. 'Apparently you are blessed in your mother.'

'I was,' she said quietly. 'But she died when I was ten.'

Lord Martin scowled. 'I think you have not met

Miss Carshalton, Huntercombe? Miss Carshalton, may I present Lord Huntercombe? He has recently married my brother's widow.'

Hunt stiffened, but he bowed. 'A pleasure, Miss Carshalton. I have met your father. Shipping, is it not?'

He watched, fascinated, as the girl—from his viewpoint she was definitely a girl—lifted her chin, a challenge in the grey eyes. Suddenly she was anything but unremarkable. 'Yes. Papa is in shipping. The Duchess has offered to introduce me to society.'

From the chin and the almost defiant expression, Hunt suspected that the Duchess's protégée was finding the going rather heavy. There would be plenty who, while outwardly polite to a girl whose father was richer than Croesus, would snigger behind her back about the smell of the shop, or, in this case, bilge water. Plenty who would miss the spark in those smoky eyes and dismiss her as a cypher with a most desirable fortune.

'I hope then, Miss Carshalton, that you are enjoying yourself and will call on Lady Huntercombe.' He gave her a polite smile. Carshalton had political ambitions, but there were whispers about his business practices, that he was none too particular about his business partners. And there was something about Carshalton himself, a streak of ruthlessness. No doubt his daughter was supposed to make a match that would further his political ambitions.

Miss Carshalton looked surprised. 'Thank you,

my lord.' She hesitated. 'I hope you won't think me impertinent, but do you still have the Donne autograph?'

Hunt raised his brows. 'I have several. Which one did you mean in particular?' And how had she known about it at all?

She flushed. 'The sonnets. You won't remember me, but my great-uncle Ignatius sold it to you.'

He stared and suddenly remembered a small girl in black with the same smoky eyes. 'You're Ignatius Selbourne's Kit, aren't you? You wrapped the manuscript up for me.' He chuckled. 'That must be ten years ago. Good heavens. How does Ignatius go on? We correspond, but I haven't seen him in the past couple of years. And, yes, I do still have that manuscript.'

Her face lit with pleasure. 'I'm glad. He's very well, my lord. I spent an afternoon with him in his shop last week.'

Hunt smiled, trying to reconcile this young lady with the sad-eyed, black-clad little girl, who had so often been in her uncle's Soho bookshop. She had usually sat in the corner with a book and Selbourne's shop cat for company. Selbourne had mentioned that his niece had died, that he had inherited her daughter. Then, some years later Selbourne had commented that his Kit had returned her father. And she was Carshalton's daughter? Good God! 'I'm sure Ignatius enjoyed that. Do give him my regards when you see him again.'

Lord Martin was staring at the girl as if he'd

only just seen her. 'I didn't know you were interested in books, Kit.'

She went very pink. 'I'm sorry. I shouldn't have said anything. Your mama does not like me talking about books, let alone Uncle Ignatius or helping in his shop.'

Lord Martin scowled. 'I think you should stop worrying about what my mother will think.' He nodded to Hunt. 'Good evening, Huntercombe.'

Hunt inclined his head. 'Lacy. Miss Carshalton—it was a pleasure meeting you again.'

She smiled, even though she cast an uncertain glance at Lord Martin. 'Thank you, sir. I hope your child is better soon.'

Lord Martin cleared his throat. 'Stepchild.'

Anger spiked in Hunt. 'That is immaterial,' he said through clenched teeth. Miss Carshalton's gaze flickered between the two of them.

Lord Martin inclined his head. 'I'm glad to hear it. I hope the child improves quickly.' From the tone of his voice one might have thought the words had been wrenched from him under threat of torture. 'Is…is it Harry or the little girl? Georgiana, isn't it?'

'Yes, it's Georgie,' Hunt said quietly. 'Very kind of you, Lacy. And you, Miss Carshalton. I'll pass your kind thoughts on to Lady Huntercombe.'

Lord Martin nodded stiffly and stalked away with Miss Carshalton.

Hunt watched them for a moment. Interesting. Keswick's Duchess, the highest of high sticklers, giving her approval to a plain—until something interested her—and bookish young woman with no connections or pretensions to gentle birth? He could think of only one reason—the Duchess saw the Carshalton fortune as a chance to establish her only remaining son in the wealth to which his upbringing had accustomed him. It was a bargain made often enough not to raise eyebrows, although it did not necessarily mean a match made in heaven.

He continued on through the throng of superfine, silk and nodding plumes. On the dance floor couples wove their paths through the graceful strains of a minuet, reminding him that the only person he really wished to see, the only woman he wished to dance with, was not here. He pulled out his watch. Nearly midnight. Well, his carriage might not devolve into a pumpkin, or Masters into a rat, but he was leaving.

Hunt opened the door to the night nursery very quietly and looked in. The only light came from the fire, but he found Emma exactly where he'd expected; in a chair by the bed. Dancing shadows made it impossible to see if she was asleep.

'Emma?' He spoke softly, hoping that if she were asleep he wouldn't wake her.

'Uncle Hunt?' Such a small, croaky voice.

'Yes.' He walked towards the bed. Georgie lay high on the pillows. Even in the dim light he could see that her cheeks were flushed, the soft curls damp with sweat.

'Mama's asleep.'

As a whisper it was less than stellar and he winced as Emma stirred. 'Not any more, sweetheart.' He laid a gentle hand on Emma's shoulder, feeling the knots and stiffness that were the consequence of sleeping in a chair.

'Hunt?'

'Yes. Are you quite comfortable there?'

'Oh, yes.'

'Hmm.' He had to admire the ready lie. 'And how is Georgie?'

Emma leaned over and set her hand to the child's forehead. 'Better, I think.'

'But I'm thirsty, Mama. And my throat still hurts.'

'Are you, love?' Emma rose, bending over the child.

Hunt nudged her back, realising what she was about. 'Let me.' He helped Georgie sit up fully and propped her against the pillows. 'There.' He sat on the edge of the bed beside her.

'Thank you, sir.' Emma set a tumbler to Georgie's lips and the child drank thirstily.

'That's nice, Mama.'

Emma smoothed damp curls back from the small brow. 'Was it? That's Mrs Bentham's special lemon and barley water. And I think some more willow-bark tea and honey might help that pesky throat again.'

'Did you go to a party, Uncle Hunt?'

'I did. A rather dull one, I'm afraid.'

'Then why go?'

He grinned. 'I get into trouble if I don't. Your

Uncle Martin was there. He and Miss Carshalton sent their best wishes for your swift recovery.'

'Who is Miss Carshalton?'

Who indeed. 'A little girl I knew once who is all grown up now. Like you are going to be.'

'Oh. Did you dance?' Georgie persisted.

He sent Emma, busy with a kettle, an embarrassed glance. 'Since your mama wasn't there, no.' Foolish of him, perhaps, but he didn't dance often and he wanted *her* to be the first woman he danced with after their wedding.

'Did you want to dance with Mama?'

He smiled at her persistence. 'Yes. Very much.' Gently he placed his hand against her forehead. The heat there sent a chill down his spine.

Looking up, he met Emma's steady gaze and saw shadowy fear behind the calm. She rose from the hearth with a small cup.

'Here we are,' she said.

Hunt slipped his arm around Georgie, steadying her.

Obediently the child sipped until all the drink was gone. 'I'm still hot, Mama.'

'I know, sweetheart.' Emma already had a damp cloth ready and Hunt watched as she set it against the flushed little cheeks.

'That's nice.' Georgie's eyelids drooped as she lay back against the mounded pillows.

Emma spoke softly. 'Keeping her propped up helps her breathing.'

Hunt nodded, looking at the child, now close to sleep. Shame flooded him that he had doubted

Emma's judgement even for a moment. He, of all men, ought to have understood her fear.

'Have you a moment?' He gestured to the door.

She looked at Georgie closely, but the child was sound asleep again and she nodded. Taking her hand, he led her out into the corridor.

'Hunt, I am truly sorry, but—'

'Don't be.'

She blinked. 'What? I'm trying to tell you—'

'You're trying to apologise, when I should be apologising,' he said. 'Is she truly better? Her forehead was burning when I touched her. Did Thompson bother to examine her? Even I can see she is seriously ill.'

She pushed a curl from her eyes. 'She is more comfortable and her breathing has eased a great deal.' She bit her lip and he had to suppress the urge to kiss the small hurt better. 'Hunt, I *am* sorry. I know being your Marchioness—'

'Sweetheart, it wasn't about being my Marchioness.' He raised his hand, traced the curve of her cheek with his fingertips, lingering at the corner of the soft mouth that could be so fiercely stubborn. 'I wanted to dance with you. Remember? Particularly the minuet.'

'You wanted—?' She stared at him as if he'd grown a second head.

'Yes,' he muttered. 'I'm not so bloody old that I wouldn't want to dance with my—'

'I did, too.'

His turn to stare. 'You did?'

'Yes. Very much.' Her tired eyes laughed a little. 'And you definitely aren't too old.'

He cleared his throat and wished he could clear his mind as easily of all the distracting thoughts that swarmed there. 'Good.' That was about the safest thing he could think of to say. 'You're staying up here again tonight, aren't you?'

Her face clouded. 'Yes. She becomes restless if I leave for long. I know it's just a cold, Hunt, but—'

He silenced her by gently setting his fingers across her mouth, felt her lips quiver. 'Don't make me feel worse than I do already, Emma.'

Caressing her cheek with his thumb, he saw the deep shadows beneath her eyes. He cursed, silently. He'd wanted to ease her worries and burdens. He set his hands to her shoulders, longing to pull her against him, hold her close. He didn't know if she would want that.

'You're tired.'

'Yes.'

He loved her directness, that she didn't bother with a polite lie to soothe him.

'Couldn't the maid sit with her while—?'

'I can't leave her.'

'I know.' He slid his hands down her arms, gathered her hands in his and held them gently. 'But you could lie down on the sofa in there until she wakes again.'

She let out a breath and, to his utter shock, stepped close, leaning against him. The sweet fragrance of her hair drifted around him. 'I'm not used to having help.'

He closed his arms around her. 'No.' She was not used to having someone take any of the load. He held her close, giving the comfort, the reassurance that she needed. 'But now that it has been pointed out to you—'

'M'lady? I heard—' There was a startled gasp. ''Tis you, milord!'

Hunt tightened his hold on Emma for a moment, then released her. He looked at the surprised maid who had come out into the corridor. 'Her ladyship is going to sleep for a little while on the sofa, if you would please sit with the child.'

'Of course, milord.'

Emma spoke. 'You will call me if she wakes, please, Jane.'

'Of course, m'lady.'

'There.' Hunt smiled at Emma as the maid slipped back into the room. 'You see how easy that was?' He only wished it could be as simple navigating the shoals of his marriage.

Chapter Sixteen

'Of course, Emma, you have never taken your proper place in society.' Letty set down her tea cup with an air of authority.

Emma inclined her head and braced herself for the inevitable lecture. In the week since Georgie's escapade either Letty or Caroline had called each day. This was the first time she had come down from the nursery to see either of them. Georgie was much better, her fever broken and the cough improving. But it had left Emma tired, her temper uncertain and she suspected her hair was somewhat dishevelled. She would have liked nothing more than to ask Bentham to tell Letty that she was still not at home to visitors, but she had not liked to send her apologies down again, nor yet keep her sister-in-law waiting while she tidied herself. Instead she had tucked her hair into a cap and come straight down.

'I did make my come-out, Letty.'

Letty waved that away. 'A dozen years ago. And the circumstances in which you have been living—' She delicately refrained from expanding on this topic. 'Naturally we can make allowances for your inexperience.'

'Thank you.' Emma examined the very pretty tea cup. It would be a shame to throw it at her sister-in-law.

'Of course, Giles's first wife was raised and trained to her position.'

'How convenient.' A very pretty cup. Did Letty imagine that Emma had been raised in a stable?

Letty raised her eyebrows. 'Yes, it was. Her father, Throckbridge, was an old friend of our father's. Both families approved the match in every way. Caroline and I, having drawn dear Anne to Giles's attention, were in alt. He married exactly as he ought.'

And this time he hadn't.

'In fact,' Letty continued, 'Giles should have remarried as soon as he was out of mourning for Anne. He needed an heir long before this.'

'But your younger brother,' Emma said. 'Gerald, was it not? Surely—'

'Our *half*-brother, Gerald,' said Letty, her expression disapproving, 'was a *most* unsatisfactory young man. Quite unsuited to the responsibility before him. Giles should have realised that and rectified the situation long before Gerald's folly got him murdered.'

Emma felt like a landed trout, gasping for breath.

Letty, apparently unaware she had dropped a bombshell, continued. 'But Giles held the foolish notion that the wretched boy would settle down. Caroline and I both told him how it would be!'

They had told Hunt that their brother—*half-brother*—would be murdered?

Emma stared and Letty seemed to collect herself.

'Well, that is neither here nor there. Giles *has* remarried and there is no question that you can bear children.' She nodded. 'In that regard he has done his duty.'

Hunt glanced up as Letty stalked into his library and laid *Paradise Lost* down carefully before he rose.

'My dear Giles, you must provide some guidance for Emma! She came down to greet me in a gown that looked as if she must have made it herself.'

'Ah.' Hunt nodded gravely. 'I'll suggest to her that when you call next she changes her dress.'

Letty glared. 'The point is that she ought to be dressed to receive a visitor in the first place!'

Hunt sought to deflect. 'Would you care for tea, Letty?'

'Thank you, no. I had tea with Emma.'

'Very lucky. I believe she gave instructions to Bentham that she was not at home to callers. So I dare say she wasn't expecting one.'

'But she *should* be!' Letty enthroned herself on a sofa. 'Giles, it is of the first importance that—'

'I'm taking her out of town for a week or so. To Isleworth.'

He should have done it immediately after the wedding, rather than remaining here in town. The house at Isleworth was far enough from town to preclude stray callers, with a park large enough for two children to run wild and get into mischief without getting into too much trouble.

'A honeymoon?'

He opened his mouth to deny that and closed it. 'Something like that. Georgie needs fresh air.'

Letty sniffed. 'Then you should begin as you mean to go on and send the children down to Pentreath.'

'But you see, Letty, I have no intention of going on in that way.' He said it with an apologetic smile. 'Shall I escort you out to your carriage?'

Letty let out a huff. 'You might as well. It's clear you won't do anything else you ought.'

Harry, accompanied by Barclay, came hurrying across the wet road from the Square, just as Hunt was about to hand Letty up into her carriage. The boy made a creditable bow to Letty, who acknowledged it with a sniff and a nod. 'Good day, Giles.' She presented her cheek. 'No doubt you will ignore all our advice.'

'Very likely.' Hunt manoeuvred around her monumental bonnet to deliver the obligatory peck on the cheek. 'It's become a habit, you see.'

Letty took an ominous breath, but got into her carriage without another word. The door closed and the carriage rolled away.

'Is she cross with you, sir?'

He glanced down at Harry. 'Naturally. She often is.' He took a closer look at his stepson. He had hardly seen the boy for the past few days. The boy's face was shuttered, he was looking at his boots, and they were back to *sir*. Barclay was standing back, probably more in deference to Letty than anything else. Hunt raised his brows questioningly with a glance at Harry and Barclay gave a slight nod.

'Would you care for some cake and milk, Harry?'

Harry looked up, surprise clear on his face. 'Yes, sir. Mr Barclay is going to send for some when we go in.'

'I meant in the library with me. I was about to have coffee.' He'd been considering brandy after Letty, but with the boy for company coffee would suffice. Barclay gave another tiny nod and went inside. Hunt knew he'd go straight to the kitchens and arrange the coffee, cake and milk.

'Oh. That would be nice. If I won't be disturbing you, sir.'

'No. My sister did that. There's no point getting back to…er…looking at my Parliamentary reports before I have to change, so you won't be disturbing me at all.' If he were to be brutally honest, he'd distracted himself with the Milton.

Back in the library he walked over to his desk,

picked up the Milton and slipped it back into its place with his other Milton editions, promising himself that he'd finish the blasted reports before he looked at it again.

Fergus got up, trotted over to Harry and thrust his nose into the boy's hand.

'Was that your report, sir?' Harry bent down to pat the dog.

He laughed. 'No, Harry. That's my vice.' He bit back a curse, wondering if the boy was too young to know what a vice was.

Harry stared at him over Fergus. 'Can a book be a vice?'

'Yes,' Hunt said feelingly. 'If you are reading it when you ought to be reading Parliamentary reports it can certainly be a vice.'

'Oh.' The boy grinned. 'Like wanting to buy a kite instead of paying for the library subscription?'

Hunt laughed. 'Exactly. Not the thing itself, but letting it lure you away from what you know you *ought* to be doing.'

Harry grimaced. 'I ought to be learning my Latin verbs, but Mr Barclay took me over to the Square because it stopped raining.'

'And now I'm tempting you with milk and cake.' Hunt looked thoughtfully at the boy. 'What's bothering you, Harry?'

The boy went very red. 'Oh. Nothing, sir. Really nothing.' Fergus sat down in front of him and lifted a paw. Obligingly, Harry shook it.

Hunt raised his brows. Amazing how *nothing* could sound exactly like *everything* depending on how it was said. 'The French call that a *mensonge pieux*.'

Harry frowned. '*Mensonge*? That's a lie, but what's *pieux*?'

'Literally, godly; or pious might be a better translation.'

Harry looked interested. 'A white lie?'

Hunt nodded. 'That's it. Now, spit it out. Are you worried about your sister?'

Harry scuffed at the carpet. 'A little. She does get colds, you know. And her breathing goes funny. And Mama worries because of Papa, you see.'

'Understandable. She is much better, you know, Harry. Ah.'

The door had opened to admit a maid with a tray.

'Master Harry's milk and cake, milord.'

He smiled at the maid. 'Thank you. Set it—' he shoved the Parliamentary reports aside '—here.'

'The coffee will be here very soon, milord.' The maid curtsied. 'And Mr John asked me to say he'll have your change of clothes ready.' She made another curtsy and left.

Hunt handed Harry the glass of milk.

'Thank you, Uncle Hunt. You're going out tonight, aren't you?'

They were attending a dinner and a ball.

The boy let out a sigh. 'I suppose Mama will go, too, since Georgie is so much better. I heard Jane the nursery maid say that Mama wouldn't need to stay with Georgie tonight.'

'Doesn't she? That's excellent. But we don't have to go out tonight.' Letty would probably kill him. 'I thought your mother and I might have supper with you and Georgie instead.' He hadn't been thinking anything of the sort.

'Really?' Harry brightened and helped himself to the largest slice of cake. 'Are you sure?'

'Absolutely,' Hunt said. 'So, apart from Georgie being better, what is bothering you?'

Harry kicked at the chair leg. Hunt, who remembered doing exactly the same when interrogated by well-meaning grown-ups, forbore to comment. Harry added a scowl to the chair kicking, but finally answered. 'It's not at all how I thought it would be. I've hardly seen Mama since we came here. Even before Georgie was sick, she had to shop and when I saw Lady Caroline the other day she said that Mama ought to be going out every evening, except she's been looking after Georgie, so Mr Barclay has been helping me with my lessons.'

Hunt blinked. Of course, he knew his secretary had more than a passing acquaintance with Latin, Greek and mathematics, but...

'I hope you behaved. Otherwise I'll have to give William a bonus.'

Harry looked slightly offended. 'Of *course* I behaved.'

Hunt didn't think there was any of course about it, not when it involved a ten-year-old and Latin, but he let it pass. 'What did you think it would be like? Your mother being married to me?'

Harry's brow wrinkled. 'I didn't think about it. I just thought it would be like it always was, except Mama wouldn't be so worried about money and she'd have more time because she wouldn't just have Bessie, but a whole houseful of servants, and we could have a dog and ponies and...' He trailed off. 'It's not like that at all. She's even busier and of course you're awfully busy. Mama says that you sit on committees for the government and have to run your estates.'

'I do.' But was he so busy that he couldn't find time each day to spend with a boy who needed a father? He'd taken Fergus for a walk this morning, as he did most mornings. He could have taken Harry with him, but it hadn't occurred to him. He'd looked in on Emma, sound asleep, visited Georgie, but hadn't spared a thought for Harry who, according to the nursery maid, had been doing his lessons. Out of sight, out of mind. With Barclay apparently.

'Are you angry with me, sir?'

Hunt realised that he was frowning. 'No. I'm angry with myself.' So he'd do something about it. 'I walk Fergus after breakfast, unless the weather is simply too bad. Would you care to come with me tomorrow?'

Fergus, having heard the fateful word, thumped his tail hopefully and Harry's face lit up. 'Yes, please.' His face fell. 'But what about my lessons?'

'We'll work around that,' Hunt said. 'We can always speak in Latin. Or Greek.'

Harry looked doubtful. 'It might be an awfully

short conversation, sir. Mr Barclay hasn't taught me quite that much.'

Hunt chuckled. 'French, then.'

After Harry had finished his milk and cake and disappeared back to his Latin verbs, Hunt continued to sit staring at the neglected report. He'd married a week ago, expecting his life to change, but absolutely nothing was as he'd envisioned it.

With a sigh, he thought back to how it had been when Anne was alive. Not like this. Not with him buried in work. Oh, he'd been busy, but he hadn't had to think about making time for his family. The time had simply been there. Then his world had broken apart. He'd tried to fill up all the empty spaces with the House of Lords, his estates, his books. Now that he looked back on it, all those things hadn't filled the emptiness, but they'd kept him busy enough that he'd been able to ignore the emptiness. Except for Gerald. But Gerald had gone off to school a year or so later and somehow he'd allowed the boy to…not so much grow up, but grow apart. He'd made mistakes with his brother. Terrible mistakes. Gerald's bitter voice echoed from their last argument when he'd refused to pay the boy's debts again…

'Do you think I don't know you'd rather Simon or Lionel had lived to inherit? That I had died instead of them?'

He'd stormed out and the next time Hunt had seen him he'd been dying from the beating Kilby's enforcers had given him.

Had he thought that? Ever? In the darkest corner of his heart? It didn't matter. Because even if it wasn't true, Gerald had been able to think that it was.

He was damned if he'd make the same mistakes again with another man's son.

'Take the children to Isleworth?' Emma stared at Hunt. She had just walked into the library after tucking them into bed.

'Yes. I have a place there.' He grimaced. 'Rather an extravagance, but it's convenient to have something close to London. We…used to use it quite a lot. William is making the arrangements. The servants need a couple of days to prepare the house, but we could leave London in three days.'

'But Parliament?'

He shrugged. 'I'll come back for a night here and there. It's only a few miles. Once Parliament rises we can leave directly from there for Cornwall.'

'And your sisters?' Letty and Caroline would be furious if she left London entirely.

'Will be busily spreading the word that we have gone on our honeymoon,' he said without a blush.

'With two children?'

'It's a big house and park,' he said. 'They—the children—need more space. I sent a note to Cambourne suggesting that Fitch might visit for a few days. And Cambourne has found a couple of ponies for me. He'll bring them over with Fitch. And, with your permission, I've written to my steward at Pentreath. There's a puppy there—Fergus's half-sister, actually. The children might like her for Christmas.'

Ponies. They had been longing for ponies. Especially since coming to live here. And a puppy. But—

'You're very generous, Hunt.' So much that she had been unable to do for Harry and Georgie. Even if Peter's money had continued after his death it would have been difficult.

Hunt frowned. 'Generous? Hardly that.' He let out a breath. 'I'm not their father. I cannot and *should* not try to take his place. But I do have to do his job as best I can. They should learn to ride. And there is a small pony carriage at Isleworth, so they can learn to drive, too.'

Oh, yes. He *was* generous. And kind, responsible. It ought to be enough.

He rose from his desk where he had been sorting through some papers and came towards her. 'Come, madam wife.'

She blinked. 'Come where?'

'An early start to that honeymoon.'

It was different this time.

She was no less heated and desperate to have his hands on her, but he refused to hurry. He escorted her into her bedchamber, dismissed her maid with a cool, *That will be all*, and stripped her with controlled expertise. By the time his clothes joined her own on the floor and he slid into her bed, she was aching. Firelight slid over hard planes, shadows etched his face as he drew her against him. Eager, she slid her arms around him, raised her knee to caress his flank.

A curse mingled with a groan and he rose over her on his elbows, cradling her face. To her surprise, rather than accepting her invitation, he straddled her, pressing her thighs together. She squirmed, but he bent to kiss her.

Deep, heated kisses that dissolved thought and protest, reducing her to a jelly. And she discovered her husband. Discovered his slow, skilled hands that learned her curves, found and teased secrets, and refused to rush. Refused to let her rush him. Discovered a strength that held them both in check, even as his wicked mouth licked and nibbled a burning path to one breast.

Her body arched and she scarcely recognised her own voice as she cried out. Need and mingled relief shuddered through her as he drew the peaked nipple into the consuming heat of his mouth.

Emma was everything he wanted and more. Such wild abandon as her body bowed up, her breast the sweetest offering, feminine curves all his.

Soft, so soft, as he learned the gentle dip of her waist, the swell of her hip and the creamy texture of her thighs. Soft and welcoming as he finally reached between them and she opened, willing and eager. Slick, lush heat, and another choked cry as he found the taut nub above her entrance.

All the tastes and scents of her body flowered and were his, and the satiny skin and muscles of her belly flickered and jumped beneath his quest-ing mouth. Her hot scent drew him and he slid lower, hard and burning.

This time she would have everything. Every-thing he could give. Everything she could take, before he surrendered to his own needs.

Beyond her control, Emma's body bucked against the rising need, was held steady by a heavy arm across her hips, even as his mouth at last found her and wild, glorious pleasure speared her. The silken caresses burned her, brought her to the edge of sanity, held her there a moment, then relentlessly forced her over into the abyss.

Hunt felt her go, felt the convulsions as she flew free. Control snapped and he surged up the length of her body and plunged into her, pleasure a dark god as her body tightened around him and she came again, gasping. He rode her through the storm, deep and sure, until his own consumma-tion bore down on him. He thrust one last time, held deep and still, shuddering as release swept through him in a white-hot blaze.

He hung there for a moment, shaking, then with a groan, let himself down, utterly sated, along the damp length of her body. Her arms came about him in welcome, and she murmured contentedly as he settled, her body giving sweetly under his weight. Some vague remnant of chivalry prodded him. He shifted, trying to ease from her, but she drew him back, sighing in contentment, pushing a sweat-dampened lock of hair back from his brow.

'I'll squash you,' he murmured and compromised, disengaging and shifting his weight to the side. He pressed a kiss to her temple, absorbing the mingled spicy scents of hot, damp Emma and sex.

'Mmm.' Contentment breathed from her. ''pology accepted.'

'What?' He raised his head with a herculean effort. 'Apology? Oh.' He'd forgotten about that. He brushed tangled curls away from her face. A sleepy sigh was followed by a change in her breathing into utter relaxation.

'Emma?'

Somewhere deep inside a laugh shook him. She'd beaten him into sleep. Deciding to take that as a compliment, he tucked her closer. He could remain for a few minutes, loving the silky warmth of her against him before he had to leave for the unwanted privacy of his own bed…or he could take the risk and stay. Wake with her in the morning, look into sleepy dark blue eyes as he kissed her awake…still thinking about it he slid over the edge into sleep.

Gerald lay, battered and bloody, in his coffin. The eyes were open, staring. His brother lay dead, yet the corpse spoke…

'It won't work. My death won't bring back Simon or Lionel. They're gone.'

'Gerald. I didn't think that. I never wanted that! Listen!'

'Too late, Hunt. I never did listen. You always said that.'

The coffin lid was closing, changing into a gravestone...

No! This time he would stop it. He wouldn't let Gerald go. If he didn't let the coffin close...

'*Gerald! Wait!*'

'Hunt! Hunt!'

He woke to Emma leaning over him, dark eyes frantic. 'Hunt, are you all right? You were struggling and you called out.'

He sat up, conscious of the usual headache and the terrible, all-consuming knowledge that he had failed Gerald. 'It's nothing. Just a—nothing.' Damned if he'd admit to a nightmare like one of the children.

'It didn't sound like nothing.'

Her worried eyes and sympathetic voice jabbed his pride. *He* was supposed to protect and reassure *her*. Not the other way round. And if he couldn't remember that, then he had no business succumbing to the temptation of remaining in her bed all night.

'I beg your pardon for disturbing you.' He pushed back the covers and swung his legs over the side.

She caught his arm just above the elbow. 'Hunt, you didn't *disturb* me.'

He freed himself gently. 'Excuse me, Emma. I should go to my own bed.'

'Why?'

Her eyes, far from being sympathetic and worried now, burned into him in the glow of the dying fire. And the time-worn excuse, that this was how a marriage in their world was conducted, withered on his lips. 'Goodnight, Emma.' He supposed it was something that he couldn't even manage a decent *mensonge pieux*. He turned to leave.

'Hunt, what happened to Gerald?'

The gentle question stabbed him.

He kept his back to her. 'He died.'

'I know. But Letty said something and you... you spoke his name. Called to him to wait.'

Forcing out a silent breath, he started for the door.

'Hunt?'

There was only one honest answer he could make. 'I killed him. Now excuse me, if you please.'

'Will there really be ponies, Mama?'

Harry could think of nothing else and had asked the same question several times. They were to leave for Isleworth that afternoon.

'Your Uncle Hunt says so.'

Harry's eyes were dreamy. 'I wonder what colour mine will be. It might a chestnut, or a bay, or...or—'

'Or a complete surprise,' Emma suggested. 'Why didn't you ask Hunt when you went for that walk with him earlier?'

'I did,' Harry admitted. 'He didn't know. He just said that Lord Cambourne had chosen the ponies, so he was confident we wouldn't get killed and that was more important.' He looked thoroughly unconvinced by this view.

'I see.' Emma folded the small riding breeches that a maid had found in a storage trunk and placed them with the other clothes for Harry.

'Were they Uncle Hunt's once?' Georgie asked. She was helping Bessie with her own clothes.

'Belonged to his lordship's eldest boy,' Bessie said, folding a very small petticoat. 'Like that little riding habit belonged to his daughter.'

'But...they died.' Georgie looked bothered by this. 'Can't we have our own?'

Emma looked across. 'Certainly. They are ordered. But they couldn't be ready by today. So if you wish to ride before they are delivered to Isleworth in a day or so, you will wear these.'

Harry looked uncertain. 'Uncle Hunt doesn't mind us wearing them?'

'Of course not,' Emma said. 'Now, can I safely leave you two to finish here? Mr Barclay needs me in the library for a few moments to look through my letters. Georgie? Are you nearly finished?'

Georgie, carefully placing Anna Maria in amongst her clothes, looked up and nodded. 'Yes, Mama. And Bessie is going to check everything.'

'That I am,' Bessie said firmly. 'You go, my lady. We're all but done here.'

Would Hunt mind the children using those clothes if he knew?

She couldn't rid herself of that question as she hurried downstairs. The servants had simply produced the clothes. Rather as they had unearthed the soldiers Harry played with, several dolls for Georgie and a great number of books.

She had no idea how Hunt would feel about Harry and Georgie using his own children's belongings. He never spoke of them. At all. It was the servants who spoke of them from time to time, always fondly. Simon, Lionel and Marianne. About Gerald, Hunt's half-brother and heir presumptive, very little was said, although she gathered that he had been of an age with Hunt's eldest son, Simon, and had been raised as another son after his own mother died. But mention of Gerald was usually in reference to one of Hunt's own children.

Gerald's folly got him murdered...

I killed him...

She didn't believe for a moment that Hunt had literally killed his brother. But somehow Hunt blamed himself. And he had closed himself away. He came to her each night, made love to her with skilled passion, but left soon after. And he thanked her. She didn't want him to thank her, as though she had passed the salt. As though what they did was for nothing more than the begetting of an heir. She wanted Hunt's child. Not merely his heir. And she wanted Hunt, not just sex.

Sex, she realised, even wonderful sex, did not necessarily mean intimacy. Hunt had made it clear that part of his life was out of bounds to her. And he kept busy with meetings, sittings in the House of Lords. Busy with managing his estates. Busy even taking Harry out for a walk with Fergus most mornings. Busy with everything but his wife.

William Barclay looked up from his ruthlessly organised desk and smiled. 'Good morning, Lady Huntercombe. You've just missed him. He's stepped out for half an hour. I have your correspondence sorted.'

He had arranged another desk for her by the fire. Emma sat down and started with the invitations. Most of them she would have to decline since they were leaving town. Those she marked with a D for Barclay to deal with. There were several letters from one-time friends who had heard of her remarriage. Those she set aside to take with her to Isleworth. One was from an elderly great-aunt, pleased to hear that Emma had repented and married to oblige her family. Emma grimaced. Typical Aunt Felicia. Better to respond to her immediately and get it over with. She glanced up at Barclay, busy with Hunt's correspondence. Discreet, intelligent and observant, Barclay was the perfect secretary. And he'd been with Hunt for years.

'Mr Barclay? You must have known Gerald Moresby. What happened to him?'

Barclay sprinkled sand on the letter he had just finished and sighed. 'Yes. I knew him before I knew his lordship. Gerald was at school with my younger brother and often came home with Reginald for holidays.'

'He did?'

'Oh, yes. They were both a little wild, always in some scrape or other, although Reginald is settling down now.' His smile was wry. 'That was how I came by this position.'

'Your brother settling down?'

He chuckled. 'No. Reg staying with Gerald for Christmas some years ago. His lordship's old secretary was retiring and Reg mentioned me as a possible replacement.'

'Well, that shows a very proper family feeling.'

Barclay glanced over his half-spectacles. 'I'm ten years older than Reg. I believe he described me to his lordship as a shocking old sobersides.'

Emma bit back a laugh. 'And?'

'His lordship wrote, very kindly inviting me to call when next he was in London.' He frowned. 'But you asked about Gerald. He came down from Oxford—he was *sent* down, actually—and fell in with a bad crowd. Got badly into debt, tried to recoup his losses in a gambling hell and was in worse trouble when he couldn't pay the fellow who had bought up his IOUs. The fellow's bruisers came after Gerald when it became obvious that he wasn't going to get his money.'

'*What?*' Emma's stomach churned. 'They *killed* him?'

Barclay nodded, his face grim. 'Yes. He died of his injuries.'

Emma felt sick, but she had to know. 'Were they caught?'

Barclay hesitated. 'I…yes. I don't know much about that. His lordship did not confide in me. But Lord Cambourne helped him track them.' He smiled. 'I believe his lordship maintains silence because of Lady Cambourne's involvement. That was how she and Cambourne met.' He cleared his throat. 'Shall I deal with those invitations for you, my lady?'

Emma smiled. 'Thank you. Yes. But is there some paper I may use for a letter?' She would need to order her own paper and visiting cards.

Barclay nodded. 'His lordship keeps paper for his private correspondence in the top right-hand drawer of his own desk. If you do not require me I have some errands to run for his lordship. Ah, all the arrangements are in place for Austerleigh Park. The baggage and servants will go late this morning, and I have ordered the carriage at two o'clock for you and the children. It's only about eight miles. Plenty of time before dark.'

'And his lordship?'

'Will drive his curricle down.'

Emma sat for a moment after the door closed behind Barclay. Her heart ached. How could Hunt blame himself for his brother's death? Had Gerald not come to him for help? She would be shattered if Harry or Georgie got into some scrape and didn't confide in her. But how difficult for a young man to admit to a much older brother that he was in over his head!

She rose and went to Hunt's large, rather untidy desk. She opened the top right-hand drawer. A stack of thick cream paper lay there. She drew it forward, surprised at the weight, and blinked when she saw the miniature lying on top.

A fair-haired lady she recognised as Anne Huntercombe smiled up at her. In her lap a small girl nestled, golden curls confined with a simple blue ribbon. A slightly older boy, his mother's arm around him, leaned close, his grin cheeky. Emma could see the likeness to Hunt in the dark hair and shape of the eyes. Another boy, taller, and even more staggeringly like Hunt, stood at his mother's other side, his hand on her shoulder, a gesture that spoke of affectionate protectiveness. Emma's breath caught at the intimacy. These must be Hunt's children, Marianne, Lionel and Simon. And there was a fourth child, a third boy. He was very like Simon, although not as tall, and stood beside him, Simon's arm around his shoulders bringing him into the group.

Gerald. The half-brother included as a loved member of the family Hunt had lost.

The memory of Peter's death slashed at Emma, a wound that could never fully heal. She let the pain wash through her, accepting it. Memories could not be stopped and they held joy despite the grief. To stop those memories would have meant denying part of herself. Love could not exist without the risk of grief.

But why was this picture hidden away? She looked at Hunt's desk again. A second miniature stood there. A very young man with waving dark hair and a slightly sulky expression. His hand rested on the neck of a chestnut horse. Her breath caught. Hunt? She could see Hunt in the tilt of the head, the shape of the jaw and nose. But, no. The

clothes were quite wrong for it to have been Hunt
at that age. This must be Gerald, probably not very
long before his death.

'Emma? William said you were— What is
that?'

Her head jerked up at the sharp tone. Hunt, his
face shuttered, stood just inside the door, hand
still on the knob.

'I was looking for notepaper,' she said.

'Really?' He closed the door. 'It doesn't look
very like notepaper to me.' His long strides
brought him across the room and he took the painting from her grasp. Very gently he laid it back in
the drawer and for one unguarded moment she
saw pain breach the ice as he closed the drawer.

'Why, Hunt?' The question was out before she
could think the better of it and she flinched at the
renewed chill in his expression.

'Madam?'

'Why hide them away and leave Gerald out?'
She gestured to the portrait still on the desk. 'That
is Gerald, isn't it?' Despite the ice in his eyes, she
laid a hand on his wrist. 'Don't put them away
because of me.'

He shut the drawer and with awful care nudged
her hand away. 'Perhaps, Madam Pandora, some
things are supposed to be private.'

She could accept that rebuke. She probably deserved it. But like Pandora, she couldn't unopen
the box. 'I'm sorry, Hunt.' She reached for his
hand, but he stepped back and she let her hand fall.
The rejection hurt more than if he'd struck her.

'If you refrain from searching my drawers in future, no apologies will be necessary.'

She took a careful breath at the lash of his voice. This was not about her. Wounded creatures could strike out. 'I'm sorry for that, too. But I meant that I am sorry you lost them.'

His mouth flattened. 'It was a long time ago.'

She shook her head. 'Not always. Sometimes it is only yesterday, or as far away as your last dream.' She knew, the moment she had spoken, that she had said precisely the wrong thing. He had dreamed of Gerald the other night...

'What would you know about it?' he exploded.

For a moment she could not answer. Something had lodged hard and tight in her throat. She choked it down. 'Everything,' she said softly. 'Hunt, you could not have prevented smallpox. And Gerald chose his own path. If he did not come to you for help—'

His expression silenced her as effectively as a blow. Hard. Bitter.

'Is that what you think? That Gerald did not ask for help?'

'Hunt—'

'He did come to me. I refused him.'

There. He'd said it. And silenced Emma's sympathy. He could imagine what she was thinking. What sort of brute would refuse to help his brother? Would send him away hurt and bitter? To his death.

'You should go, Emma.'

She hesitated. 'That is truly what you want?'

'Yes.' It ought to be.

'Then I'm sorry. And I wish with all my heart that you had not lost them.'

Hunt watched her cross the room. Pain, as raw as his last dream, twisted inside him, mingled with shame. 'You wish then that we hadn't married?'

She shook her head. 'No. Never that. Excuse me. I must finish packing.'

He cursed as he realised that he'd nearly forgotten why he'd needed to speak with her in the first place. 'I am very sorry, but we will need to put off our departure to Isleworth. There is some business that I should attend to first. A couple of committees I must attend, including one in an hour.'

'I see.' Her hand was on the doorknob. 'If you do not object, Hunt, I will take the children to Isleworth this afternoon as planned.' The pallor of her face tore at him.

'By yourself?' Anne had taken the children to Cornwall early when he had to remain in London. He had never seen them again. He wanted to roar a protest, but he swallowed it. 'No, I have no objection. I will follow in a day or so.'

Something unreadable flickered across her face. 'If you wish. But if you find that you cannot, it is not of any consequence.' She hesitated. 'The servants—they found riding clothes for the children. Do you...do you mind?'

For a moment he couldn't think what she meant. 'No. God, no. Of course not!' How could she think that?

'Then, Hunt…' her voice was gentle, but distant as the moon as she opened the door '…put them back on your desk. They deserve better than to be hidden. Keep them all in the light.'

The door closed. Gone. She was gone. Because he had lost control and driven her away. As he had driven Gerald away that last time. He sat heavily in his chair, gazing at his brother. He had driven Gerald away and he had let Anne go alone.

I wish with all my heart that you had not lost them.

He had wished that, too. Over and over, beating in him like a sore tooth. He had thought he still wished it. But it was pointless, something that could never be. Time could never be reversed. Even a clock could not be truly turned back. It had to go forward. And if you did manage to force Time itself back, would something break? The way a clock was damaged if you forced the hands widdershins? You could stop the clock, but even then, if you stopped it for long enough it wouldn't work properly until someone mended and regulated it.

Who regulated Time?

Slowly Hunt opened the drawer, lifted the picture out and set it back where it had always stood. There was no point in wishing that Time and its Regulator had done this or that. All you could do was make your choices according to what you had been given. If your choice was to stand still and refuse the gift, bitter though it might seem at first, then you would wither, just as the clock would seize up. To wish the past undone was to wish Emma, Harry and Georgie away. He couldn't bring himself to wish that. Not for the first time he wished one of his parents was still alive to give advice. And smiled at the thought. He'd been thirty before he'd realised how good his parents' advice had been.

He stared at his father's portrait above the fireplace. The old man, a hand resting lightly on his setter's head, gazed out across the library. Tradition decreed that the last portrait of the previous Marquess always hung there. One day his own portrait would be there. Would his and Emma's son gaze up at it hoping for guidance?

'Play the hand you're dealt...'

He could almost hear the crusty old man's voice. He had played that last hand with Gerald so badly. But Fate had dealt him a new hand with Emma, Harry and Georgie. He just had to work out how best to play it.

Chapter Seventeen

$\approx\!\!\!\sim\!\!\!\sim\!\!\!\sim\!\!\!\sim$

Emma wondered if her erstwhile mother-in-law ever planned to leave. The Duchess had arrived, with Lord Martin and the Miss Carshalton Hunt had mentioned, at one o'clock, a perfectly respectable time to call. Unless of course your hostess intended to leave London within the hour.

She had given Bentham instructions that she was not at home, but upon being confronted with the Duchess of Keswick, he thought it better to check. She had miscalculated badly in deciding to see the Duchess. Most calls of ceremony lasted twenty minutes, but the last time Emma had managed a surreptitious glance at the clock over the fireplace it had been half past one.

The Duchess had insisted upon seeing the children, so Georgie and Harry were arrayed in their best clothes and seated upon footstools close to the Duchess—whom they had been graciously invited to call *Grandmother Duchess*. Not that she had exchanged above two sentences with either child, or even seemed to notice them unless Georgie wriggled.

The arrival of Louisa had only entrenched the Duchess in her position as the two grandmothers sniped at each other with barbed elegance. Louisa arrived and upon Miss Carshalton being presented to her, said with her sweetest smile, 'Oh, yes. The shipmaster's daughter.'

Miss Carshalton inclined her head and agreed that she was.

Lord Martin stood in moody splendour by the fireplace, responding in monosyllables to Emma's attempts at conversation. As he moved slightly, she caught a glimpse of the clock. Nearly quarter to two. They should be leaving shortly. Darkness closed in so early at this time of year and the last thing she wanted was to be travelling after dark.

'Impatient to be shot of us, ma'am?'

Lord Martin's soft voice was edged with ice.

Emma flushed. 'Not at all, Lord Martin,' she lied. 'It must always be a delight to see my children's relatives.'

His dark brows shot up. 'Not yours?'

She met the mocking gaze with hauteur. 'No, sir. Not mine. That was made evident long ago.'

Lord Martin grimaced and inclined his head. '*Touché*. As well females don't fence. You'd hit something painful.' He pushed away from the chimney piece. 'Mother, we should be taking our leave. Lady Huntercombe is casting meaningful glances at the clock and I must escort Kit…er, that is, Miss Carshalton, home.'

Louisa closed her eyes, saying in pained accents, 'Really, Emma, have you forgotten all conduct?' She gave the Duchess a sweet smile. 'Such a relief to see her well settled! A mother always worries about the choices her children make. So pleasing when they listen to reason, is it not?'

The Duchess's eyes turned flinty. She spoke in tones that dripped condescension. 'Indeed. I am pleased to say that, unlike his poor brother, Lord Martin has been most dutiful in that regard. We shall shortly be making an Interesting Announcement.'

Miss Carshalton blushed crimson.

It was hard to say if Louisa looked more intrigued or chagrined, but good breeding prevented her from saying anything more than, 'How charming!'

Emma contrived to look suitably delighted. 'Congratulations, sir.'

He eyed her coolly. 'Optimistic when you have not been furnished with the lady's name.'

In light of Miss Carshalton's heightened colour, Emma thought she had been furnished with all that was needful. 'I am sure if the Duchess approves, that the lady is all that is amiable.'

His mouth quirked. 'Thank you. She is.' He glanced at Miss Carshalton, an odd expression on his face. 'Miss Carshalton has done me the honour to accept my hand.'

The Duchess preened a little, reaching out to

pat Miss Carshalton's hand. 'Dear Katherine. Such a modest, unassuming girl. *Just* the sort of bride a mother wishes for her son.'

Emma turned to smile at Miss Carshalton. And wondered. The younger woman's blush had faded, leaving her pale and wan. 'May I wish you happy, Miss Carshalton?' What had Lord Martin called her? Kit? At least that suggested some affection, but—

If anything the girl paled further. 'Thank you. You're very kind.' Her voice was slightly husky and Emma thought the gloved hands trembled.

Georgie looked up from the book she had supposedly been absorbed in. 'Are you going to be married, sir? To Miss Carshalton?'

Emma blinked. Georgie had been listening a great deal more carefully than she would have thought.

Lord Martin looked surprised, too, but that might have been at being directly addressed by his niece. 'It seems so.'

Georgie frowned. 'Don't you *know*?'

Lord Martin grinned, looking more like Peter than ever.

'Yes, I am very definitely getting married.'

'Like Mama,' Georgie said. She favoured Lord Martin and Miss Carshalton with the angelic smile that warned Emma she was up to something. 'When Mama got married Harry and I gave her away. At least we can keep her, but we share her with Uncle Hunt now.'

'Uncle Hunt? Do you call him that?'

Georgie nodded. 'Yes, sir.'

He cleared his throat and crouched down beside her. 'This *sir* business could become tedious. Why don't you just call me Uncle Martin? I *am* your uncle, you know.'

Harry nodded. 'Mama explained. And…you look like Papa.' He flushed. 'At least, I think so. It was a long time ago.'

Lord Martin's face was expressionless. 'Yes, it is. You do not have a picture of him?'

Harry shook his head. 'No, sir. That is, Uncle Martin.'

'I see.' Lord Martin hesitated. 'Well, I think—'

'Sir—Uncle Martin?' Georgie tugged at his cuff. 'Would you like us to give Miss Carshalton to you?'

Louisa made a pained sort of sound, but a low chuckle broke from Miss Carshalton. 'Thank you, Georgie. That's very kind, but I think my father will do that. However, I am sure there would be some flowers you could carry. In fact, I shall see to it.'

Georgie looked positively smug at this and Lord Martin looked as though he were trying not to grin. He glanced at Emma. 'Perhaps Miss Carshalton and I might take the children out one day soon? They might like ices at Gunter's.'

'That is very kind of you, sir, but—'

'Mama would like an ice, too,' Georgie announced. 'She could tell Miss Carshalton about being married. But we're going to live somewhere else this afternoon.'

Lord Martin blinked. 'Somewhere else?'

Emma fought back a laugh at his obvious confusion. 'I am taking the children out to Huntercombe's house at Isleworth this afternoon, sir.'

'Just yourself and the children?' The Duchess sounded like a seagull swooping on a particularly smelly piece of fish. 'Huntercombe does not go?'

Emma stiffened her spine. She would *not* be baited by this woman. There was *nothing* unusual in a husband and wife being apart for a few days. 'Huntercombe has commitments here in town. He will join us in a day or two.' *She hoped.*

'Of course.' Seagulls didn't usually coo, but somehow the Duchess did it, and Emma could just imagine the whispers spreading out in widening ripples.

Poor Huntercombe. I hear Emma Lacy is quite impossible these days. They say he has lost no time in bundling her off to Isleworth with her children. One wonders exactly how *she caught him. Of course, he* does *need an heir...*

Speculative eyebrows would lift and everyone would be counting on their fingers the moment any Interesting Condition was confirmed...

The Duchess rose, held out a gracious, beringed hand to Emma, her expression saintly. 'Good day, Lady Huntercombe. We shall not delay you further.' She glanced at her son. 'You must deliver dear Katherine home in good time, Martin.' She smiled at Miss Carshalton. 'And we must discuss our engagements for this evening, my dear.' She inclined her head to Louisa. 'Dear Louisa, I do compliment you on your confidence in wearing that *particular* shade. So many women would consider it ageing.' On this parting shot she sailed from the field of combat, colours flying, Lord Martin leaping to open the door for her and Miss Carshalton, who uttered a breathless farewell and hurried after her mother-in-law-to-be.

Louisa, eyes flinty, also took her leave, her gracious air showing signs of wear around the edges. 'I think, Emma dear, that your place should be with your husband. I am sure the children will settle quite readily without—'

'Mother, you must excuse me.' Emma hoped a sweet smile would cover the interruption. 'Goodbye. It was lovely to see you.'

Sometimes a small lie could be justified, but judging by Louisa's disapproving mien, this one had been wasted. She took her leave, not bothering to say anything to the children.

Emma breathed a sigh of relief as the door closed behind her mother. 'Harry, take Georgie up to the nursery. Ask Bessie and Jane to get you into your travelling clothes quickly. I'll order the carriage to be brought around.'

'Yes, Mama.'

Hunt stared at his travelling carriage in disbelief as he alighted from his town carriage behind it. He glanced up at the sky, but clouds hid the sun, so he pulled his watch out. Three o'clock. The light would start to fade in half an hour and it was likely to take half an hour to clear London.

Even as he strode towards the carriage, Emma came out of the house with the children and two footmen piled with rugs.

'Look, Mama!' Georgie tugged at Emma's hand and pointed. 'It's Uncle Hunt.' She gave Hunt her most enchanting smile. 'Are you coming with us? Mama said you couldn't.'

'My lord.' Emma looked somewhat frayed around the edges as she lifted Georgie into the carriage. 'You will excuse us if we keep going, I hope.'

'My dear.' He caught her hands. 'It's far too late to leave now. It will be getting dark soon.'

'There is still time if we do not delay,' she said, flushing. 'I know we should have left over an hour ago. My mother called *and* the Duchess of Keswick.' She glanced at Harry. 'I could hardly refuse to see them, or kick them out when they remained longer than I expected.'

He could certainly understand that. But still... 'Emma, leave in the morning. Surely—'

'Aren't we going after all?' Harry asked. 'Mama said there would be time.'

'There is,' Emma said. 'If we leave now.'

He could override her and order Masters to put the carriage away. He didn't want to do that. Certainly not after the way he'd left things this morning. He looked again at the sky. 'Masters?'

'My lord?'

'Is there time to reach Austerleigh before dark?'

'If we leave now, my lord. Horses are fresh. Luggage went on ahead, so it's just my lady and

Master Harry and Miss Georgie. We'll make good time, never you fear.'

If Masters said it was all right, then it was. And yet… Hunt fought down the urge to order Emma and the children straight back into the house.

'Very well.' He offered Emma his hand. 'Up with you.'

She laid her hand lightly on his and stepped into the carriage. 'If you cannot come the day after tomorrow—'

'I'll be out tomorrow afternoon.' He gripped her hand. 'You won't mind?' He wouldn't blame her if she did.

She stared. 'Of course not. But your meetings—'

His fingers tightened on hers. 'I have one here tomorrow morning.' No one else knew that yet, but they would as soon as he sent notes around. 'I'll come mid-afternoon.' He tucked one of the carriage rugs around her. Essence of Emma surrounded him, sinking deep, and he brought her hand to his lips, pressing a kiss to the inside of her wrist. Soft. Silky soft. And not just her wrist. She was soft and silken everywhere— He broke off, realising he had an interested audience. 'Are you warm enough, Georgie?' The child was buried in a veritable sea of furs.

'Yes, Uncle Hunt.' A dimple flashed. 'I'm a bug in a rug!'

He laughed. 'Are you? You're certainly snug enough. Harry.' He turned and held out a hand to the boy. 'Look after your mother and sister for me.'

Look after your mother and little brother and sister for me...

Harry gripped his hand. 'Yes, sir.' Pride blazed in the boy's face and for a shattering instant time reversed and Hunt saw that other boy's shining eyes as he set out on his last journey. Harry lowered his voice. 'Can I ask you something?'

'Of course.'

'Do you think I could sit up on the box with Masters and Jem?'

Pain stabbed at him. Simon, Lionel and Gerald had taken turns sitting up with Masters and the groom. 'Emma?'

She smiled, a little lopsidedly. 'If Masters doesn't mind.'

Masters chuckled. 'Never knew a lad wouldn't rather sit up here than inside. Come along, young master.'

Hunt boosted Harry up, passed up a carriage rug Emma handed to him. 'Use it. If you catch cold your mother won't let you do this again.' He looked back at Emma. 'I'll see you tomorrow. And we'll talk.'

He stepped back, allowing the footman to put up the steps and close the door.

On the box, having tucked the rug around Harry, Masters touched the whip to his hat. 'We'll take care of them, my lord.'

Hunt nodded, curbing the nagging fear, the memory of seeing Anne and the children off on that last journey eleven years ago. Lightning didn't strike twice. And in case it did, he'd made enquiries—there was no sickness or disease near Austerleigh. They were safe.

Emma sank back against the squabs. There had been something in Hunt's voice, in his eyes, as he'd tucked the rug around her. Something in the way he'd said, *we'll talk*. Something that had made her long to suggest that he just got into the carriage and came with them. But she must not. A wife must not demand her husband's attention. She must not be forever expecting him to dance attendance on her.

The courtship, such as it had been, was over. They were married. But...*we'll talk*... Perhaps he wanted to reiterate the terms of their marriage. But his eyes, tired and haunted, hadn't been saying that at all.

She glanced at Georgie, occupied with looking out the window. Both children were thrilled to be going on what Harry had described as another adventure. Logically she knew it was the best thing for them. There would be time and space for them to adjust to their new life. Lord Cambourne's young brother-in-law would arrive tomorrow for a few days. There would be far more for the children to do while she set about the task of interviewing and engaging a governess. Hunt had already written to a couple of potential tutors for Harry.

All very logical and sensible. Like her marriage. Only she wasn't being very logical and sensible about that.

* * *

Hunt stared unseeing at the document he was supposed to be reviewing. He'd read it three times and nothing had lodged in his brain. His mind was miles away—literally—thinking about where Emma and the children must be by now.

Barclay cleared his throat. 'Sir?'

Hunt gave himself a mental shake. 'Right. It seems to me—' He searched for something to say that would suggest he had actually retained something on the subject of the war with France.

'Sir? Don't you think you would concentrate better at Austerleigh?'

He narrowed his eyes at Barclay. God knew he allowed William a great deal of licence, but—

'May I remind you that I have a meeting here tomorrow?'

'Oh, be blowed with the meeting, sir!'

Hunt blinked. How very unlike the responsible, dutiful William. 'Are you suggesting that I should take French leave?'

Barclay looked shocked. 'Certainly not, sir. I'll cancel it.'

Despite himself, Hunt laughed.

'Sir, you have been married a week. No one will think it wonderful that you have left town briefly. I'll reschedule the meeting for early next week and you can ride in for it.'

Why the devil was he arguing? Hunt rose. 'Right. Are you coming? Happy to ride?'

Barclay smiled, gathering papers. 'I'm packed

already. I just need half an hour to make sure I have all the documents.'

'Are we nearly there?'

Emma supressed a groan. The charms of the passing scenery had already faded for Georgie and they were barely a mile past the Knightsbridge turnpike.

'No. Are you warm enough?'

Georgie scowled. 'If Harry is then I am. Why can *he* sit up with Masters? Why can't I sit up there, too?'

'Because Masters has enough to do with the horses and there isn't room. And Harry asked if he might first.' She knew better than to mention Georgie's recent illness.

'But I didn't know I could ask!'

'What do you think we should call the puppy?'

'Puppy?'

She had delayed telling them about the puppy. 'Uncle Hunt says there is a puppy for you and Harry at his—*our* home in Cornwall. A little girl. We need to think of names.' Hopefully Georgie wouldn't suggest something appalling. 'Several names that we can discuss with Harry and try out on the puppy.'

Georgie forgot the injustice of not sitting up on the box in the cold. 'Will she be brown and white like Fergus?'

'I don't know,' Emma lied. Hunt had said the puppy was black and white. 'That's why we need lots of different names. Uncle Hunt did say she was very pretty. What's French for pretty?'

Puppy names in French and Italian got them through another half-hour. Outside, Emma could see that the dusk was deepening and darker than she would have expected. The carriage pulled up.

Georgie brightened. 'Are we there?'

The trap opened and Masters's face appeared. 'Rain coming, m'lady. I'm sending Master Harry inside.'

'Thank you, Masters.'

The door opened and Harry scrambled in. 'Masters let me take the ribbons,' he announced.

Forestalling an explosion from Georgie, Emma said, 'We have been thinking of names for the puppy.'

'Puppy?'

Emma let Georgie explain.

Harry looked pleased. He grabbed a rug and wrapped himself up in it. 'It was jolly cold up there.' He looked at Georgie. 'I asked Masters if I could drive next time and he said I could, unless you wanted a turn. Of course, girls don't drive, so—'

Emma cleared her throat. 'I can.'

Harry stared. 'I didn't know that.'

'And I do want a turn,' Georgie said.

'Oh.' Clearly deflated, Harry changed the subject. 'What shall we call the puppy?'

A reasonably amicable discussion of more puppy names carried them over another couple of miles, as the light faded. The rain stopped, but neither Harry nor Georgie asked about joining Masters on the box, for which Emma was deeply grateful. She could see that the clouds were thinning, but the light was fitful and Masters would have enough on his mind.

'Mama?' Georgie was looking out the window. 'Do you think Masters and the footman are—?'

Crack!

The carriage jolted to a halt.

'Stand and deliver!'

Chapter Eighteen

Hunt could see the glow of the carriage lamps ahead from time to time before the road bent, but in the rapidly fading light he didn't push the pace. He felt settled, right in himself. He'd been a fool to let her go at all. A fool and a coward, hiding behind duty and not letting himself see the truth. Just as long as he hadn't messed it up completely… somehow he thought Emma was the sort of woman who would give a muddle-headed husband a second—

The pistol shot shattered the night.

He froze, checking his gelding. Beside him, Barclay swore. Hunt barely glanced at him before he'd sprung Petrarch into a gallop.

'Drop yer barkers, cullies!' The rough voice carried clearly. 'I got more'n one left and the next won't be no warning shot.'

'Mama!' Georgie clambered into Emma's lap, clinging to her.

'Shhhh.' Emma hugged her close. 'It's all right. He'll want money and jewellery. Then he'll be off.' She didn't have a great deal of money or jewellery with her, but she couldn't help that.

'You'll bloody regret this.' Masters's growl was followed by several thuds as he and the footman threw down their pistols.

'Right.' The highwayman's voice came again. 'Everyone out!'

'Mama! No!' Georgie's voice was muffled in Emma's shoulder as she clung, frantic.

Gently, Emma pried her loose, fear churning in her gut. 'Shhh, Georgie.' She kept her voice very soft. 'I have to.'

'Hurry up in there or your coachman gets a hole in 'im!'

'Mama, he'll hurt Masters!' Harry's voice shook, but he kept it low.

'Just jewellery and money,' Emma repeated. 'Nothing important. I'm coming!' she called. She set Georgie gently on the seat. 'Harry, stay with her.'

'Mama!'

White-faced, Harry nodded and Emma snatched up her reticule, trying not to hear Georgie's terrified screams as she opened the door and got down. Just beyond the yellowish glow of the carriage lamps she could make out a horse and rider.

'Took yer time, didn't you, me fine lady?'

'Here.' She pulled off her betrothal ring and

earrings and fumbled at her throat for the pearls Hunt had given her. She dropped them all in the reticule, held it out. 'That's all I've got. There's money there, too.'

'Get both them brats out, bitch.'

Hoofbeats sounded, faint at first, but coming fast.

'What? No!' Fear, sharp and metallic, soured her mouth. 'This is what you—'

'Get 'em out, and hurry it up or you'll have a dead coachman!'

'Bugger that!' Masters snapped. 'There's someone coming. Tell 'em to stay—'

'Mama.' Harry's voice shook. 'We're here.'

She whirled to see Harry helping Georgie down, keeping her behind him.

'Damn it, boy!' Masters roared. 'Get your sister back inside!'

'Shut it, old man! Less you want her dead!'

Georgie screamed. *'Mama!'* The hoofbeats were closer, but Emma knew they weren't close enough...

'You. Boy. Bring me that fancy bag.'

Horror shot through Emma. 'No!' She stepped in front of Harry. 'I'll bring it to you.'

There was a click and she froze. He'd cocked the pistol, was pointing it directly at Masters.

'Stay where you are, bitch. The boy brings it or I use this.' His voice mocked. 'Reckon I'll take a look at yer whelp.'

'Mama, I can do it.'

Before she could stop him, Harry had taken the

reticule from her shaking hand and had stepped away from the carriage, away from the shelter of her body, and was walking towards the highwayman.

The man gave a low laugh. 'That's it, boy. Closer now. Don't be shy.'

She didn't know what warned her. The satisfied croon in the man's voice, or the steely glint as his pistol shifted...she sprang, flattening Harry in the mud as the pistol roared amid the thunder of the approaching hooves.

At the second shot Hunt forgot about steadying Petrarch for the last bend. He drove his heels into the gelding's flanks and urged him on, Barclay close behind. He heard Masters's furious roar, the crack of a whip and the terrified scream of a horse. They thundered around the bend into the flickering yellow light of the lamps and his heart stopped, the whole world ended.

Emma lay still on the ground, covering Harry with her body.

Too late. Too bloody late.

Time slowed and his veins iced with pure cold rage as he spurred straight at the highwayman. For an instant he met the man's eyes, saw shock there, before Petrarch's shoulder struck the plunging cob. The impact jarred every bone in Hunt's body and, with another scream, the horse and man crashed to the ground. Petrarch stumbled slightly but Hunt kept his seat, held the horse together with hands and legs, barely bringing him to a halt before he was out of the saddle and running to where Emma struggled to rise.

He dropped to his knees in the mud, lifted her into his arms. 'Stay still!' He ran shaking hands over her, his heart stuttering back to life when he realised that her gown was wet with mud, not blood.

'Hunt?' She sounded dazed.

'Yes.' His voice shook. Would he ever be able to hold her long enough to believe she was safe? 'Are you hurt?'

'N-no. Harry?'

Harry was sitting up, his face pale. He stared at Hunt. 'I'm all right. But I... I don't understand... Why did he—? I was *taking* him the stupid reticule!'

'*Mama!*'

Georgie flung herself on Emma, sobbing. Emma's arms closed around the child.

'I thought he killed you!' Georgie wept into Emma's shoulder. 'And Harry.'

Harry patted her awkwardly on the back. 'I'm all right, Georgie. We're both all right. Uncle Hunt came.'

Emma looked up from the children and met his gaze. Her mouth trembled. 'Yes. We're all safe now.' She stretched out a hand, touched his cheek as if to reassure herself that he was there.

At the touch of those shaking fingers, words jammed, useless, in his throat. Instead he leaned forward, brushed his lips over hers, got his arms around all three of them and held on tightly, his cheek resting on Emma's dishevelled curls, just breathing her in, the sweet Emma scent of her. He heard William take command and left him to it. In a moment he might believe that he hadn't been too late, that she was alive. Right now he kept seeing her body in the mud as he charged, thinking she was dead. It was no thanks to him that she wasn't. He'd failed her. Failed to protect her, failed to protect the children.

'Come, sweetheart.' He rose, taking Georgie on one hip and helping Emma with his free hand. He noted with shamed pride that Harry scrambled up at once, helping his mother. 'Let's get you all back in the carriage so we can go home.'

Barclay came up and cleared his throat. 'We've got the bast— the fellow tied up, sir.'

Hunt lifted Georgie into the carriage. 'Put the rug around you.' He turned to Barclay. 'He's alive?'

Barclay nodded, his mouth grim. 'Yes. Still unconscious. And his horse is lame. Strained foreleg and Masters's whip cut her face. We've tied him on to my horse instead. Do you want him taken straight to Newgate?'

It was his first instinct. He thought it through. 'No. We'll take him with us.' The fellow could have an accomplice lurking somewhere. He couldn't risk Barclay alone with the prisoner and there was no other available horse for the groom to go. Even if there were, he wouldn't risk his men's lives over it. 'He can be secured in one of the cellars with an armed guard outside. I'll send for a magistrate in the morning.'

'Will he be hanged?'

Hunt glanced at Harry. If he could ask the question… 'Very likely. In with you.'

Harry bit his lip. 'Mama?' He held out his hand to Emma.

Hunt heard her shuddering breath as she set her hand in the child's and permitted him to help her in.

He gripped the boy's shoulder. 'Good lad. *Now* in with you.'

Harry scrambled in, sitting as close to Emma as he could. Georgie was already in her lap, the rug bundled around them both.

'You've got everything under control, William?'

Barclay nodded. 'Oh, yes. He won't get away.' Vicious satisfaction edged his voice.

'Good.' Hunt leaped in, adjusted the rug around Harry and gathered them all close.

They covered remaining distance to Austerleigh swiftly. After seeing Emma and the children into the care of his shocked staff, Hunt went down to ensure the prisoner was secured. The man had regained consciousness, but appeared dazed. He had walked into the house under heavy guard, his hands tied behind him, and been escorted to the cellar.

Hunt found Barclay coming out of the butler's pantry. He raised his brows. 'You put him in *there*?

What about the silver?' He could see Bentham having apoplexy at the thought of locking a felon up with the family silver.

Barclay snorted. 'Well, I know, sir. But it's the only room, even down here, with absolutely no way in or out save the door. There's no window *because* of the silver. And we all helped Bentham move that for the night, as well as anything else that might be used as a weapon. We didn't light the fire either.'

Hunt gripped his shoulder. 'Good thinking. We'll alert the magistrate first thing.'

Barclay looked slightly shamefaced. 'Already done, sir. Masters insisted on riding over himself with the message.'

Despite everything, Hunt laughed. 'I should have known. William—' He gripped the younger man's hand. 'Thank you. If you hadn't nudged me into following them…' He couldn't say it.

Barclay flushed. 'Rot. You were going to make that choice anyway. I could see it a mile away. Anyone can see what Lady Huntercombe means to you.'

Hunt swallowed. They could? Although he himself had been wilfully blind? Without returning an answer, he opened the pantry door and glanced in. The highwayman, bruised and dishevelled, glared at him. He was bound hand and foot and further tied securely in a very heavy chair. Satisfied, Hunt closed the door and locked it. 'Who's on guard first?'

Barclay's jaw hardened. 'I am. With a couple of

grooms, just to be sure. There'll be at least three of us here armed all night. Jem and Griffin are loading pistols and they'll be along.' He jerked his head at the door. 'That goose is well and truly cooked!'

Hunt found Emma coming out of the night nursery.

'Hunt!' She hurried to him and he opened his arms, gathered her close.

'Are they all right?'

He felt her nod against his chest. 'Yes. But Harry wants to see you. Do you mind?'

'Mind?' He pushed down the hurt that she could think he'd mind. 'No. Of course not. I was coming to see that they were settled anyway and reassure them the fellow is safely locked up.'

Emma flushed. 'I'm sorry. I didn't mean that the way it sounded. It's not about the highwayman being locked up. Harry seems to think you'll be angry with him, but he won't say why. Just that he needs to say sorry.'

Hunt shut his eyes. *He* was the one who ought to be apologising. He should never have let them go. He took a deep breath. 'Very well. Let's see what it is.'

Harry and Georgie were in the same room, each sitting up in bed. When Georgie saw Hunt she flung back her covers and scrambled out, running to him. 'Uncle Hunt! Is he in the dungeon?'

He swung her up and balanced her on his hip where she clung like a limpet. 'Close enough. He's under guard. Mr Barclay and two of the grooms are on guard.'

'With pistols? Will they shoot him dead?' Georgie demanded.

How the devil should he answer that? 'Very unlikely. But they'll do whatever needs to be done.' He looked at Harry. The boy's face was nearly as white as his own sheets and his eyes were red-rimmed. 'Georgie, why don't you take your mama to sit by the fire in the other room for a few minutes?'

'No,' Harry said at once. 'They…they should stay.'

Hunt nodded slowly. 'Very well.' He sat on the edge of Harry's bed, settling Georgie in his lap. 'What's bothering you, Harry?'

The boy flushed, shot Emma an anguished look as she sat on the other side of the small bed. 'I… I didn't do as you asked. I didn't look after them!'

'Harry—' Emma began.

'Yes, you did.' Georgie looked up at Hunt seriously. 'He held my hand getting out of the carriage and made me stay behind him.'

Hunt pressed a kiss to the child's forehead. 'Thank you, Georgie. What do you mean, Harry?'

'When the man said for me to bring him Mama's reticule—'

'*What?*'

'I was taking it to him.' Harry whispered. 'I thought I was doing the right thing,'

Hunt focused on the boy, who was blinking back tears, and gripped Harry's hand on the coverlet. 'He told *you* to bring it to him?'

'Yes.'

Everything in Hunt stilled. 'Then you did exactly the right thing, Harry.'

'But he shot at us anyway.' The boy's hand turned under his and clutched. 'I... I must have done something wrong and that's why he pointed the pistol at me.'

'He pointed the gun at *you*? While you were taking him the reticule?'

Harry bit his lip, looked at Emma.

She reached out, touched his cheek. 'Just tell Uncle Hunt exactly what happened.'

Harry nodded, looked back at Hunt. 'I...he told me to bring him the reticule. Mama said no, she would take it, but you had said to look after Mama and Georgie, so I... I took it and started towards him. Masters was awfully cross, and he— the highwayman—laughed, sort of.'

'He did,' Georgie said, wriggling closer. 'He had a horrid laugh.' Hunt held her tighter, feeling the small body trembling.

Harry went on. 'He'd been pointing the gun right at Masters, sir.' His eyes pleaded for understanding. 'That's what he said to make me do it— that he'd kill Masters. And he'd threatened Mama to make Masters shut up when he told us to get back in the carriage. We could hear you and Mr Barclay coming then, only we didn't know it was you. He might have had a friend.'

'Go on.' Hunt's brain worked furiously. Any sane thief would have covered Masters, not a boy who was no possible danger.

'I don't really know what happened next,' Harry admitted. 'The gun went off and I was on the ground. I thought he'd shot me, but—'

'I thought he'd shot Mama.' Georgie's voice was muffled in Hunt's waistcoat and he held her close. 'She sort of fell on Harry and they were on the ground. And then you and Mr Barclay were there and your horse simply *crashed* into the other one.'

'I didn't do as you told me.' Harry's voice was low, his gaze averted. 'You said to look after Mama and Georgie. I... I didn't look after Mama.'

It was a punch in the gut to hear a ten-year-old boy blaming himself for something he could not possibly have prevented. Hunt took a careful breath. 'Harry, you could not have stopped the carriage from being held up.'

'No, but I didn't protect her.' Harry's cheeks were wet. 'I'm nearly eleven and you trusted me.'

He bit back a curse at himself. He'd wanted the boy to feel important, on his way to manhood. What he'd done was lay a man's responsibility on a child's shoulders.

'Harry, when I said that, I meant for you to do things like help your mother in and out of the carriage. I didn't expect the damn carriage to be held up!' He'd never considered the consequences if the boy was actually called on to live up to impossible expectations.

Georgie sat up. 'You said *damn*. That's a bad word. Mama doesn't let us say it.'

Oh, hell! 'And nor should I,' he said. 'Not in front of ladies. I apologise, Georgie.' He looked at his stepson. 'Harry, a hold-up is a matter for grown-ups. You were not in any way responsible.'

'Then I shouldn't have tried to take the reticule to him?'

Children were a quagmire. He wanted to tell Harry that he should have stayed in the coach with Georgie, no matter what the threat. But it sounded as though the fellow might well have shot Masters, or even Emma, to enforce obedience. Then Harry would be blaming himself for that. Sometimes there was no right answer. Only the right thing. And despite his responsibility to Peter Lacy, he thought the boy's father would be proud of his son.

'No. You did the right thing, the honourable thing, Harry. You acted exactly as your father would have done. The problem is—' How on earth did you explain this to a child? He tried. 'Doing the right and honourable thing doesn't always have a happy ending.'

Harry blinked. 'It doesn't?'

'No. But that doesn't let us off doing it. I might wish you'd stayed in the carriage and your mother certainly would have preferred that, but we understand why you didn't.'

'But—'

'No buts, Harry. And the highwayman is securely tied up under armed guard and he'll be taken away in the morning.' After he'd answered a few very pointed questions.

'And…and you think Papa would have been proud of me?'

Hunt's answer came straight from the heart.

'No. I think he *is* proud. Just as I am. Even if we both wish it hadn't been necessary.'

Georgie wriggled. 'He must be a very stupid highwayman. I mean, once he'd shot Harry he wouldn't have got anything, would he?'

'No. He wouldn't,' Hunt agreed. He rose, lifting Georgie. 'Time for both of you to be tucked up.'

'It's funny, though,' Harry said.

Hunt glanced at him as he lowered Georgie into her bed. 'Funny?'

'Odd, funny. Not funny, funny,' Harry said. 'He must have known all about us.'

Hunt frowned. 'Known what about you?'

'That Mama had two children. He told her to get us out. *Both* of us.' He scowled. 'I mean, how did he know *I* was there? He'd know about Georgie—' He looked apologetic. 'Sorry, sis, but you *were* making an awful noise.'

'I was *scared*!' Georgie's voice, muffled in her pillow, remained defiant.

'Me, too,' Harry admitted. 'Anyway, it's funny.'

Hunt met Emma's shocked gaze, saw horrified speculation. He shook his head very slightly. Better not to discuss the implications here. He straightened, went to her and brushed a kiss across her mouth, knew the fierce urge to deepen the kiss, sweep her from the room and assure himself in the most primitive way that she was safe. His. He stepped back. That was not possible. Tonight, of all nights, Harry and Georgie needed her. 'We'll talk in the morning.'

Chapter Nineteen

Hunt left Emma tucking the children in and went to his own rooms. He didn't bother ringing for a servant, but shrugged out of his damp coat and let it fall, followed by his waistcoat. Someone had come up and lit the fire and left a brandy decanter on the wine table by the fire. He'd need help with his boots eventually, but that could wait.

He sat down by the fire and poured a generous measure of brandy. If what he suspected was true, then Harry had had a very narrow escape. Twice. Because the more he thought about it, the less the house fire seemed like an accident. If Emma and the children had been there… He shuddered, took a swallow of brandy. Somehow he had to protect Harry. Because if he was right, the danger was not over. He was not even perfectly sure where the danger lay precisely…and it was possible this had not started with Harry. There was also poor Thirlbeck's death…

* * *

He was still sitting there half an hour later when the clock chimed midnight. He should go to bed, but he was far from sleep. More brandy would do the trick, but that wasn't what he wanted. What he wanted, being a thoroughly selfish and inconsiderate type, was his wife. In his bed and...

'Hunt?'

His heart quaked. Emma stood in the open doorway that led to her own rooms, her face pale against the darkness of the room behind her, her slender form swathed in a dark blue silk robe.

'I thought you might be asleep. May I come in for a moment?'

Only for a moment? When she was in this room? Where she belonged. Where he wanted and needed her. He found his tongue and some of his wits. 'You're not with the children?'

Obviously not, as she was crossing to the fireplace.

She smiled as she sat down in the other chair. 'No. They both said I should go to bed. That they were quite safe with you here.'

He let out a bitter laugh. 'Safe because I'm here? Emma, my stupidity—'

'Your *what*?'

'My stupidity,' he repeated. 'I should never have let you leave so late. Or if I did I should have sent outriders, or gone myself!'

She nodded. 'I've been kicking myself for leaving so late, too. It wasn't just your decision. And

I suppose we could dismiss Masters for being wrong. Is there another glass?'

'What?' He was still getting past the idea of sacking Masters. 'Oh. I've had enough. Take this one.' He poured brandy into his glass and handed it to her.

She accepted the glass, sipped. 'If you're blaming yourself, Hunt, then you've had more than enough. You came.'

'Nearly too late.'

'You came,' she repeated. 'And we're safe.' She let out a breath. 'Hunt, the fire? Could that—?'

'It's possible,' he said. 'I think very likely. He knew you were there that night.'

Emma let out a breath. 'Martin. Who else could want Harry—?' She shut her eyes. 'I don't think I mentioned it to you—there was no reason—but he knew we were coming here, too. He was there this afternoon.'

Hunt felt a small click as the piece dropped into place. 'Was he now?'

Emma looked sickened. 'Yes. Escorting his mother and Miss Carshalton.' She clenched her fists. 'Hunt, they are *betrothed*. You know her, don't you?'

Hunt let out a breath. He'd suspected as much at the Westerfolds' ball the other night. Why else would the Duchess of Keswick sponsor the chit? 'I knew her as a child. She is the great-niece of a man I admire and respect very much, and the only child of a very wealthy ship owner, the perfect bride for a penniless younger son who wanted more and didn't see why a nephew should stand in his way.' His mouth hardened. 'Or a brother. Thirlbeck was killed in a hold up. At the time it caused a deal of talk—outbreak of lawlessness and fears about revolution, because it seemed he had been deliberately targeted according to witnesses.' He let out a breath. 'Perhaps there was a simpler motive. And now we have a second hold up. A pattern.'

'But can we prove any of this?' Emma whispered. 'If we can't, Harry may never be safe.' The glass rattled as she set it down.

'There may be a way.'

'What way?'

'If the magistrate agrees to offer clemency to our prisoner in return for information.'

'Clemency?'

'Transportation.' He didn't much like it. He wasn't usually bloodthirsty, but in this instance, he'd like to pull the lever himself. 'He's committed a capital offence and there are enough witnesses to ensure that he'll hang. But if he turns King's Evidence, then his testimony would at the very least cast a heavy shadow on whoever was behind him.'

Emma nodded slowly. 'You don't think it might be Keswick? All that fuss about custody might have been to make it easier to get rid of Harry.'

He'd considered that. Looked at it from every angle. 'It's possible. I wouldn't rule it out just yet, but it's unlikely. He might have *preferred* Martin to inherit, but I doubt he'd want to kill an heir.'

'An heir,' Emma whispered. 'Not a grandson.'

She glanced at the clock and rose. 'I'm sorry. It's late. We can deal with this in the morning.'

'Yes.' He stood up and held out his hand. 'Come to bed?'

She stared at him, clearly surprised, and he could have groaned out loud and kicked himself. Of all the clumsy, inarticulate *oafs*. 'I meant, you must be exhausted. Stay with me tonight. To sleep.' It shook him to his very foundations, but he wanted *that*, that simple intimacy, more than he wanted *her*. And he wanted her more than his next breath. However, on this occasion he was going to be a gentleman, and—

'Are you inviting me to your bed?'

He took a careful breath. 'Do you need an invitation?'

'Don't I?'

She did while he didn't. That was the way aristocratic marriages worked. A gentleman visited his wife's bed when it pleased him, and left when it pleased him. He had been very careful to establish that pattern. Always going to her bed. And the other night, after he'd woken from the nightmare, he'd pushed her away, left her bed. 'Emma, when we discussed marriage initially, what we both wanted—'

'I don't want that anymore.'

Emma gathered every scrap of her failing courage and took a deep breath. 'Hunt, I can't hold to the terms of our marriage.' She met his shocked gaze. 'I've fallen in love with you.'

'*Love*, Emma?'

Oh, God! What had possessed her to tell him? *Love*. The one thing neither of them had wanted either to give or to receive. Why had she never understood that love could perhaps be ignored, but never commanded or forbidden?

His eyes were unreadable. Did he view it as a burden? Something to feel guilty about if he could never return it? Would he opt for a kindly lie?

She groped for words, for a coherent thought, to fling into the bubble of silence that engulfed them. Somewhere beyond the silence the fire danced and crackled. 'It is a gift, Hunt.' She went to him, laid her fingers in his outstretched hand, raised her other hand to his face and cradled the shadowed jaw. Her palm tingled at the rasp of his stubble. 'A gift, free and clear. It requires no recompense, no guilt. It just *is*. And it isn't inconvenient.'

He said nothing at first, but his gaze pinned her, searching.

'You believe that?' he asked at last. 'Even though we agreed love was against the rules?'

'Yes,' she said. 'I can't help how I feel and it's your fault anyway.'

His brows shot up. '*My* fault?'

'How was I supposed to resist you?' she demanded. 'You're kind, honourable, you make me laugh and you're excellent in bed.' He actually blushed and she charged on, desperate to lighten the moment. 'Besides, don't you know that telling a woman something is forbidden is guaranteed to make her *do* it?'

His slow smile, the one that left her breathless and turned her insides to jelly, curved his mouth. 'Of course. Bluebeard. That's me. So—' Heat crept into his eyes. 'If I absolutely forbade you to strip off your robe and—' Her robe hit the floor between one breath and the next.

His eyes darkened, narrowed. 'I see. And your nightgown—if I forbade you to unbutton it, *very* slowly—'

She released him, stepped back and her fingers shook at the heat in his gaze, her nipples peaking in an aching rush as she reached for the first dainty pearl button. Carefully she slipped it free, heard something very like a strangled groan. Heat pooled liquid in her belly and lower, between her thighs, at the knowledge that he wanted her. She kept her eyes on his. They burned in the glimmering firelight, dark and hungry. This, then, was power, feminine and glorious. Another button and he clenched his fists. As if it were all he could do not to reach out and rip the gown away. Wicked delight spread through her at the thought and she licked her lips as she freed the third button, heard his soft curse.

Hunt's mouth dried. Three buttons and he was harder than granite. 'You're playing with fire, wife,' he whispered. It wasn't just the buttons. It was that half-smile that told him she knew just how hot the fires were burning. That she intended to stoke the blaze.

More buttons slipped free until the demure linen hung open to her waist and firelight danced with gilded shadows in the sweet valley between her half-revealed breasts. Heat rose, her fragrance wove through him, temptation incarnate. Desire scorched in every vein, his cock ached, his whole body burning with the need to tumble her to the bed, hike up her nightgown and ravish her. He held back. How bold would she be? And would he survive it?

He took a careful breath and a step back. 'Shrug it—' God! His voice was little more than a growl! 'I mean, you are absolutely forbidden to shrug it off one shoulder.'

Laughter, old as Eve, glimmered in her eyes as she twitched one shoulder and the nightgown slid away. At the same time she reached up, tugging the ribbon from her braid, sliding her fingers through it so the silk of her hair cascaded in a dark river over her naked, rose-crested breast.

He clenched his fists. 'That's enough.' He barely knew his own voice, harsh, strangled. Any more and he was likely to lose all control.

Her smile, utterly female, all challenge and invitation, said she knew it as well as he and with a twitch of her other shoulder the nightgown fell away. She stood naked, the once-demure creamy linen in a froth about her feet. Not Venus arising from the sea-foam, this sultry seductress, but Diana the huntress, in a pool of moonlight. And he was her prey.

His breath came in hard. 'The bed. Now.'

She didn't move. But the deepening curve of her smile would have lured an angel to damnation.

On a sound that was half-curse, half-laughter,

he took one swift stride and swept her up into his arms. An instant later he tumbled her on to the bed, following her down and rolling until they ended in the middle of the vast expanse of blue counterpane.

Emma found herself gazing up into Hunt's storm-dark eyes. Somehow her wrists were caught above her head. 'Weren't you going to forbid me your bed?' she murmured.

His mouth crushed hers briefly. 'Are you trying to drive me insane, woman?'

She wriggled, savoured the hard, delicious weight of him pinning her to the bed, his hips cradled between her thighs. Somehow the fact that he was still in his shirt, breeches and boots was even more erotic. 'Is it working?'

She cried out as his hand slipped between them, found the aching wetness where she wanted him.

'God, yes.' His voice was ragged and his fingers were gone and she could feel his fierce haste, unbuttoning his breeches, shoving them down. And then he was there, pushing inside, stretching her. She gasped at his invasion and he stilled. 'Emma?'

'Yes.' She tilted her hips, accepting, demanding.

She saw his eyes darken as the last of his control snapped and he surged in. Deep, so deep that she cried out in an agony of pleasure. Her body leapt to flame and she wrapped her legs around him, matching him stroke for stroke, taking him as he took her.

His hand slid beneath her, tilting her into his thrusts, and she came on a scream of unrestrained pleasure. He rode her hard and deep, so that she came again, and he surged, pumping hard and fast, until he broke on a groan and collapsed over her, heavy and sated, his heart pounding in time with hers.

Eventually Hunt came back to himself. Beneath him, Emma was warm, soft. Her fingers idly caressed his nape and to his disbelief he felt a renewed stirring of interest. A little more of his brain re-engaged. He'd taken her in his breeches and boots, for God's sake!

'Emma—'

'How closely are you related to the Churchills, Hunt?'

He found the strength to lift his head and look down at her. Her eyes were still closed a contented smile curving her lips. 'Ah, third cousin, once removed, to Marlborough on my mother's side. Why?' Hell's teeth, but he had to lose the boots—

The smile tilted up at one corner. 'Explains the boots.'

Laughter shook him. The first Duke of Marlborough had famously returned from a military campaign and pleasured his Duchess without removing his boots. 'I was going to apologise for that.'

One eye opened. 'Not necessary.'

'No?'

'No.'

Reassuring, but even so, he was getting his boots off before he had her again. Preferably his breeches, too. He rolled to the side, taking her with him so she nestled snugly in his arms, exactly where he wanted her. Not just in his arms, but in his bed, his heart. Where, apparently, she wanted to be. 'Nevertheless, will you excuse me for a moment while I get rid of them?'

'Mmm. If I must.'

Emma sank to her knees in mud and rain-washed darkness, lifted the small, limp body. Rain mingled with the salt of tears.

'Give him back! Kill me! Kill me instead!'

Her screams were silent agony.

In the yellow flicker of the lanterns she looked up from Harry's body, saw the gleam of the pistol barrel levelled at her. She didn't care if she died. Her life for Harry's...

But the barrel swung away...to Georgie...

'No! Not Georgie! Not Georgie!'

And again her voice echoed in the silence of her mind and the pistol glinted...

'Emma! Emma! You're dreaming. Emma, come back. Come back to me!'

She fought, struggled to win free of the arms that held her. Georgie! It was too late for Harry and the pain sliced to her soul.

But gradually the deep, tender voice penetrated. 'No, sweetheart. You saved Harry. They're safe. Come back.'

She came back to herself fully, half in Hunt's lap as he rocked her in those powerful arms, but the shreds of nightmare still clung, scored her.

'Hunt?' Her own voice, raw and shaking, full of tears. She would have crawled inside him if it were possible.

'Yes.' His arms tightened, his lips against her temple. 'They're safe. I swear it. Come. I'll take you to them.'

Five minutes later she stood, Hunt's arm close around her, in the doorway of the night nursery. Harry and Georgie—both in Harry's bed—lay sound asleep in the flickering light from the candle Hunt held. Georgie clutched Anna Maria and Harry's fist held a toy soldier.

'There.' Hunt's lips pressed against her hair.

She nodded, dragged in a trembling breath. Tears still clogged her throat, but she held them back, leaned on Hunt, husband and lover, as she pulled the door gently closed again.

In the glow of the fire, Bessie smiled at her. 'Reckon they're still sleeping, me lady.'

Emma nodded. 'Yes. I… I just needed to see.'

Bessie got up, poked the fire and added some wood. 'Course yer did. I've been in a couple of times. Seems Miss Georgie got scared—you saw she's in with Master Harry. When I looked in she was sound asleep and Harry was nearly asleep, but he said she was fine there.'

Emma managed a wobbly smile. 'He's looking after her then.'

'Aye.' Bessie's eyes crinkled. 'An' you should let his lordship do the same with you. Go on. I'll send if needs be.'

Hunt's arm tightened. 'Would you rather stay, love? There's Georgie's bed and I can bring a chair in.'

She turned in his arms. 'A chair? For you?'

His tender, crooked smile turned her heart upside down and inside out. *Had he called her love?* 'Where else would I be?'

Nowhere, she realised. He'd be with her. With her children. *Their* children. They would always be Peter's, but now they were Hunt's, too, in every way that mattered.

She looked back at the door. 'I think they'd rather we didn't. They have each other and perhaps when he arrives today, Fergus's basket might go in there. Just for now? They would love that and Harry won't feel embarrassed.'

Hunt's whole body shook as he snorted out a laugh. 'Very well. But I give you fair warning— that basket is only for show!'

He took Emma along the dark, silent hallways, shatteringly aware of her slender body leaning against him. This was how it should be, this sweet acceptance and care of the one for the other. The simplicity of being able to give again. How on earth had he ever thought he could maintain any other sort of marriage?

They reached his room and he shrugged out of his robe. He turned to Emma, drawing her into his arms. In a moment her robe lay on the floor as well. He found her mouth, kissed her gently, deeply. It wasn't about sex. He tasted the salt of tears still on her cheek, felt the deep tremors in her body as he scooped her up into his arms.

'Hunt! You'll hurt yourself!'

He snorted. 'I'm not so bloody old I can't still carry my woman to my bed.' He suited the action to word and settled her exactly where she belonged—in his bed. He got in with her, drew the covers up around them and breathed a sigh of utter contentment when she snuggled into his arms and laid her head on his shoulder there in the quiet shadows of his bed. *Their* bed. He desperately wanted it to be that.

'You don't want me to go back to my own bed?'

He looked down at her in the dim glow of the fire. 'Ouch.'

'Ouch?'

'Yes. Ouch.' He pressed a kiss to her temple. 'I was an idiot the other night.' Like an all-conquering hero, he'd not wanted to show any weakness. He'd been afraid to accept her comfort; instead he'd made her feel unwanted. Because he'd wanted to do all the giving, all the bestowing and all the protecting. Not because she might think the less of him, but because he hadn't wanted to admit that he needed *her*, needed their marriage to be more than merely convenient.

'I want this to be *our* bed that we share,' he said. '*Not* because I want you convenient for sex, but because I want *you*. Just you. To sleep with me. To wake up with me.' He took a very deep breath. He'd come this far… 'The other night… It's always the same dream, Gerald is dead and he begs me for help. I try. I try to stop the grave closing, but I can't. And he can't hear me, because when I speak there's no sound.' Heat burned his eyes and he rested his cheek on Emma's hair. Her arms came around him in wordless understanding and entwined they slept safe and secure.

Chapter Twenty

Hunt, dressed and shaved, hurried downstairs, praying that Emma would remain asleep. He wanted the prisoner interviewed and gone and his family safe. He found Barclay and Masters on guard duty in the below-stairs corridor, sharing a pot of coffee. He shook his head as he approached. Masters. He might have known it. The man would have taken last night's attack as a personal insult.

Barclay greeted him with a tired smile. 'Good morning, my lord. Our man is secure.'

Hunt nodded. 'Good. Have you two been here all night?'

'And where else would I be?' Masters growled.

Barclay shrugged. 'We were spelled, but we were here for most of it. Chap's awake, but not very happy. Will you interview him now?'

'Yes.' He was going to have some answers. 'I'd like you there to note the entire interview, William. And you, Masters. In case he tries anything.'

Masters scowled. 'Reckon I hope the bastard *does* try something. Then I could put a ball in him like he deserves for trying to kill the boy.'

Hunt caught his breath. 'Harry told me what happened. Was he the target?'

Masters nodded grimly. 'That would be my take. He knew those children were in the coach, my lord. Both of them. Sure Miss Georgie was wailing, but he said, clear as day, for them *both* to get out. How'd he know? And why waste the time if all he wanted was her ladyship's purse? No, he wanted the boy.'

Barclay looked grim. 'We talked it over. Not hard to think of someone who might want Harry dead.'

'Then we need him to turn King's—'

'Hunt!'

He swung around to see Emma hurrying towards them.

'Sweetheart.' He caught her hands. 'You should not be here.'

Her hands tightened on his. 'Yes, I should. If he is the same man who followed me about those last few weeks I lived in Chelsea, then I can identify him. That's more evidence—'

'For God's sake, Emma!' Hunt exploded. 'You're not going anywhere near that bast—' He broke off, fought down the panic. 'Sweetheart, I want you safe.'

She put her hand on his arm. 'I know, but… please, Hunt. I need to do this. To help keep Harry safe.'

And there was the bottom line. For both of them. Harry. Her courage had saved the boy last night. She had every right to be here now.

'Very well.' He caught her face between his hands. 'But I don't like it.' He took his own pistol from the pocket of his coat, checked the load and cocked it. He looked at Emma. 'Behind me.' At her mutinous expression, he said simply, 'If I have to use this, you can't be in the line of fire.'

Her face cleared. 'All right.'

He nodded to Barclay and Masters. 'Ready.'

Exchanging glances, Barclay and Masters checked and cocked their pistols. Hunt unlocked the door, opened it and looked in. 'Right. He's not going anywhere.' He stepped into the room.

Emma dragged in a breath, and fought down the fear, the nausea, as she walked into the room.

The highwayman, bound hand and foot, was tightly secured to a heavy-framed chair. Bruised and dishevelled, he glared at Hunt, then his gaze swung to herself. She saw the jolt of shock, heard the sharp intake of breath.

Rage flooded her, engulfing fear, as she recognised him. 'You didn't expect me,' she said. 'You were masked last night, but I've seen you before. You're the man who used to follow us.'

He snarled as she turned to Hunt. 'If you ask around Chelsea you will likely find others who saw him. Perhaps even on the night we left. Maybe he knows something about the house.'

The man's jaw clenched. 'That fire wasn't—' He broke off.

Emma smiled coldly. 'Fire? Did I mention a fire?'

The man glared at her in sullen silence.

Hunt laid his hand lightly on Emma's shoulder. 'Well done.' He spoke directly to the man. 'Your name?'

'Go to hell!'

Hunt shrugged. 'It's you that's slated for hell, via the gallows. Who sent you?'

The man sneered. 'Help you? Why?'

'To save your neck.' Hunt's voice held a winter chill. 'Holding up a carriage carries the death penalty. And you deliberately fired on a child? They'll line up ten deep to watch you swing.'

There was a moment's silence while that sank in.

'Or,' Hunt said quietly, 'I could see that you are transported. If you tell me who gave you your orders. Come! Why swing for someone who was too cowardly to do his own dirty work?'

The man snarled. 'Reckon I don't know that's a trap?'

'It might be,' Hunt acknowledged. 'But what do you have to lose? You're dead already. Without your information I'll push for execution. Speak, or swing.'

The prisoner swallowed. 'You want a name?'

Hunt inclined his head. 'I want two names. Yours and your master's.'

'Riley. My name's Riley.'

* * *

Ten minutes later, having extracted as much information as possible, Hunt left the room with Emma. Hunt turned to Barclay. 'William, I'll leave you and Masters in charge here. Make sure there are sufficient armed men on hand when the wagon arrives.'

William's nodded grimly. 'Believe me, my lord, he won't escape.'

They continued up to the ground floor.

'Hunt?' Emma sounded as sickened as he felt. 'Do you think it can be proved?'

'The connection? Yes. Enough to protect Harry.' They were crossing the front entry hall, on the way to the library. 'Whether or not the information was passed deliberately—who the devil is that?'

The footman on duty in the hall hurried to open the door as the knocker fell silent.

Hunt glanced at Emma. 'We'd better see who it is and make sure they leave without any hint of—*bloody hell*.' His eyes widened at the unexpected visitors.

Emma pulled herself together and went forward. 'Lord Martin. Miss Carshalton. How surprising.'

Lord Martin looked faintly embarrassed. 'Lady Huntercombe. I didn't expect to see you. I merely wanted…that is, I was driving out with Miss Carshalton and, ah, thought to leave this.' He held out a small package. 'For the children. Something Harry said yesterday led me to think they might—' He broke off, cleared his throat. 'Look, we didn't mean to intrude.'

'You aren't intruding, Lacy.' Hunt didn't bother to hide the steel in his voice. 'Your arrival is opportune actually.' He shot a look at the footman. 'Have our other *guest* escorted to the library before he leaves, if you please.'

'My lord.' The footman scurried off.

Lord Martin frowned. 'Huntercombe, if you have a visitor—'

Hunt gestured towards the library. 'I insist, Lacy. I think you'll both find this very interesting.'

Lord Martin looked annoyed. 'Now see here, you may have a quarrel with me—I'm fully aware that I behaved badly to Lady Huntercombe. But there's no need to subject Kit—that is, Miss Carshalton to any unpleasantness.'

Emma watched, curiously detached, as he turned to the girl at his side. 'Kit, wait by the fire here in the hall. Huntercombe can say his piece and—'

'I think, Lord Martin,' Emma said quietly, 'that Miss Carshalton should hear what Huntercombe and I have to say.'

The younger woman's chin went up. 'It's all right, Martin. I'm sure whatever it is can be sorted out amicably.'

'Amicable,' Hunt said coldly, 'is not what I had in mind.'

The library fires did nothing to dispel the chilly atmosphere. Hunt set a chair for Miss Carshalton and she sat, eyeing him warily.

'What is this about, Huntercombe?' Lord Martin demanded.

Hunt shot Emma a glance. 'Let me begin.' He'd used the short walk to the library to refine some sort of strategy. He wanted the truth here.

'Lacy, the night after you and your father called on Lady Huntercombe, or Lady Emma Lacy as she then was, in Chelsea, I responded to those threats—'

'I didn't threaten her, Huntercombe!' Lord Martin sounded as though his back teeth were jammed together. 'Whatever my father may have said, I was merely concerned for the children's distress if they were forcibly removed by the magistrate.'

Hunt inclined his head. 'That is one interpretation. However, I responded by removing Lady Emma and her family to my own house. We found out later that *her* house burned to the ground that same night.'

'What?' Lord Martin's voice was hoarse. 'Are you suggesting *I* had something to do with it? Why the *hell* would I—?'

'Bear with me,' Hunt snapped. 'Last night the coach bearing Lady Huntercombe and the children was held up.'

Lord Martin paled. 'You can't be—' He dragged in a breath. 'But surely…no one was hurt? The children…that is…' He clenched his fists. 'Go on, Huntercombe.'

Hunt waited a moment. Then, 'Yes. The children. An interesting point, Lacy. But before we get to that, remind me—how did your eldest brother, Thirlbeck, die?'

Lord Martin looked as though he might be ill. 'A hold up. Beck was ordered out of the coach by the highwayman and he…he was shot.'

Hunt nodded. 'Precisely. Before he'd handed over any valuables, he was shot and the murderer fled. And somehow last night the highwayman was fully aware that there were two children in the coach. Despite Emma's willingness to hand over all valuables, he demanded that the children, both of them, get out.'

If Lord Martin had been pale before, he was grey now. 'Huntercombe—'

Hunt flung up his hand. 'Tell me, Lacy, apart from yourself, who gains from Harry's death? From Thirlbeck's?'

Lord Martin swallowed. 'Huntercombe, please—is Harry…?' He shut his eyes, then seemed to force himself to open them. 'Tell me—'

'The shot missed, Lacy. And the man was captured.' Lord Martin seemed to sag and Hunt continued. 'That being the case, I offered him a chance for transportation if he gave me the name of the man who wanted something so badly he'd arrange the murder of a child to get it.'

'No!' Horrified denial burst from Miss Carshalton. She rose and stepped to Lord Martin's side, grey eyes blazing, a flush scoring her cheeks. 'You *can't* think Martin would—'

'Kit, wait—'

She shook off Lord Martin's restraining hand.

'No! Don't be an idiot, Martin! The man would say anything to save his neck!'

Hunt inclined his head. 'I agree, Miss Carshalton. And I was very careful *not* to give any hint of the name I expected.' He glanced at Lord Martin. 'And, yes, I fully expected Lacy to be the culprit.'

The door opened and a footman came in. 'We've got the prisoner here, my lord. Wagon is out the front, but they said you wanted him brought here in first.'

Hunt steeled himself. 'Thank you. Bring him in.'

'For God's sake, Huntercombe!' Lacy moved abruptly to stand in front of Miss Carshalton as Riley was shoved into the room, hands bound behind him. 'If you must—'

Miss Carshalton gasped. 'But that's...' Her voice shook and she seemed to struggle for words, even breath as she went bone white.

'Kit!' Lacy slipped an arm around her, but she gathered herself and fended him off, turning to face Hunt, her head high.

'You recognise him then, Miss Carshalton?' He couldn't afford to feel pity. Not with Harry's life at stake.

She didn't bother looking at Riley again. 'You must know I do. His name is Jonas Riley. He works for my father.'

'Kit—'

She stepped away from Lord Martin, her face blank.

Hunt glanced at the sullen prisoner, then at the

men guarding him. 'Take him away. Inform Sir John that I will ride over later to discuss the case.' He waited until the door closed and said quietly, 'Apparently, Miss Carshalton, your father's political ambitions run deeper than marrying you to a mere younger son.'

'God damn you, Huntercombe!'

Miss Carshalton ignored Lord Martin. 'Apparently so.'

Hunt had to admire her calm, but he pressed on. 'One question remains: how did your father know that Lady Huntercombe and the children would be travelling out here yesterday, let alone that they would be late on the road? You knew, did you not?'

Miss Carshalton's breath came in audibly and she looked briefly at Lord Martin before facing Hunt again. 'Yes. I knew.' Even as she spoke, she tugged a ring from her finger. She set it down on the desk and turned to Lord Martin. 'I'll save you the embarrassment of requesting that back, my lord.'

Lord Martin's face was cold. 'You are saying that he did know? That *you* told him, Kit? Deliberately?'

Her breath jerked in. 'How else could he have known?'

Hunt nearly missed it, but he saw the girl's eyes flicker and realised she had avoided a direct answer. 'Miss Carshalton—'

'I'll bid you all a good day.' Miss Carshalton's voice was as brittle as her expression and she moved awkwardly, as if unsure of her footing.

'Damn it to hell, Kit!' Lacy exploded. 'Where the devil are you going?' He caught her arm and she flinched.

'Please, let me go, Mart—my lord. I'm going ho—back to London.'

'I drove you out here in my gig!'

Lord Martin's knuckles whitened as his grip on the girl's arm tightened.

She jerked free. 'I'm not such a fine lady that I can't walk!'

'Walk?' Lord Martin stared. 'To *London*?'

She went straight past him, her eyes wide and blank, opened the door and was gone. Lord Martin started after her, cursing, but Hunt stepped into his path.

'No, Lacy. Let her go.'

Lord Martin clenched his fists. 'She's not going to—'

'No, she isn't,' Hunt said. 'I'll see to it.'

Lord Martin turned away on a blistering curse. 'Go, then.'

Hunt hurried out, remembering what he'd told Harry: *Doing the right and honourable thing doesn't always have a happy ending.* It didn't make him feel any better.

Emma watched as Lord Martin walked across to the desk, still carrying the brown paper parcel. He set it very carefully on the desk and picked up the ring Miss Carshalton had removed. He stared at it blindly for a moment, before slipping it into his pocket.

'I beg your pardon, Lady Huntercombe.' He spoke stiffly. 'I'll relieve you of my presence.'

'Lord Martin—' Emma did not know quite how to broach the subject, but she had to try. 'Have you…have you considered that Miss Carshalton might simply have mentioned it to her father in all innocence?'

His face hardened. 'Irrelevant, Lady Huntercombe.' Each word was like flint. 'She could be as innocent as a babe in arms and it would make no difference.'

'She defended you!' Emma felt sick, seeing again the blind look on the girl's face as she left. 'And you won't stand by her?'

Martin's knuckles whitened. 'Carshalton has powerful friends who won't like being embarrassed,' he said quietly. 'The word of a felon is unlikely to convict him. How safe do you think Harry would be if I married his daughter?'

That silenced her.

His mouth twisted. 'Exactly. It's all I can do to protect Peter's son.' He gestured to the parcel. 'That's for the children. Something Harry said yesterday… Good day to you.'

'Martin?'

He stopped. 'Yes?'

'Will you call again? So they can thank you?'

His lips curved in a travesty of a smile. 'I would like that, but it will be better for everyone if I don't.' He hesitated, then said, 'Peter was a very lucky man. Goodbye, Emma.'

The door closed behind him with a click and

Emma sank into a chair, shaken. They had the truth and Harry was safe. But if Miss Carshalton was innocent… Did Martin believe that, or not? Whichever it was, Emma suspected that he had cared about her more than might have been expected in a betrothal supposedly arranged between rank and fortune.

Her gaze fell on the parcel he had left on the desk. For the children he had said. With an aching heart she rose and went to the bell pull by the fireplace. The least she could do was let them open their own present.

Chapter Twenty-One

'Miss Carshalton!'

She was halfway across the entrance hall and her steps faltered, but she didn't stop, let alone turn.

Hunt lengthened his stride and came up with her as she reached the front doors. 'My dear, I can't possibly permit you to walk all the way back to London.'

That did stop her. She faced him and he saw with a pang that her eyes were wet with tears she had not allowed to fall. Despite that, they still blazed. 'You are not my father! You have nothing to say in what I do!'

He took a careful breath. 'No. I am not your father. But I knew you as a child. Will you not permit me to have the carriage brought around for you? For my own peace of mind. I count Ignatius Selbourne a friend. What do you think he will say to me when he finds out I let you walk home from here?'

Her mouth trembled. 'I...very well. Thank you.'

Hunt beckoned to the footman on duty who looked as though he were trying very hard to melt into the wall. 'The carriage for Miss Carshalton. Immediately.'

He turned back to her. 'Shall we wait in the Long Gallery?'

She swallowed. 'You don't need to wait with me.'

'Yes, I do,' he said quietly.

She was silent a moment, then let out a breath. 'Very well.'

He showed her into the gallery at the back of the house and closed the doors. The fires had not been lit and he saw her shiver.

'Why did you avoid Martin's question, Miss Carshalton?'

She stiffened. 'Avoid? What are—?'

'You didn't answer directly when he asked if you had deliberately passed information to your father. He was upset enough not to notice, but I did. Why?' he demanded. 'Why hurt him by letting him suspect you did it deliberately. You didn't.'

She faced him defiantly. 'You can't know that.'

'Yes, I can. *Why?*' He saw her mouth tremble and realised just how close she was to breaking. 'Kit, my—'

'Don't call me that!'

'Why not? Because Martin did?'

She nodded, her throat working.

'Kit,' he spoke very gently, 'if you think it will make it easier for him believing you involved, you are very wrong.'

She shuddered. 'Better that, than—' She caught herself.

'Better than what? The truth?' He was beginning to suspect what she was hiding and it sickened him. 'Kit, if you know something, tell me. A child's life is at stake here. You can't protect Martin by hiding the truth.'

She stared at him for a long moment. 'You're right. I'm sorry. If…if anything happened…and I hadn't spoken, he'd hate me even more.' She bit her lip. 'I didn't speak to my father yesterday afternoon, beyond greeting him. But Martin's mother did.'

He'd suspected it from the moment he realised Kit was hiding something from Martin. What he couldn't see was *why*.

Kit turned away. 'She…she's besotted with him, you know.'

He looked at her sharply. 'The Duchess? With Martin?'

'Yes.' There was a moment's silence and when she continued her voice was low and taut. 'She used to talk sometimes about what a shame it was that Martin would never be the Duke. That he was meant for great things, that he alone of his brothers knew his duty. Thirlbeck, at nearly forty, had not married. Lord Peter had married to disoblige his family and, worse, had spawned "a brat"—her words—who might not even be legitimate.'

'He is,' Hunt assured her.

'That's not the point!' She turned back to him and the pain in her eyes was like a blow. 'She *wanted* Harry to be illegitimate.' Her voice broke. 'I... I have no idea if Thirlbeck's death was my father's doing and, if it was, if she knew. But my father came into the hall yesterday as we entered the house. She told me to...to *"Run along, Katherine, and order tea."'* Her imitation of the Duchess's condescending accent was pitch perfect. 'She wanted a word with my father about...about the wedding date.'

She turned abruptly away and went to stare out into the wintery gardens. Pity stabbed at Hunt. There was nothing he could say, no comfort to offer. All he could do was pretend he hadn't seen those first tears fall.

'Uncle Hunt!' Georgie ran to grab his hand as he entered the library after seeing Kit into the carriage fifteen minutes later. 'Come and see! We've got a present!'

'A present?' His mouth curved, despite the ache in his heart. Somehow being dragged across the library by an excited child lifted all weights, reminded him that there could always be hope. 'What is it?'

'Come and see!' Georgie repeated.

Harry, seated on the arm of Emma's chair, held

a small object. As he drew, or was dragged, closer, Hunt saw that it was a miniature. And he knew.

Harry held the painting out for his inspection. 'It's Papa. Mama says it's a very good likeness.' The boy looked up at him with shining eyes. 'Uncle Martin left it for us.'

He managed another smile. 'I'd better have another made so you have one each.'

'*Could* you?' Harry asked. 'It wouldn't be too expensive?'

Hunt shook his head. 'No. Not at all.' He smiled at Emma. 'Shall we go for a walk? By the lake?'

'Can we come, too?' Georgie bounced on her toes.

'Certainly, if you promise not to fall in until late next summer,' Hunt said.

Georgie's brow wrinkled. 'Why late next summer?'

Harry rolled his eyes. 'Because the water will be jolly cold now and you can't swim yet!'

Georgie scowled, and then said, 'But am I going to learn? I thought girls weren't—'

'If you're going anywhere near my lake you learn how to swim.' Hunt held out his hand to Emma, drew her out of the chair. 'Come along. Fergus has arrived. He's in the stable yard. We'll go that way.

With the children and Fergus racing ahead, Emma listened in dazed horror to what Hunt told her. 'The *Duchess*? But, she's—' She couldn't say it.

Hunt did it for her. 'Yes. Harry's grandmother.'

'Are…are you sure?'

'Yes,' Hunt said. 'I had to drag it out of Kit.'

'She *knew*? But why let Martin think—?' Emma's heart cracked. 'She was protecting him?'

'Yes. I think though, even if I hadn't pushed just now, she would have contacted me with the truth when she realised her silence left Harry in danger. The poor child was thinking only of Martin.'

Emma shut her eyes. 'He'll have to know.'

'Yes.' Hunt's eyes were shadowed. 'I'll see him and Keswick tomorrow. Keswick will have to find a way to keep his Duchess in check and the fact that Martin's betrothal is broken should nullify Carshalton.'

'What should we tell Harry and Georgie about it?' Emma asked. Hunt had slipped his arm about her waist and they walked in easy step together.

'Nothing,' he answered. 'I doubt we can bring Carshalton down over this. But the broken betrothal will protect Harry. Carshalton will not waste his time on something that brings him nothing.'

She rested her cheek on his shoulder. 'Poor Kit. Her reputation, when the broken betrothal becomes known—even if we can't prove her father's involvement—'

'It's more than that, sweetheart.' He let out a breath. 'I think she made the mistake of falling in love with Martin.'

Remembering her own pain at initially refusing Hunt, Emma swallowed. If Martin also loved Kit…

They reached the lake and walked around it towards a grove of willows, whose bare branches dipped and swayed over the water in the chill breeze. On the far side of the lake a small structure was built out over the water. The children came tearing back.

'Uncle Hunt! Is that a *boathouse*?' Harry skidded to a halt, breathless. 'Can we go in? Please?'

Georgie wasn't far behind. 'Please, Uncle Hunt? If we promise faithfully not to get in the boats or fall in until next summer?'

'Faithfully?' Hunt asked, raising an eyebrow.

Georgie nodded vehemently, and Harry said, 'I'll mind her, sir. We'll just look.'

Hunt chuckled. 'Very well. The boats are out of the water for the winter, but the dock will be slippery. Stay well back from the edge.'

'Yes, sir!'

They were gone in a flash, Fergus with them.

'Harry is very like his father, isn't he? Except he has your eyes.'

Emma caught her breath. 'Yes. Very like. He, that is, Harry told Martin yesterday that he didn't remember Peter very well. So—he brought the miniature. There was a note with it. He had it done after Peter's death from a painting at Keswick Hall. You don't mind?'

'Mind? That Harry and Georgie have something to help them remember their father?' He regarded her quizzically. 'As you minded the painting of Anne and the children?'

She managed a wobbly smile. 'Not at all, then.'

Hunt's arm tightened, drawing her on and, as they rounded the willows she saw their destination.

A headstone rose out of the turf close by, twenty feet back from the lake on a little rise. Her breath jerked in. 'Oh, Hunt. Gerald?'

'Yes. He and my sons used to play here in the willows. He loved this spot.' He pulled something from his pocket, bent down and placed it at the foot of the headstone. Her throat tightened. It was a tiny sprig of rosemary.

He straightened, removed his hat and stood silently, gazing down at his brother's grave. It was a very simple headstone. Just Gerald's name and that he was the beloved son of Lucius and Susan, beloved brother of Giles, Letitia and Caroline, followed by the dates of his birth and death together with a line from a psalm—*He leadeth me beside the still waters and maketh me to lie down in green pastures.*

From the boathouse, fifty yards away, the children's voices floated back, bright and happy. Emma had not bothered with a bonnet, but she pushed back the hood of her cloak and said nothing. He wanted her here with him. That was enough. She rested her cheek against Hunt's shoulder and waited. Several swans sailed on the lake as the wind sifted through the willows, whispered across the water, and brought small waves dancing home on the shore.

His arm came back around her. 'I'd paid Gerald's debts when he was sent down from Oxford.' His voice was very quiet, almost as if he spoke to himself. 'They were…staggering. Not just unpaid bills, but gambling debts.' The break in his voice tore at Emma, but there was nothing she could say. Nothing she should say. Now was for listening. He went on. 'I was worried. Worried that he was spending heedlessly, and showing all the signs of becoming a habitual gambler. Fox ran through a fortune in our youth, unable to stop, and I saw Gerald going the same way. Watching Fox was bad enough, but if Gerald did that…' She turned slightly, slipped her arms around him, and felt the tremor that ran though him. 'And the estates, my tenants, so much depended on him. *I* depended on him. Maybe too much.'

She held on. They were coming to it now. 'Of course you depended on him. You needed to know he would be able to accept his responsibilities.'

'It wasn't just that. Losing my own children, along with Anne—Gerald was the closest family I had left. I wasn't just worried about his responsibilities; I was worried about *him*. I *loved* him.'

Her heart broke a little for him. 'I know. What happened?'

Hunt swallowed. 'I knew he was under the hatches before he came to me. I'd come up with the perfect plan. You see, he was still under age, only twenty. No decent man would have allowed him to play for more than chicken stakes. So I told him I'd pay the bills in return for his word of honour that the gambling would stop. He'd never broken a promise to me and I was more worried about tradesmen who might be ruined than gamesters who should never have taken a boy's vowels.'

'The gaming debts?'

The steel band clamped around his heart, his guts. 'I refused to pay them. At that point he stormed out.'

She was very still for a moment. 'At that point? Then you still had something to say?'

'That I had drawn up the deeds to transfer one of the unentailed properties to him in trust. He would not be able to sell it, but he could use the income to pay off his gambling debts.' Why hadn't he said that *first*? Why—?

Her lips brushed his cheek. 'So he chose not to listen when you called him to come back?'

'How do you know I called him?'

She pulled back a little, raising her hands to cradle his cheeks, and met his gaze, her eyes wet. 'Because I *know* you, Hunt. You loved him. So you would have gone after him.'

'Yes. But he was shouting at me, incapable of hearing anything. I'd done that, made him so angry, that—'

Her fingers pressed gently against his lips. 'Hunt, stop. Don't do this to yourself. Gerald made his own choices. Not good ones. And no parent can foresee everything.'

They stood quietly for a while. Eventually he said, 'This is the first time I've been here since we buried him. I kept the miniature on my desk. But I couldn't come here. To him.' And it felt easier now that he had. Grief remained, regrets, but not the endless weight of guilt. That was gone, as if it should never have been.

The future, without that weight, beckoned. He reached out, brushed his fingers over the marker in farewell and they walked on towards the boat-house and the children's laughter.

'Each year on Peter's birthday, I take the children to visit his grave. I tell him about the children and they tell him about me. We leave flowers. Silly, but—'

He silenced her with a gentle kiss. 'No. No, it's not. Would you…would you permit me—?' He broke off as her eyes filled with tears. Perhaps he shouldn't even ask. 'No. I'm sorry. Forget—'

'You'd come with us to Peter's grave?' A tear spilled over, slid down her cheek.

His heart flooded. With joy. With sorrow. With love. Sometimes those things became inextricably entwined. 'Yes. Before we go to Pentreath? I'd like the chance to assure him that I have you and the children safe.'

Another tear slid to join the first. 'He'd like that. I'm sure he knows anyway, but he'll like that you came. He made me promise him something at the end.'

'Tell me.'

'He made me promise to be happy again. To love again and…and to find someone to love me. And he said, *"No regrets, Emm."'*

A soft laugh shook him. 'Anne didn't have the chance, but she would have said something very similar. I'm glad I finally obeyed her on all counts. Perhaps you might like to tell her?'

He knew the moment she understood, the moment his words and their implication sank in. She stopped dead in her tracks to stare up at him, her heart and his future in her eyes.

'Hunt? Are you saying—?'

He covered those trembling lips with his own, folded her close and kissed her deeply. After a moment he broke the kiss and smiled into her eyes. 'That I love you? Oh, yes. So very much. I thought there was nothing left in me and perhaps there wasn't. But somehow you—you and the children—have filled me up again. I had no idea what it was at first. Just that I felt complete again.'

'You didn't want that,' she whispered.

'No. But it happened,' he said. 'And I may be a fool on occasion, but I'm definitely not fool enough to refuse love when it finally hits me over the head.'

'Then our marriage of convenience is not, after all—'

'Convenient?' he suggested. 'Oh, I wouldn't say that at all. I find being in love with my wife, and having her love me in return, perfectly convenient.'

Late November 1804

Hunt took the main stairs of Pentreath Hall two at a time, Fergus at his heels, not bothering to shed his greatcoat and gloves.

He walked quietly into the nursery, waving Bessie to silence, and just looked his fill. It was a sight he could never tire of—Emma, seated in a rocking chair by the window, their child at her breast. Two weeks away, and little Piers had grown again. He'd forgotten how fast they grew. And Emma, his Emma, cradling the baby, a tender smile curving her lips.

Fergus rushed forward, wriggling in joy, and Emma looked up, her smile blooming to outright joy. 'Hunt! We didn't expect you for another two days. Harry and Georgie are out riding with Masters.'

He hadn't expected himself for another two days. 'I missed you,' he said simply, dragging a chair over to them. 'All of you. No need to ask how *he* is.' He stroked his son's cheek and was rewarded with an annoyed glare at the disturbance. 'Piglet!'

Emma laughed. 'He's sleeping through the night now, thank goodness. How was Mr Selbourne?'

'He says he's dying.' Hunt sat down. 'His heart.'

Emma's smile faded. 'I'm sorry. And Kit?'

'I didn't see her, but she's still with him. He hasn't told her. He has promised me that he will.' He hesitated. 'Emma, he has left everything to her.'

Emma switched the baby to the other breast. 'Well, of course. Surely he didn't call you up to town just to tell you that?'

'No.' Hunt let out a breath. 'He's appointed me executor and Kit's trustee. She's nearly twenty-two, so not a guardian as such.'

'Oh.' Emma thought about that. 'Will she continue to run the bookshop?'

Hunt nodded. 'Yes. He says he's taught her nearly as much as he can, that she will manage perfectly well, but he wants me to act as trustee until she's thirty. He doesn't trust her father.'

Emma snorted. 'And Martin? Any news of him?'

Hunt nodded. 'Yes. He's back. Limping badly, but safe.' Martin Lacy had disappeared within a month of the broken betrothal. Very few had known that he had volunteered for a covert mission to the Continent. 'Oddly enough Ignatius seemed to know all about it.'

Emma stared. 'How?'

Hunt shook his head. 'I've no idea. The only thing I can think is that Martin told him. That he's seen him.'

'Then he did care about her,' Emma said softly. 'Poor Martin. And poor Kit.'

Hunt sighed. 'Yes. But at least she has Ignatius. And I have you.' He leaned forward to kiss her tenderly. 'And our family.'

She returned his kiss. 'Yes. You have us and we have you.'

He had everything. Everything he had lost and thought never to feel again. He had always known that to truly receive you had to give. Now he understood the equal truth: that to be able to give with a whole heart you had to be prepared to receive in turn.

* * * * *

If you enjoyed this story, you won't want to miss these other novels from Elizabeth Rolls

IN DEBT TO THE EARL
LORD BRAYBROOK'S PENNILESS BRIDE
A COMPROMISED LADY

MILLS & BOON®

& HISTORICAL

AWAKEN THE ROMANCE OF THE PAST

MILLS & BOON®

Coming next month

THE MARQUESS TAMES HIS BRIDE
Annie Burrows

'Don't be ridiculous. I am not your fiancée. And I don't need your permission to do anything or go anywhere!' Clare said.

'That's better,' Rawcliffe said, leaning back in his chair, an infuriatingly satisfied smile playing about the lips that had so recently kissed her. 'You were beginning to droop. Now you are on fighting form again, we can have a proper discussion.'

'I don't want to have a discussion with you,' Clare said, barely managing to prevent herself from stamping her foot. 'Besides, oh, listen, can't you hear it?' It was the sound of a guard blowing on his horn to announce the arrival of the stage. The stage she needed to get on. 'I have a seat booked on that coach.'

'Nevertheless,' he said, striding over to the door and blocking her exit once again, 'you will not be getting on it.'

'Don't be absurd. Of course I am going to get on it.'

'You are mistaken. And if you don't acquiesce to your fate, quietly, then I am going to have to take desperate measures.'

'Oh, yes? And just what sort of measures,' she said, marching up to him and planting her hands on her hips, 'do you intend to take?'

He smiled. That wicked, knowing smile of his. Took her face in both hands. And kissed her.

And just as she was starting to forget exactly why she ought to be fighting him at all, he gentled the kiss. Gentled his hold. Changed the nature of his kiss from hard and masterful, to coaxing and…oh, his clever mouth. It knew just how to translate her fury into a sort of wild, pulsing ache. She ached all over. She began to tremble with what he was making her feel. Grew weaker by the second.

As if he knew her legs were on the verge of giving way, he scooped her up into his arms and carried her over to one of the upholstered chairs by the fire. Sat down without breaking his hold, so that she landed on his lap.

Continue reading
The Marquess Tames His Bride
Annie Burrows

Available next month
www.millsandboon.co.uk

LET'S TALK
Romance

For exclusive extracts, competitions
and special offers, find us online:

f facebook.com/millsandboon

⊙ @millsandboonuk

𝕏 @millsandboon

Or get in touch on 0844 844 1351*

For all the latest titles coming soon, visit
millsandboon.co.uk/nextmonth

Want even more
ROMANCE?

Join our bookclub today!